CAJUN FRIED FELONY

JANA DELEON

Art attribution: Design and derivative illustration by Janet Holmes using images from Shutterstock.

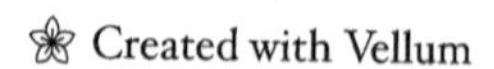

Miss Fortune Series Information

If you've never read a Miss Fortune mystery, you can start with LOUISIANA LONGSHOT, the first book in the series. If you prefer to start with this book, here are a few things you need to know.

Fortune Redding – a CIA assassin with a price on her head from one of the world's most deadly arms dealers. Because her boss suspects that a leak at the CIA blew her cover, he sends her to hide out in Sinful, Louisiana, posing as his niece, a librarian and ex-beauty queen named Sandy-Sue Morrow. The situation was resolved in Change of Fortune and Fortune is now a full-time resident of Sinful and has opened her own detective agency.

Ida Belle and Gertie – served in the military in Vietnam as spies, but no one in the town is aware of that fact except Fortune and Deputy LeBlanc.

Sinful Ladies Society – local group founded by Ida Belle, Gertie, and deceased member Marge. In order to gain membership, women must never have married or if widowed, their husband must have been deceased for at least ten years.

Sinful Ladies Cough Syrup – sold as an herbal medicine in Sinful, which is dry, but it's actually moonshine manufactured by the Sinful Ladies Society.

CHAPTER ONE

WHEN I HEARD the car horn, I ran out my front door and jumped into Ida Belle's SUV. Gertie was already in the back seat, looking entirely too excited given that it was Saturday morning and we were on our way to exercise.

"I wore my new running shoes all day yesterday," I said. "I hope they're broken in good."

Gertie's eyes widened. "You're participating? That's awesome!"

I looked at her, then Ida Belle, wondering what I'd missed.

"It's for charity, right?" I asked. "Town tradition. Every Thanksgiving."

"Oh yes," Gertie said. "It's a total hoot. Every year I think I'm going to win and then there's always some sneaky junior high student who dashes all my hopes of taking home that trophy."

I stared for several seconds. "I am so confused. You said this was a turkey run. Like a race for charity? Why are you this excited about running? You hate running. And why do junior high students win a marathon on a regular basis?"

Ida Belle chuckled. "It's not that kind of turkey run."

"What other kind is there?" I was almost afraid to ask.

Ida Belle grinned. "The kind where the volunteers turn loose a bunch of wild turkeys in the schoolyard and those who signed up for the race try to catch one with their bare hands."

I stared at her in dismay. "And you participate in this?"

"Heck no," Ida Belle said. "At least not the running and catching part. I help, uh, prepare the turkeys for transport home."

"She whacks them," Gertie explained.

"Can't fry them if they're still flapping around," Ida Belle said.

"I'm not chasing wild turkeys," I said. "Not even for charity. And I'm not whacking them either. I got out of that business."

"But you have no trouble eating them," Ida Belle said.

"Of course not," I said. "Well, wait, are we going to be eating whatever Gertie catches?"

"Lord no," Gertie said. "I bought a Butterball when they were on sale a week ago. Wild turkey tastes different than tame turkey."

I sighed. "I am so confused."

Ida Belle nodded. "Goes with the territory."

"Which territory?" I asked. "Sinful or Gertie?"

"Both," Ida Belle said. "And it's nothing to worry about, anyway. Gertie is 0 for 10 on actually catching one of those birds."

"But this year, I've got expensive running shoes," Gertie said. "And I've been working on my arm speed. I might get lucky."

"And what happens if you do?" I asked. "I mean, you and Butterball already have a date on Thanksgiving."

"I'll give it to another family," Gertie said. "Not everyone can afford a turkey. The Sinful Ladies try every year to get birds out to families we know can't spring for the cost, but some of them are too proud to accept the help. But if I won the bird fair and square and wasn't going to use it myself, they wouldn't want to see it go to waste."

I smiled. The more I learned about these women, the more thankful I was that we were friends. "Then I hope you get lucky. Carter told me he was working the run as well. Is he chasing or working with Ida Belle on the whacking team?"

"Neither," Ida Belle said. "He's there to make sure the protest doesn't get out of hand."

"Protest?" I stared. "Don't tell me there's a save-the-turkey movement in Sinful."

"Good Lord, no," Ida Belle said. "This is Louisiana. You can't make noise about protecting meat here. If you even tried, the South would rise again."

Gertie nodded. "There's people in Sinful who probably haven't ever eaten a vegetable."

"I'm almost afraid to ask," I said, "but then what is the protest about?"

Gertie rolled her eyes. "Everyone's favorite pain in the butt, Celia, protests me competing in the turkey run. She says it's only supposed to be for kids."

"I've made the logical argument about age being relative," Ida Belle said. "But you know Celia."

"Doesn't the event have organizers?" I asked. "Rules?"

"Sure," Ida Belle said. "The Baptist church organizes the event. I'm the committee chair. Marie and Gertie are my committee."

I laughed. "Now I understand. So why don't the Catholics organize their own turkey-catching fun?"

"Oh, don't think she didn't try," Ida Belle said. "But the wild-turkey catchers wouldn't sell to her. They said they'd rather eat turkey for a year than help Celia out."

Gertie grinned. "That first year she tried it and she couldn't acquire the turkeys, she attempted to do the same thing with pigs."

I frowned. "I love bacon as much as the next person, but that doesn't exactly say Thanksgiving."

"I was *very* thankful," Gertie said. "The guy who delivered the pigs got the address wrong and stopped by Celia's house to ask for clarification. While he was talking to Celia, the latch on the trailer failed and all ten pigs ran straight for the farmer, who dashed into Celia's house to avoid the stampede."

"Leading them straight into Celia's living room," Ida Belle said.

I let out a laugh, the visual of pigs running through Celia's house clear in my mind.

"It took the fire department, the delivery guy, and six neighbors over an hour to get the pigs back into the trailer," Gertie said. "They destroyed her entire downstairs. Broke every table and chair and left a mess—the unmentionable kind—all over the floors. Celia was so distraught the paramedics had to come and sedate her."

"She couldn't find a cleaning crew in the entire state that would handle the mess," Ida Belle said. "Finally ended up hiring a forensics cleaning crew out of New Orleans. Cost her two thousand dollars to have the pig crap removed from her floors."

Gertie shook her head. "Two thousand dollars would buy an awful lot of dynamite. I mean, really, tie a rag around your nose and get to work, right?"

"Right," I said. "About the cleaning part. Not so much the dynamite."

"Anyway," Ida Belle said, "thus ended Celia's attempt to host an event counter to ours."

"What happened to the pigs?" I asked.

"Celia refused to take delivery," Gertie said, "and the farmer refused to issue a refund. She sued but the judge said she either took the pigs or shut her yap."

"I can't imagine she did either," I said.

"She bitched to the moon and back," Ida Belle said. "But the judge's order held. The farmer was so fed up with Celia by then, he rewarded the pigs by making them all breeding stock."

I grinned. "I love a happy ending."

Ida Belle nodded as she pulled into the parking lot of the elementary school. "Then let's hope for another one. I'd really like this event to go off without a hitch. I've been praying for a quiet holiday."

Gertie rolled her eyes. "Boring. There's been no excitement since we came back from vacation. I'm still bummed the DEA wouldn't let us investigate that barrel of money and skeleton."

"I don't think it required much of an investigation," I said. "A barrel of money with a dead person buried on a known drug lord's former property. Seems pretty straightforward to me."

"Well, they could have at least called and given us an update," Gertie said. "Or maybe a stack of that cash as a reward."

"You mean the blood money that had been housed for God knows how long with a dead person?" Ida Belle asked.

Gertie shrugged. "It still spends. And my having some wouldn't make the guy any deader."

"More dynamite?" I asked.

"A girl's gotta have a hobby," Gertie said.

"You should concentrate more on a legal one," Ida Belle said.

"Like what?" Gertie asked. "Stamp collecting? Bird-watching?"

Ida Belle nodded. "Either. Your purse would be a lot safer."

"She'd climb a tree to bird-watch," I pointed all. "That lends itself to all manner of chaos."

"No bird-watching then," Ida Belle said as she parked. "You can take up watching grass grow."

I looked at the crowd gathering in the fenced playground and now understood the wisdom of holding the event at the school. It offered a decent-sized fenced area for the turkey-chasing fun. We all climbed out of the SUV, and Ida Belle went to the back and collected her rifle and a hatchet.

"Let's get this over with," she said, and headed off for the crowd.

I spotted Carter standing next to a horse trailer with cages stacked in the back. I could hear the turkeys gobbling in unison. It wasn't an altogether pleasing sound and I wondered why he had chosen to stand in that particular location. Then I saw a local young woman standing just a bit away, staring wistfully at him.

Five feet four. A hundred twenty pounds. Limited muscle tone. Cell phone permanently attached to her hand. Gertie could take her.

I'd seen her before around town but only once close-up. It was at the General Store and I'd issued a greeting, as I'd been instructed was the polite thing to do in a small Southern town, but her response had been a scowl and then she'd stomped off. I'd meant to ask Ida Belle and Gertie about her but had forgotten.

Now I had a good idea what all the scowling and stomping was about.

I walked toward Carter, keeping a side-eye on her to test my theory. As soon as she caught sight of me headed his way, her eyes widened, then she whipped around and hurried off toward a group of mothers with young children.

"You got a stalker I need to know about?" I asked as I stepped up.

He looked over at the retreating woman and sighed. "That would be Ashley Prejean. She graduated from college last year and came back home to Sinful. I'm pretty sure her original plan was to nab a husband while she was in school and never come back at all, but apparently, that didn't pan out."

"So she decided to turn her attention to the most eligible bachelor in Sinful."

"*Former* most eligible bachelor."

"Maybe she didn't get the memo."

He grinned. "Jealous?"

"I'm pretty sure if you'd had any interest in the local women, the eligible title wouldn't have been in place when I arrived."

He shook his head. "You're going to be really rough on my ego if you're never threatened by a pretty young woman."

"You and your ego will have to get over it. Given my former profession, it's hard to feel threatened by scowling and stomping."

"She scowls at you?"

"She did when I spoke to her in the General Store one day, but that was before everyone knew my real identity. This time she just looked frightened and hurried off."

He laughed. "Your reputation precedes you."

"People say that a lot." I glanced at the trailer load of noisy birds. "So why are you standing over here, anyway?"

"Because I avoid pretty young stalkers and old complainers that way. They don't like the noise."

I grinned. "I assume you're referring to our friend Celia?"

"That's your friend, not mine. I swear, if that woman moved away, I could cut my working hours by ten percent."

"If Gertie moved, you could cut them by fifty."

"Yeah, but it wouldn't be as interesting. And if you tell her I said that, I'll deny every word."

"What are her odds on this turkey-chasing thing?"

"Of not injuring herself or actually catching a turkey?"

"Both?"

"Slim and none. But the entertainment possibilities are high."

"Goes without saying."

I heard a loud whistle and looked over to see Walter standing on a picnic table.

"There's our cue," Carter said.

I pulled out my cell phone as we headed for Walter. I wanted to make sure I got the entertainment portion of the day on video.

"Welcome to the annual Sinful Turkey Run," Walter said as the crowd gathered around him. "You all know the drill, but I'd be remiss if I didn't give you a reminder. When we get ready to start, everyone but the competitors will exit the playground and will remain behind the fence until the event is over. When the competitors are staged, the handlers will turn the birds loose in the playground. I'll put five minutes on the clock. When I sound the bullhorn, it's time to run."

"My group is here to protest," Celia shouted from Walter's right.

"No one cares," a woman shouted.

"Get a life," another woman yelled.

"Preferably in another state," a man added.

"Someone needs to send her some pigs and give her something else to do," another man said.

"I see Celia's making her usual strides with the community," I said.

Ida Belle nodded. "Like a broken record."

"If everyone will please leave the playground except for the competitors," Walter continued.

Celia stomped up to where Walter was standing and looked up at him. "As a citizen of Sinful, I have a right to protest anything that isn't in the best interest of this community. And I don't think letting a grown woman compete against children is in our best interest."

"The children are quicker and more limber," Walter said. "Seems fair enough to me. You know the rules of this event. If you don't like the rules, then take them up with the event coordinator."

Celia glared. "You mean the woman who enables Gertie to be an insult to our society."

"That would be the one," Walter said and waved his hand, trying to get parents out of the playground.

"I don't waste my time with people who don't listen," Celia said.

"Funny," Walter said. "You're doing it now."

"Oh, for Christ's sake!" Sheriff Lee stomped over to the picnic table and pointed his finger at Celia. "Woman, if you don't shut your yap and get out of the way, I'm going to arrest you for being an affront to human beings."

"You will do no such thing," Celia retorted.

"Try me and you'll spend a night in jail just so this town gets twenty-four hours of peace," Sheriff Lee said.

Celia put her hands on her hips. "I am *not* the problem here."

"You've been the worst problem this town has had since your birth," Sheriff Lee said. "You're a wart on the butt of humanity and if one more thing comes out of your mouth, even a sigh, I swear to God, I'm pulling out the handcuffs."

I raised an eyebrow. I'd never heard Sheriff Lee sound that aggravated. Celia must have drawn the same conclusion, because she'd gone silent. Finally she gave him a disgusted look and stomped off for a spot along the fence where her cronies were clustered. Sheriff Lee waved at Walter.

"Well, get on with it," Sheriff Lee said. "We're burning daylight."

"What's up with Sheriff Lee?" I asked. "He's always been direct but not quite that honest."

Ida Belle frowned. "I have noticed a difference lately. I wonder if he's hitting that late stage in life that a lot of people do."

"What stage is that?" I asked.

"The one where you stop filtering anything before you say it," Ida Belle said.

"Ida Belle hit that stage before she started talking," Gertie said.

"All contestants, please enter the playground," Walter yelled again.

"Wish me luck," Gertie said and headed off.

"I'm wishing for a miracle," Ida Belle said. "You know, the kind where things don't end with Gertie visited by the paramedics."

"Unless a bear or a bad guy with a gun starts chasing her, she'll run herself out quickly."

Ida Belle nodded. "There is that."

I watched as Sheriff Lee left the picnic table and stomped in our direction, then I elbowed Ida Belle. "Here comes Mr. Sunshine."

I waved at him as he approached. "Good morning, Sheriff Lee. Everything okay?"

He scowled. "Same crap, different day."

"Are you feeling all right?" Ida Belle asked.

"Why do people keep asking me that?" Sheriff Lee asked.

"Maybe they're worried about you," I said.

"Another waste of time," Sheriff Lee said. "I can take care of myself. Young woman, do you know how old I am?"

"No, sir," I said.

He frowned. "That's too bad. I don't either."

He shook his head and headed for his horse, who was tied to a fence post about twenty feet away. I looked over at Ida Belle.

"I got nothing," Ida Belle said. "Something's definitely up with him, though."

We watched as Pastor Don approached Sheriff Lee, a concerned look on his face.

"Sheriff Lee," Pastor Don said, "you appear distressed. Is there something I can do to help?"

Sheriff Lee threw his hands in the air. "There's nothing wrong with me. I don't need any help. Maybe you should spend your time praying for the people that woman harasses, because I don't think it will do any good to pray for her. She's been batting for the wrong team for a long time."

Sheriff Lee stomped off, leaving Pastor Don staring after him, a dumbstruck look on his face.

"Maybe he shouldn't be riding a horse with a loaded weapon and that attitude," I said.

"You want to tell him that?" Ida Belle asked.

I shook my head. "Guess I'll just let Pastor Don get on with the praying."

"Good call," Ida Belle said. "In the meantime, I'll see if I can figure out what's stuck in Sheriff Lee's craw. But don't tell Gertie. She'll be on it like we were hired to investigate."

"Handlers," Walter called out. "Bring in the turkeys."

CHAPTER TWO

IDA BELLE and I hurried to the fence with our cell phones. I wasn't about to miss one second of this. Gertie and eleven kids, ranging in age from around ten years old to fourteen, stood in a long line at one end of the playground. The handlers carried in the crates of turkeys through a gate about thirty feet away.

Twelve contestants. Ten turkeys. Five minutes on the clock.

Each handler leaned over a crate and prepared to let the turkeys exit. Walter lifted a bullhorn and a couple seconds later, a huge blast of sound ripped through the playground. The handlers opened the crates, and turkeys ran out of their confinements and into one another, trying to get away. The contestants ran straight for the turkeys, which led to more flapping and gobbling and general disarray as the birds tried to get away from the children.

And Gertie.

The kids were faster, of course, but Gertie was giving it everything she had. She sprinted—sort of—at the frantic birds, but every time she got within two feet of one, it zigged and she zagged. The kids weren't faring much better. They all scrambled one direction then the next, tripping over one another and falling, then jumping up and trying again. Some of them even gave it the full commitment and dived at their target.

A few of the birds headed toward the playground equipment, probably in an attempt to find a place to hide. One of them tried to run up the slide but kept sliding back down. As a young boy reached out to grab it, the turkey let out a cry, flapped its wings, and managed to leap to the top of the slide.

"I didn't think turkeys flew," I said.

"Wild ones can in short bursts," Ida Belle said. "A lot of them sleep in trees, but they can't sustain it over a distance."

I smiled. "So they can get just enough lift to give them an advantage over the runners."

Ida Belle nodded. "That's why we use wild ones instead of tame. It takes a bit for the hunters to trap them, but it's worth it."

The boy scrambled around the slide and up the ladder, snagging the bird by the feet. The turkey flapped furiously, but the boy managed to get it tucked in his arms and jumped off the ladder, still clutching the angry bird.

"He got it!" I yelled.

"Now all he has to do is get the bird over to one of the cages," Ida Belle said as she pointed to a spot inside the playground near where Walter was standing. "They'll put his name on the cage."

The boy half jogged a bit sideways, clutching the struggling bird. He managed to get it into the crate and the door shut, a huge grin on his face. A man standing close to the fence let out a giant hoot and started high-fiving with the other men standing nearby.

"The father, I presume?" I asked.

Ida Belle nodded. "He won four years running when he was a kid. Probably even happier now, as we had a retailer donate a prize this year. First one to snag a bird gets a hundred-dollar gift card to Fisherman's Headquarters. I see some new fishing tackle in father and son's future."

"Oh look!" I said and pointed. "Gertie's close to one!"

Gertie had chased a turkey onto the merry-go-round and was just about to attempt a grab over one of the bars, when one of the other contestants ran by and gave the merry-go-round a good shove. The round disc began to whirl and Gertie fell backward onto her rear. Another kid ran by and gave the wheel another shove, laughing as he passed, and the turkey flapped wildly, trying to maintain its balance as it inched toward the outside of the whirling playground equipment.

Realizing the turkey was getting away, Gertie managed to get onto her hands and knees and started crawling toward it, Gertie and the turkey swaying like two drunks. The wheel was starting to slow so both picked up speed as they approached the edge. Gertie reached out with one hand, ready to snag the bird, when another kid gave the wheel a whirl. Gertie and the turkey flew off the side of the merry-go-round and crashed into the dirt.

The bird immediately righted itself and started off away from Gertie, weaving as it went. Gertie managed to get onto her feet and staggered after it, both of them moving like extras from a zombie movie. She made it three steps before tripping and falling onto the bird. I heard a squawk and cringed, then let out a sigh of relief when Gertie rolled over, clutching the struggling turkey.

Ida Belle looked over at me and laughed. "You know that turkey's fate is the same, one way or another."

"Yeah, but being tortured on a piece of playground equipment, then crushed by a spin-drunk contestant doesn't seem a very dignified passing."

"Nothing about this is dignified, but I get your point. If she gets that bird in a cage, she'll finally be one of the winners."

"Maybe she'll give it up then."

"Ha! Not if we have another gift card up for grabs. She'd rise from the dead for a shot at free fishing tackle."

"She sorta looks like she just did," I said, and pointed at Gertie as she stumbled across the playground, clutching the angry bird. "You think she's going to make it to the cage?"

"I wouldn't put money on it."

I started cheering, hoping my yelling would give Gertie additional strength or balance, and Ida Belle and the crowd took up the cry with me. Everyone was laughing and cheering and having a great time watching Gertie wrangle the turkey.

Except Celia.

Satan's right-hand woman stood at the fence line in front of the cages, glaring at Gertie as she stumbled her direction. Gertie looked up as the cheering started and grinned, and that's when things went the way things with Gertie tended to go.

All the way south.

She stumbled on a patch of uneven ground and lunged forward. She was too far off balance to keep herself from falling, so she did what most people do when they're about to crash into the ground—throw their arms forward to break their fall.

The bird took advantage of the liftoff boost and flapped its wings, determined to get away from the crazy woman who had almost killed it on playground equipment. But with its limited flying capabilities and still in recovery from its bout on the merry-go-round, its flight path was as sketchy as Gertie's walking had been. The extra boost from Gertie flinging it had allowed the bird to get decent lift and distance, and it headed straight for the fence. It clipped the top of the metal fencing and pushed off again, but without Gertie's thrust behind it, couldn't gain the same height as before. I'd been so focused on the bird that I hadn't looked ahead, but a bloodcurdling scream had my gaze shifting right.

Just as the bird flew directly into Celia's face.

Celia, as usual, was wearing a ridiculously huge hat with flowers on it, which had probably prompted the panicked turkey to think she was shrubbery. The scream let the bird know it had grossly miscalculated. It scrambled on her head in a tangle of straw hat, fake flowers, and hair as Celia whirled around in a circle, trying to get the bird off her head.

I glanced over at Ida Belle, who was still filming.

"This is getting good," she said, answering my unasked question of whether or not we should attempt to help. I looked around and realized that everyone with a cell phone had it trained on the turkey fiasco. Carter, Sheriff Lee, Walter, and even Pastor Don were in on the action.

Gertie scrambled up and yelled at Celia to stop assaulting her bird, then ran for the hurricane fence and started to climb over. Her ascent was wobbly, but she managed to get to the top rail and then sorta slid off the other side onto the ground. But a little bruising wasn't stopping Gertie on her quest to nab the turkey.

The crowd parted and she pushed herself up and half jogged, half staggered toward Celia just as the turkey managed to get itself free from her hair and leaped off her head with one of its feet shoved clean through the straw hat. Between the merry-go-round, Gertie's capture, the fight on Celia's head, and the hat, the turkey was so panicked it had no idea what to do anymore. It attempted flight, but the hat seemed to prevent liftoff, so it resorted to running, the leg with the hat on it flung out a bit to the side, which sent it off at an angle.

Celia yelled at the turkey about her hat, then took off after it. Gertie was hot on her tail and seemed to be maintaining a semi-straight line. The turkey took off toward a section of the playground that was under construction. I'd been told the half court for basketball was completed earlier that year and had been such a success that they were now working on a sand volleyball court. A small bulldozer sat nearby, ready to clear the ground the next week while the kids were out on holiday.

Gertie inched up next to Celia and then either stumbled or pulled a hockey check on her. Either way, Celia came out the loser. She flew off to the right and tackled some guy filming the whole event, and they both fell into a thick hedge. I could hear her screaming as she went. Probably, people in Alaska could hear her. Or maybe it was the guy. I couldn't be sure.

The turkey was oblivious to the shrubbery crisis behind it and continued its mad dash for freedom. Gertie closed in on it as it reached the construction area. The bird must have sensed that it was in the crosshairs again because when it got close to the bulldozer, it turned on the afterburners, then gave flight one more chance. This time, the hat dislodged from the turkey's foot as the bird took off, and it hit Gertie in the face. She whirled around in a circle, clutching the hat, and finally managed to fling it behind her.

Where it caught Celia just as she staggered out of the shrub. She must have been disoriented by the fall, because she threw her hands up in front of her and batted the hat away, yelling for someone to shoot it. I assume she thought the turkey was coming at her again. Unfortunately, this was Sinful, so a guy who'd been standing next to the shrub when Celia made her entrance pulled out his pistol and blasted a hole through the hat, sending Celia screaming backward again into the bush.

From the shrub, I heard a feeble cry for help that was definitely male. I glanced into the shrub as I hurried past and saw the guy who'd been filming flat on the ground, an angry Celia on top of him.

"Assault," he called out.

"You wish!" Celia yelled.

I was sure that about this time, film guy was probably regretting living in Sinful, much less coming to the turkey run, but I couldn't stop to rescue him. I had to catch up with Gertie before things went to that whole other level that things often did where she was concerned. Besides, I wanted to see how it ended.

The turkey had managed to reach the cab of the bulldozer and Gertie scrambled up after it. The bird hopped onto the driver's seat and was preparing to exit the cab when Gertie made a lunge for it. Just as she was about to latch onto its foot, the turkey made a leap down and disappeared on the other side of the dozer. Gertie fell onto the driver's seat and then slid off onto the metal floorboard.

And then the dozer started to move.

It was sitting up on a tiny incline, and dislodging the brake was all it took to send the heavy machinery down the slope. Everyone started yelling and several of the men sprinted for the runaway dozer. Gertie popped up and scrambled to get upright and grab the brake, but she couldn't reach it in time. The dozer slammed into the basketball goal, pushing the entire thing over and bringing up a huge hunk of the court with it.

"You moron!" Celia yelled as she pulled leaves out of her hair. "I want her arrested for the destruction of taxpayer property! And my hat!"

"Your hat is ugly," Ida Belle said. "And the court is insured."

Gertie staggered down from the dozer, clutching her head with one hand. The turkey poked its head around the hunk of raised cement, took one look at the descending mob, and set off for the woods. At least five people pulled out guns and started firing. Without even thinking, I dived behind a park bench and pulled out my pistol, ready to return fire.

"Stop shooting!" Carter yelled, waving his arms at the shooters.

Ida Belle looked over at me, clearly amused. "If you're still inclined, there's a couple of them that people wouldn't miss much."

I shoved my pistol back in my waistband and stood. "Former occupational hazard."

"At least retirement hasn't slowed your reaction time."

"I don't know. I didn't pull my weapon on the guy who shot the hat."

"Only one guy and you were looking at him when he drew. Doesn't count."

"What happened to the turkey?"

"He got away. The people shooting couldn't hit the broad side of a barn."

I felt a little guilty at how happy that made me. The part where the turkey got away. Not the part where a bunch of clearly unqualified people decided to start firing while standing in a crowd. But that was Carter's business to sort out.

Ida Belle and I headed over to Gertie, who had ducked down behind a dozer wheel when the shooting started, but was now creeping out, a bit unsteady. We clutched her arms, trying to help her balance.

"Are you all right?" Ida Belle asked. "What's your name?"

"Depends on who you're asking," Gertie said.

"She's fine," Ida Belle said. "Probably just a good knock on the head."

I waved the paramedics over and pointed to Gertie. "Check her out, please."

A crowd of people gathered around the raised cement, trying to assess the damage. Some of the men were already arguing about the best way to repair it. Carter whistled to get everyone's attention, then waved at them.

"I need everyone to move away from this area and back to the playground," he said. "It's a holiday, people. Let's all try to get through it without injury."

"What about my hat?" Celia ranted. "What about the damage to the school's property? That woman is a drain on this community. What are you going to do about it?"

"Well, let's see," Carter said. "I could cite her for chasing a turkey. No, wait, that's what she was here for. Or maybe you'd rather I cite the turkey? Because Gertie didn't tear up your hat, and if the turkey hadn't run out of bounds and through the dozer, then Gertie wouldn't have followed him. Seems to me that all this trouble comes back down to that bird."

Sheriff Lee stepped up beside him and nodded. "I need all available men to form a posse. I'm going to deputize the lot of you to go after that turkey. Wanted dead or alive."

Celia glared as everyone began chuckling. I grinned and stepped past the crowd as they began to wander away, wanting to get a closer look at the damage. The chunk of concrete that the basketball goal had lifted out of the ground was a pretty good size. At least eight feet square. As I didn't know much about playground construction, I had no idea whether it could be repaired or if the whole shooting match had to be redone. Either way, no one was playing basketball anytime soon.

I caught a glimpse of something pink underneath the lower edge of the cement and bent down to get a closer look. I frowned and got down on my hands and knees, then crawled under the chunk of cement.

"Are you crazy?" Carter's voice sounded behind me. "That could break off from the pole at any minute. Get out of there."

I pulled my phone out and took a shot before crawling back out and rising up to look at an aggravated Carter.

"What the heck were you doing?"

I leaned close to him and accessed my pictures. "We have a problem."

Then I showed him the patch of hot-pink cloth with a skeleton hand sticking out of it.

CHAPTER THREE

While Gertie had been off on the wild turkey chase and setting free bulldozers, the kids had managed to wrangle the remaining turkeys into cages. A couple of the local men helped Carter rope off the court to prevent people from getting too close, then he'd headed back to the playground. Obviously, he was hoping to get the crowd dispersed before he attempted to retrieve the body under the concrete.

Gertie had apologized nine ways to Sunday to everyone attending, but no one seemed to be overwrought about the court destruction except Celia. But the first time she went to open her mouth and complain, Sheriff Lee pulled out a pair of handcuffs and dangled them in her face. She'd turned beet red, then huffed off, finally realizing that retreat was sometimes the best option.

Ida Belle had immediately caught on to the fact that something was wrong but had been called off to turkey preparation duty before she could pull me aside. Carter tried to keep his expression blank, but there was no hiding the set of his jaw or his constant glances toward the court as the contestants and spectators wrapped things up and trickled off. Finally, only Ida Belle, Gertie, Walter, Carter, and I remained.

"You might as well spit it out," Ida Belle said, glancing back and forth between Carter and me. "It's clear as day that something is horribly wrong, and I don't think that upended court is what has you two straining for normalcy."

Gertie and Walter narrowed their eyes and stared at Carter and me, looking almost offended that they hadn't clued in to the same thing Ida Belle had.

"By God, she's right," Gertie said. "You two look practically constipated."

Walter nodded. "Whatever it is won't be a secret for long, and it's possible we can help. Out with it."

I pulled out my phone and showed them the picture I'd taken under the lifted concrete. They all stared blankly for a moment. Then their eyes started to widen, and Walter gasped.

"Is that...is that a hand?" he asked.

"I'm afraid so," I said.

"I've called for a forensic team and a couple of guys that can help remove the concrete," Carter said. "Hopefully they can get it up without damaging the body any further, although I have serious doubts on that one. It being buried in concrete didn't do me any forensic favors."

"The size looks like a woman's hand," I said as I enlarged the image to study it better. "As does the choice of clothing color. Hot pink. And there's something shiny...hold on. I think it's a charm bracelet. There's something dangling. It looks like maybe a skull?"

Gertie sucked in a breath and Ida Belle frowned.

"You know who it is?" Carter asked.

"I can't be sure, of course," Gertie said, "but Venus Thibodeaux had a charm bracelet with a skull."

Ida Belle nodded. "And her preferred color for everything was hot pink."

Carter frowned. "I thought Venus went back to New Orleans."

"That's what her dad said," Walter confirmed. "Rumor is she took up with some undesirables when she was there before. He figured she'd headed back to it."

"And maybe she did go back to New Orleans," Gertie said. "But she's the only person I can think of that fits those two items. Not saying I'm right..."

"It gives me a place to start with identification once the body is removed," Carter said. "I'd appreciate you guys keeping this under wraps."

"We can do that," Ida Belle said. "But once those contractors catch sight of the body, they'll be on their phones ten seconds later."

Carter sighed. "I know. But hopefully none of them will know Venus's favorite color and jewelry preferences. I don't want that particular suggestion making it around to her father before I know for sure and get a chance to talk to him myself."

I shook my head. Most people thought law enforcement in a small town was an easy job, but it came with issues that cops in big cities didn't deal with. Like a gossip train that moved at the speed of light. Like personally knowing the victims and their families.

Like personally knowing the perps.

And ultimately, the worst of it came down to that. All the trouble Ida Belle, Gertie, and I had managed to stumble onto —or let's be honest, run toward on purpose—had produced villains that were currently part of or had been part of the Sinful community. It was an added layer of difficulty in delivering bad news and in investigating.

"Is there anything we can do?" I asked, already knowing the

answer, but unable to keep myself from asking the question. I was one of those people who took action to fix things. That wasn't likely to change even when I knew I had nothing to contribute to the situation.

Carter shook his head. "No. This is all on me and the forensics team. Once I get a positive ID, I'd appreciate hearing any gossip that might have passed your way, but that's it."

His directive was clear. If Ida Belle and Gertie had any suspicions, they needed to give them up. They did not need to enroll me in launching our own investigation. And I was okay with that. No one I cared about was at risk of being inserted into the middle of a murder investigation, and no one had hired me to poke my nose into it. But I'd be willing to bet that Gertie was already mentally packing her purse with detective supplies. Whatever that entailed.

"I don't know how long this will take," Carter said to me. "I'll call you later if I think I can swing by tonight, but don't go to any trouble with dinner."

Ida Belle raised an eyebrow.

"He means don't heat up one of those frozen casseroles that Gertie gave me," I said.

"Ah," Ida Belle said. "Well, give us a call if you need us. We'll be at Fortune's for a bit planning Thanksgiving dishes."

I managed to keep a straight face, as did Gertie, but we both knew that as soon as we sat down at the kitchen table, we'd be discussing nothing else but the body under the basketball court. At least, I hoped that's what we'd be talking about. I didn't have much to contribute to a discussion on cooking, and creamed corn wasn't nearly as interesting as crime.

Gertie cast a glance at the woods and sighed. "I almost had one this year."

I patted her back. "Look at it this way—you lost the turkey but exposed a murder."

Gertie perked up. "You always know the right thing to say."

Carter shook his head and walked away. Walter watched him for a moment, then looked back at us.

"You three be careful," he said.

I SLID into a chair at my kitchen table and grabbed a chocolate chip cookie from the plate in the center of the table.

"Spill," I said.

Gertie's lips quivered. "Well, I thought I'd make a nice chicken dressing and some deviled eggs."

"Don't give me that crap," I said. "You've had the Thanksgiving menu planned for the last forty years."

"Maybe longer," Ida Belle said.

"So out with it," I said. "You think the hand belonged to this Venus Thibodeaux."

"I do," Gertie said.

"Any relation to Myrtle?" I asked. Myrtle Thibodeaux was one of Ida Belle and Gertie's closest friends and a dispatcher at the sheriff's department.

"Not that I know of," Ida Belle said. "There's a million Thibodeaux in Louisiana. Same as Hebert."

I nodded. "So what do you know about her?"

"The problem isn't what we know," Gertie said. "It's where to start."

Ida Belle nodded. "Venus was one of Sinful's more...uh, colorful teens."

"That's saying a lot," I said. Sinful seemed to produce far more than its share of colorful individuals. If Venus was topping a list, then she had really worked overtime. "Do I need to break out more cookies?"

"We might still be here for breakfast," Ida Belle said.

"Then give me the highlights," I said.

"That's still going to take us back a ways," Gertie said. "Because to get a handle on Venus, you have to know about Starlight."

I stared. "Starlight?"

"What could loosely be called her mother," Ida Belle said.

"Starlight and Venus," I said. "I'm sensing a disturbance in the force already. I was hoping Venus was a nickname."

"Venus is her given name," Ida Belle said. "Starlight is from New Orleans, so I can't speak with conviction about her parents and their potentially fanciful naming conventions. But I'm going to hazard a guess that Starlight is not written anywhere on her birth certificate."

"Stage name?" I asked.

"If you consider seedy bars, casinos, and street corners in New Orleans the stage, then sure," Gertie said.

"Starlight was a prostitute?" I asked.

"She was a hustler," Ida Belle said. "But her hustling extended in several directions. She'd been busted for petty theft, extortion, pickpocketing, and soliciting. At least, that's what a friend who clerked in the New Orleans Police Department told us."

"You had her checked out?" I asked.

Ida Belle nodded. "As you can imagine with just that little bit of information, Starlight didn't exactly fit in Sinful. After she arrived, Gertie and I thought it might be prudent to get the skinny on our newest resident."

"Basically, she looked like trouble," Gertie said. "And she was."

"So why did she come to Sinful?" I asked. "There's only so many people to hustle around here before everyone is talking about it down at the café or in church. It doesn't seem like much of a career move."

"Definitely not," Gertie said. "The simple answer is a man brought her here."

"Is it someone I know?" I asked, running down a mental list of which men would be foolish enough to think someone like Starlight was a catch and actually bring her home to Mom. Turns out the list was rather long.

"Percy Thibodeaux," Ida Belle said. "You would probably recognize him if you saw him but he's not much of one for talking. He's a welder. His handiwork can be found on most every commercial shrimp and fishing boat in Sinful."

"He's a heck of a welder," Gertie said. "Took after his daddy on that one."

"But not in the picking women department," Ida Belle said. "Percy is a hard-core introvert. Would probably happily convert to hermit if he didn't need to work."

Gertie nodded. "You know how some kids are different and get picked on in school? Percy was so quiet he was practically invisible. I'll bet some kids he went to school with don't even know who he is."

"That's quite an accomplishment in a place as nosy as Sinful," I said.

"And unfortunately, it proved to be his undoing," Gertie said. "If you don't spend time around people, you don't get to know how they think. And Percy definitely wasn't ready when Hurricane Starlight hit him."

"How did they meet?" I asked, completely intrigued by the relationship between a hermit and a sorta hooker.

"New Orleans had a huge bridge repair project and needed the best welders they could find," Ida Belle said. "A former Sinful local worked for the city and threw Percy's name out. The city contacted him and offered him a ton of money for a couple months' work, so he packed a bag and headed out."

"This is when things fall to rumor," Gertie said. "But the

story goes that some of the guys Percy worked with convinced him to hit the casino with them one night and Starlight was there working the crowd. With money in his pocket and 'naive' practically tattooed on his forehead, Starlight probably zeroed in on him as if he were lit up in neon."

"By the time the job was done and Percy was due to return to Sinful, he was hooked," Ida Belle said. "So he asked her to marry him."

I shook my head. "Okay. All of that makes sense up until the point where she must have said yes. Why in the world would she marry a mark and head to Sinful?"

Ida Belle shrugged. "No one knows for sure. I suppose Percy might have eventually figured it out or Starlight threw it in his face at some point, but if he knows, he's never said. She wasn't wanted for anything at the time, so the hiding-out theory doesn't really work. At least not in regard to law enforcement."

"I always wondered if maybe she was trying to do the normal thing," Gertie said. "Maybe she took a look at Percy and thought, 'Here's a decent guy with a good job, and maybe I should give the whole happy housewife thing a try.'"

"I take it her attempt at domestic bliss was a failure," I said.

"On all fronts," Gertie said. "It was clear from the start that Starlight was no June Cleaver. Her clothes were too tight and her makeup too thick, and she had a habit of making most everything she said somewhat vulgar. But she did appear to be making an attempt at the whole 'dog and white picket fence' thing. Albeit half-heartedly."

"That's true enough," Ida Belle agreed. "She settled in, for what it was worth, for about a year before she came up pregnant with Venus. And I think that's when all her pretending ran out of juice."

"I'm surprised she didn't just fix that situation," I said. "I can't imagine the type of person you described wanting a child."

"Oh, no way she wanted a baby," Gertie said. "But one of the Sinful Ladies was a nurse at the clinic where Starlight went when she wasn't feeling up to snuff. Turns out she'd never been regular in a female sort of way, so by the time she headed to the doctor, she was already six months along."

"Holy crap," I said. "And she had no clue?"

"She'd been on birth control because of the regularity problems so I guess it never occurred to her," Gertie said. "She'd been feeling a bit sick to her stomach for some time, but she assumed it was a flu bug that she couldn't kick."

"We figured it was more likely a hangover she couldn't kick," Ida Belle said.

"True," Gertie said. "But this was one of those rare times we were wrong. Well, partly. I'm sure the drinking didn't help matters, but it was a particularly bad year for flu in Sinful. You know how it goes. You think you're feeling better so you move on. But in Starlight's case, it kept coming back, so finally she broke down and saw the doctor."

"So how did Percy take it?" I asked.

Gertie frowned. "I think by that time, the rose-colored glasses had slipped completely off, and Percy realized what a mistake he'd made. Rumor was he'd gone to New Orleans to see a divorce attorney just a couple weeks before, but I don't know that for a fact."

I whistled. "And then he finds out he's going to be a parent."

"With Starlight," Ida Belle said. "The man looked sicker than Starlight, truth be told. The fishermen said he barely spoke when he came to work on the boats. Mostly just nodded or grunted."

"Then Starlight kept getting sicker," Gertie said. "And next thing you know, Percy whisked her off to New Orleans to see some specialists. Percy never talks about it and Starlight wasn't exactly one for hobnobbing with the locals, so all we know is she was hospitalized for the rest of her pregnancy."

"That sounds serious," I said.

Ida Belle nodded. "It's not usually done unless both the baby and the mother are in danger, so Starlight must have been in a bad way."

"Given the way she'd lived up until then, there's no telling what that baby had been exposed to," Gertie said. "Percy took up work in New Orleans and got a place to stay there, and that's where they remained until a good while after Venus was born. She was still tiny when they came back to Sinful a month later, so my guess is the baby had to stay in the hospital a while."

"They didn't say?" I asked.

"No," Gertie said. "Percy was never one for talking anyway, especially about personal business. And after she had Venus, Starlight became as close-lipped as Percy."

"We had a baby shower and all," Ida Belle said. "Like we would for any resident, but it was clear from the beginning that Starlight had no interest in the baby. As much as she could pawn her off on one of the church ladies, she did."

"In Starlight's defense, Venus was a difficult baby," Gertie said. "Always sickly. I figured the doctors probably got the dates wrong and she was born a bit premature."

"Why did Starlight pawn her off?" I asked. "Sinful isn't exactly a mecca of entertainment." I paused and sighed as I considered Starlight's past and the local options. "The Swamp Bar."

Ida Belle nodded. "Percy tried to reel her in, but once Starlight got two feet planted firmly back into her old life, there was no chaining her to a baby that cried more than not and all the domestics that came along with taking care of a household. One day when Venus was about three months old, Percy came home and realized that Starlight had cleared out. Took all her things and every stitch of money in their bank account and disappeared."

"Word got around that she'd headed straight to New Orleans," Gertie said. "Back to the same thing as before. Percy got an attorney who managed to track her down and get a divorce finalized. Not only did she not want custody of Venus, she signed over all parental rights as long as Percy would forgo child support."

"That's seriously cold," I said. "So Venus never knew her mother?"

"I'm not sure about that," Ida Belle said. "Certainly Starlight had nothing to do with raising her daughter and we never saw her in Sinful again after she left. But Venus ran off to New Orleans about four years ago, the second after she turned eighteen. I've always suspected she tracked down Starlight."

"Looking for a mother-daughter reunion?" I asked.

"Something like that, I suppose," Gertie said. "The truth is, Venus was always a hundred percent Starlight and none of Percy. She was trouble from the time she could walk. I'll give Percy credit for trying as best he could for a good many years, but after a while, I think he gave up as well. Teachers spent a countless number of hours trying to get her on the right path. I was still substitute teaching back then and beat my head against that wall for a solid year. There was simply no getting through to her. Maybe none of us were qualified to help. Or maybe DNA won out. I honestly don't know."

"Venus went out of her way to cause problems," Ida Belle said. "Problems at school, with Percy's clients, with local business, with boys...if there was some way to twist somebody into a knot, she seemed to revel in how much turmoil she could cause. It was a game to her. I guess as she got older, she realized the Sinful pond was too small and moved on to a bigger set of fish."

"Percy didn't try to find her?" I asked.

"Not that I know of," Gertie said. "To be honest, I think he was relieved."

I nodded. As horrible as it sounded, I sort of understood. "Then if she left and never came back, why would she show up dead under a basketball court?"

Ida Belle narrowed her eyes at me. "Oh, she came back."

"When?" I asked.

"This past spring," Ida Belle said. "Waltzed into town like she owned the place. Drove right to her father's house and let herself in—he'd never changed the locks. Had already unpacked her suitcases and was watching television and drinking his beer by the time he got home from work."

I stared. "Wow. That is some serious cojones."

Gertie nodded. "Venus never did anything without flair."

"What did Percy do?" I asked.

"He called Sheriff Lee and had her arrested for trespassing," Ida Belle said.

"I did not see that one coming," I said.

"Neither did Venus," Gertie said. "And she raised holy hell down at the sheriff's department. Managed to rip apart the mattress in her cell and threw the stuffing everywhere. When no one responded, she started screaming at the top of her lungs and told the two other guys in jail that they should sue for having to listen to her."

"I can't imagine Carter fell for that one," I said.

"He didn't," Ida Belle said. "At least, not in the way she hoped. Instead of letting her loose, he let the other two guys go. Couple of drunks who'd been fighting at the Swamp Bar, so nothing that would come back on him, but it eliminated the leverage Venus thought she had."

"She didn't stop the noise, though," Gertie said. "She started singing loud then. Myrtle said you could hear her all the way to the front desk. She stuffed cotton in her ears when she came on shift and told Carter to go on home. The phone lights up when it rings, so no worries there."

"And did Percy follow through with pressing charges?" I asked.

Ida Belle shook her head. "Carter convinced him to go talk with Venus the next day. After Percy had a chance to wrap his mind around things. I don't know what all was said, but he finally agreed to let her move back in with him until she figured out what she was doing next."

"That worked out about as well as you could expect," Gertie said. "She was supposed to get a job or enroll in school —those were the options Percy gave her. She asked around a couple places about employment, but everyone in Sinful knew better than to take on Venus. And Lord knows, the girl was never suited for school, so that was never a real option. Ultimately, she ended up doing what we all figured she would."

"Causing trouble? Undesirable man?" I guessed.

"She managed both at the same place," Ida Belle said. "Took a job waitressing at the Swamp Bar and started dating Whiskey."

I frowned. "Seriously? He's got at least ten years on her."

"Closer to fifteen," Ida Belle said. "But Whiskey came along with a job that offered a place for her to get into trouble and he paid her to do it on top of it. Bar fights soared as soon as she started working there. My guess is she flirted with men to get into their pockets and then incited them to fight over her. I'm sure it amused her."

"How could one girl cause so much trouble?" I asked.

"The thing we never covered was that Venus was gorgeous," Gertie said. "'Could have been on a magazine cover' gorgeous. She had those tall, thin, runway model looks but with her mother's chest size. High cheekbones, big blue eyes, puffy lips, blond hair, dark tan, and she knew how to work every inch of it."

"So I assume she was popular with the boys but not the girls," I said.

"Got that right," Gertie said. "She managed what she considered a friendship with two girls back in high school. One was a troublemaker but not up to Venus's level. She needed Venus to help her take things up a notch. The other was what we'd call a wilting flower back in my day."

"Why in the world would someone like that want to hang out with Venus?" I asked.

"Because Venus paid attention to her when no one else did," Gertie said. "It was definitely for Venus's benefit. She used the girl for doing her homework and to bum money off of her, but Venus also stopped the other girls from picking on her."

"So this girl felt beholden," I said, still trying to understand teen angst. My own teen years were a blur of forgotten memories. Sometimes one broke through and I saw things clearly, but so far, it seemed to be one big dull nonevent. I supposed I should consider myself lucky to have never drawn the attention of one of the warring factions of girl groups.

"I'm sure feeling beholden was part of it," Gertie said. "But beyond that, I think she looked up to Venus. She wanted that strength for herself."

I sighed. "That's all sorta sad. So back to present day—how did Venus get from raising hell at the Swamp Bar to being dumped into a construction site?"

"That is the sixty-four-thousand-dollar question," Ida Belle said. "Venus took off again shortly before you arrived. Percy said he came home one day and her car and all her stuff were gone. He got a text from her saying she was going back to New Orleans."

"You think he's telling the truth?" I asked.

"Why would he lie?" Gertie asked.

Ida Belle shook her head. "Because someone buried Venus in that construction site before they poured the concrete."

CHAPTER FOUR

It was getting toward 9:00 p.m. when Ida Belle and Gertie finally called it quits and headed home for their bedtime routine. I'd gotten a brief text from Carter a couple hours before saying not to wait up. I wondered if Carter had found something that gave him positive ID, but no way was I asking. One of the first things I'd figured out about Carter was that he was more forthcoming with information if he thought I wasn't interested. If I played my cards right, he might just give up something when I saw him again, especially since I had no reason to get in his way on this one.

I will be the first to admit that my curiosity had been piqued. Why wouldn't it be? A troubled girl who left town, then came back, then supposedly left again, but might have turned up dead instead. And after everything Ida Belle and Gertie had told me about Venus, if that body turned out to be hers, I wanted to know how things had gone down. Not because I had any ties to her, and Ida Belle and Gertie had no personal emotional trauma over the situation, but the fact still remained that someone had put a body in that hole and covered her with dirt, knowing that a court would be poured over it.

And that person was likely a Sinful resident.

That's when the lines of civilian life and law enforcement started to blur for them and for me. Until the body was identified, we didn't know it was Venus. But even if it wasn't Venus, it was someone with a connection to Sinful. Granted, until we knew cause of death, we couldn't even be certain the person in the concrete was murdered. It might have been an accident and then someone panicked and covered it up. But if that body did turn out to be Venus, then the cover-up was fairly elaborate. The missing clothes and car and the text were indications of an elaborate scheme to ensure that no one thought twice about Venus being gone.

If someone had gone to that much trouble, they had a lot to lose.

I shook my head and blew out a breath. I was letting my imagination run wild with me. The reality was, regardless of what interesting stories my creativity could spin, all the speculation was useless until we knew who the body was and whether or not it was murder. All I really knew for certain was that I was clearly bored and needed to find more ways to occupy my mind until I got some clients.

I was just headed upstairs to shower when there was a knock at my front door. I skipped over to it, recognizing the strength and cadence of the rap, and let Carter in. I'd given him a key but he had told me straight out that no way was he letting himself into my house unannounced unless he was sure I wasn't home. He wasn't interested in acquiring any more bullet holes in his body. I was fairly certain I wouldn't just open fire without looking first, but I wasn't ready to fault his prudence on the matter.

"I have some roast beef left over," I said. "You want a sandwich?"

He leaned over to give me a quick kiss and nodded. "That would be great. I haven't had anything since lunch."

We headed to the kitchen and I pointed to a chair as I grabbed him a beer from the refrigerator. I passed it to him, then pulled out the roast beef and some bread and started making him up a sandwich.

"Was it hard to get the body out of the concrete?" I asked as I assembled.

"It took some maneuvering. Had to make sure that piece was really secure before we started lifting. I didn't want it falling back."

I nodded. The crime scene had already been compromised enough by the pouring of the cement and when the bulldozer lifted up the hunk. Carter was doing everything possible to preserve any evidence that might be available.

I slid the sandwich onto the table and took a seat across from him. "Was the forensic team able to extract the body?"

He took a bite of the sandwich and nodded. "There was enough dirt separating the body from the concrete so most of it wasn't encased. The concrete guys had to cut around some of it and they collected all the concrete around the body in case there was anything to find."

"Makes sense."

"What's the local gossip?"

"Ida Belle got the call around seven. A nephew of one of the Sinful Ladies was one of the contractors who helped lift the concrete. He didn't give much in the way of details. Just told her that he'd helped pull a body out from under the court. A couple of other calls came in after that. Word was filtering around, all originating with the construction guys."

"I figured as much," Carter said. "I asked them not to mention anything, of course, but I knew it was going to happen anyway. Any speculation yet?"

"If there is, it didn't make it to Ida Belle. But then, I'm guessing construction workers probably wouldn't clue in on the bracelet or the hot-pink clothes and be able to make a logical guess like Gertie did."

"Good. I don't want word getting back to Percy before I know for sure. And if it turns out it's Venus, that's not the sort of thing a parent should hear via the local Sinful talk."

"Do you think Gertie's right?"

"I'm sure she's right about Venus having a bracelet like that and the hot-pink thing. She's always noticed those sorts of things, and she doesn't forget much when it comes to other people, often to their dismay."

"I'll bet."

"Forensics could see enough after the extraction to give me an estimate of height and said the body was female and adult but young. That's not official, of course, since none of them are doctors, but they've seen enough bodies to know that much. Since there's no one else who fits all that criteria and also disappeared from Sinful around the time that court was poured, then I'm inclined to believe Gertie got it right."

"How long do you think it will take for the medical examiner to make a positive ID?"

"I left him a message with the information Gertie provided. There's only one dentist in town. But it will all have to wait until Monday. The body's been in that cement for months. No reason for the ME to rush in on a Sunday for this one. I imagine he'll get the records first thing Monday morning and assuming it goes the way I figure, I'll be talking to Percy shortly after."

"I wonder how he's going to take it." At his curious look, I waved my hand in dismissal. "Gertie and Ida Belle filled me in on the Venus gossip."

Carter nodded. "She was a handful, that's for sure. Percy never really stood a chance with Starlight, and Venus was her mother made over, except a bit more clever."

"Which only made her more trouble."

"I'm afraid so. She managed to cause trouble with more than one couple in Sinful when she targeted boyfriends. Stuck around long enough to get money out of them, then moved on to the next target while the boys were left behind with no money and angry girlfriends. The population of young women in Sinful probably heaved a collective sigh of relief when Venus left."

"And probably started making voodoo dolls when she returned."

"It wouldn't surprise me if they did."

"So what you're saying is that you'll have no shortage of suspects if this turns out to be murder."

"I don't know. I'm sure there's plenty of people who won't shed a tear at her passing, but it's hard for me to imagine someone killing her years after the fact over teenage silliness."

"Someone put her in the ground. Knowing that concrete would be poured."

He sighed. "Yeah. But that doesn't automatically imply a local. I have no reason to believe that Venus cleaned up her act in New Orleans. And her return here was abrupt and completely unexpected. Makes me think she was running from something."

"You think someone could have followed her here to take care of some unfinished business in New Orleans?"

"Sure. Why not? The construction on the school grounds

was readily visible. Even someone passing through would have seen it."

"Then wouldn't someone have seen when the body was buried?"

"Not at night. The playground doesn't have any lights at all, so it would have been pitch-black after dark. And even if someone saw headlights, sometimes teens park there to make out."

I nodded. "I guess the biggest challenge with cases like this is that a lot of enemies means a long list of suspects."

"Yeah, it does."

He sounded tired when he said it and he looked as tired as he sounded. I knew his exhaustion went deeper than just this case. I knew Carter had made the decision to return to Sinful and become a deputy partly because of all the things he'd seen and done while serving in the Marine Corps. He wanted to get away from those things and had thought Sinful was the place to do it.

Unfortunately, even Sinful had caught up with the criminal times.

"Did you ever think that maybe it's always been this way?" I asked. "I mean, allowing for the era."

He stared at me for several seconds then finally nodded, and I knew he understood what I was asking.

"Yeah, I think maybe it was," he said. "Allowing for the times, as you said."

"So basically, the crimes have grown in scope and severity as society has declined, but the number of people who chose that life over the other remains the same."

"I believe so."

"That sucks."

"Yeah, but I keep reminding myself that there are just as

many good people as there were before. And we're doing everything we can to level the playing field."

"The other team is playing dirty."

"They always have."

LOUD, unusual noise woke me the next morning and I bolted out of bed, trying to focus on the source. It sounded like barking dogs and since I didn't own one dog, much less a pack of them, I was confused. I was also still half asleep. I finally located the culprit of the barking and grabbed my cell phone, already guessing that Gertie had changed my ringtone to play a joke on me. The chuckling I heard when I answered confirmed it.

"I will get you back," I said. "And what the heck is so important at..." I checked my phone. "Good grief. It's eight o'clock. Church doesn't start until eleven."

"I was hoping you were lounging in bed with sexy man-candy," Gertie said. "But I saw Carter's truck at the sheriff's department when I picked up some muffins from the café, so my fantasies for you were dashed."

I perked up. "You have muffins?"

Gertie sighed. "The fact that you're more excited by muffins than the sexy man-candy fantasy means we've still got a lot of work to do."

"The man-candy part of my life is in place. My breakfast is not. Can I assume you're headed my way with those muffins?"

"Nope. You're heading my way. I have a surprise for you and Ida Belle at my house. It arrived by special delivery first thing this morning."

"It's first thing this morning right now."

"For you, maybe, but for the delivery guy, 7:00 a.m. was

first thing. He'd been driving all night. So get your butt over here as soon as possible. I can't wait!"

The call disconnected and I stared at my phone, frowning. A special delivery at 7:00 a.m. on a Sunday? Gertie sounding as though she'd just won the lottery? Something that we needed to go to her house to see?

All of that sounded like trouble.

A minute later, my phone rang again. Ida Belle.

"I'll pick you up in two minutes," Ida Belle said. "I don't know what the heck that woman is up to now but it can't be good."

The call dropped and I hurried to pull on clothes and shoes and rush downstairs. Ida Belle was already screeching to a stop in my driveway when I reached the front door. I paused only long enough to lock the door behind me, then practically ran to her SUV.

"Any ideas?" I asked as she took off down the street.

"Plenty, and none of them good."

"I know. It can't be dynamite because she gets that all the time. And I was thinking it must be something big if she can't haul it over to my house."

"Big and likely illegal and she doesn't want everyone to see it."

"Yeah, that's the part that worries me. I keep thinking submachine gun or something equally as lethal."

"Well, she can't fit a tank in her garage, so at least that's one thing off the list."

"Grenade launcher?"

Ida Belle gave me a pained look. "I swear my blood pressure is through the roof. I'm too old for this crap."

I grinned. "I don't think it's going to stop. You might want to ask your doctor for a pill or something."

"Maybe something I could slip into her drink."

"I meant something for *your* blood pressure, but the other is a viable option."

Ida Belle pulled into Gertie's drive, and we watched as Gertie ran outside and started hopping up and down while clapping. Ida Belle looked up and I could see her lips moving. I assumed she was praying. Probably not the worst idea.

We got out of the SUV and Gertie started motioning for us to come inside.

"Hurry up!" she yelled. "You two are dragging butt."

"God, I hope it's not something that's set on a timer," Ida Belle mumbled.

"Surely she wouldn't blow up her own house."

"Not intentionally. But there was this one time she thought she would put a new well in out back and didn't want to wait for the backhoe."

Ida Belle picked up her pace so that I was practically jogging to keep up with her. Then I remembered that the siding on one side of the back wall of Gertie's house had always looked a little newer than the other side. I went ahead and kicked things up to a full jog. Hopefully, if anything about Gertie's surprise required a lit fuse, she was waiting for us to get there.

Gertie had disappeared into her house and we rushed through the open door, scanning the house for the source of the potential disaster. Then we saw Gertie standing next to a huge wire cage in the corner, beaming at us as she struck a Vanna White pose indicating the giant parrot inside.

Ida Belle and I drew up short and glanced at each other, neither of us knowing how to handle this complete turn of events. We'd been expecting a weapon of mass destruction and we'd gotten a bird.

"That's...that's a parrot," Ida Belle said finally.

Gertie nodded. "A green-winged macaw. Isn't he wonderful?"

"This is the surprise?" I asked, wanting to make sure that something far more sinister wasn't tucked away in the garage or the coat closet.

"Of course," Gertie said. "What did you think?"

I gave her a sheepish look. "Well, given your propensity for unusual weaponry..."

Gertie waved a hand in dismissal. "I'm all stocked up on the lethal stuff. You don't have to worry about me on the private investigator end of things. I'm well prepared."

That statement had the opposite effect on me than what Gertie intended but she didn't seem to notice my look of dismay. She was too enthralled with her new housemate.

"The vet estimates his age at thirty," she said. "He'll live another thirty or forty years, so eventually, I'll have to face the loss, but I think it's still worth it."

Ida Belle shook her head but wisely remained quiet.

"Why a bird?" I asked, still confused.

"You two keep harping on me about getting a hobby," Gertie said. "I even joked about taking up bird-watching yesterday but of course, it was an inside joke."

"Far inside," Ida Belle grumbled.

"At least no trees are involved," I said. "So how does one acquire an, uh, green-winged macaw?"

"There's breeders, of course," Gertie said. "But it's really expensive to get a young bird. Mostly, you have to find someone who kicked the bucket and doesn't have any family that wants to keep them. But I got Francis through a police auction."

"Francis?"

"Police auction?"

Ida Belle and I both spoke at once.

Gertie nodded. "Apparently, he must have escaped his first home when he was fairly young. He was found by a nun and lived in a convent for the first ten years of his life. They named him Francis after Saint Francis of Assisi because apparently, he used to preach to birds."

I laughed. "You have a Catholic bird?"

"Don't blame Francis," Gertie said. "He's no more responsible for where he was raised than those orphans the church takes in."

"No, of course not," I said, feeling as if I'd entered a dream state. Despite having a pretty good imagination, I couldn't form a visual of a parrot in a convent.

"Besides," Gertie said, "I plan on talking to Pastor Don about converting him."

Ida Belle shook her head. "The more important question is where Saint Bird went after the convent and how he ended up part of a police auction."

Gertie shrugged. "They wouldn't really tell me that. Said it was all part of an ongoing investigation and couldn't be discussed. All I know is that Francis was seized along with some other property, and since they couldn't exactly stick him in a warehouse with the money and weapons, they got permission to sell him."

I raised an eyebrow. "Money and weapons?"

"Yeah," Gertie said. "But the weapons weren't for sale. I checked."

"Of course you did," Ida Belle said.

I took a couple steps toward the cage and leaned forward, eyeing the bird as he stared at me. "So...does he talk?"

"They said he has a large and colorful vocabulary," Gertie said.

"Colorful?" Ida Belle asked.

"Yes, well," Gertie said. "He called the delivery driver a few colorful names when he banged the cage against the door hauling it inside. But he did offer to pray for him before he left."

I eyed the bird again. "Hello, bird."

The bird cocked his head to one side. "My name is Francis. You're pretty."

I glanced back at Gertie, somewhat surprised. "He *does* talk."

"Of course he talks," Gertie said. "Why do you think I got him?"

Ida Belle frowned. "I think this was a bad idea."

"Why?" Gertie asked.

"I think this was a bad idea," Francis said.

Ida Belle pointed. "That's why. He's liable to repeat anything he hears."

Gertie waved a hand in dismissal. "We do all the good talking when we're plotting something illegal. And that's all at Fortune's house."

Ida Belle didn't look convinced. I could see her point but wasn't sure it was as big a risk as she seemed to think. A knock on the door interrupted my thoughts and we all looked at one another.

"Did you invite anyone else over to meet Francis?" Ida Belle asked.

"No," Gertie said. "And it's a little early for visitors."

Ida Belle headed for the front door and swung it open. Carter was standing outside.

Gertie leaned toward me and whispered, "It's like we said the word 'illegal' and summoned him."

I nodded as Ida Belle waved him inside.

"Is something wrong?" I asked.

"No," he said. "I mean, no more than usual. I got positive ID this morning. Gertie was right. It was Venus Thibodeaux."

"How in the world did you manage ID that fast and on a Sunday? Did the overnight at the ME's office know the dentist and get the records?"

"Didn't need them," Carter said. "Apparently Venus had some cosmetic work done and the overnight knows someone at the manufacturer..."

Gertie looked over at Ida Belle. "I told you her boobs were bigger when she came back. Of course, I heard her tell someone in the café that it was a push-up bra. I knew that wasn't a push-up bra. She lied about everything."

"Your knowledge of bras and fake boobs is astounding," Ida Belle said. "But I think there's a more important point here."

"Anyway," Carter said. "I was on my way to Percy's and saw Ida Belle's vehicle here, so I thought I'd let you guys know. It's going to spread fast enough once I make a statement and I'll be doing that after church."

"Should do it before," Ida Belle said. "It would be a more efficient way to spread it around. You know, save all the locals the time of having to make excuses to drop by and call people when they really just want the scoop."

"I'm not really worried about making Sinful more efficient at spreading gossip." He frowned. "Speaking of which, should I even ask what you guys are doing over here this early?"

"Said the word 'illegal' and summoned him," Francis said.

I struggled to maintain a straight face. Ida Belle didn't even try. She broke out in a huge I-told-you-so grin.

Carter's eyes widened as he finally realized Gertie and I were standing in front of a huge cage. "What's that?"

Gertie stepped aside, beaming. "This is Francis. My new housemate."

Carter stepped up to the cage and peered in at Francis. "Good morning."

Francis cocked his head to the side. "Good morning. We're plotting something illegal."

Carter turned around and narrowed his eyes. "What are you plotting?"

Ida Belle bent over the recliner, laughing so hard she couldn't stand up anymore. I lost all ability to remain neutral and started laughing as well.

"Gertie thought it would be a good idea to buy the bird from a police auction," I said, creating cover for today and every day in the future. "Apparently, they didn't want to keep the bird as evidence, but they were okay with the weapons and money. Who knows what he's going to say."

"She lied about everything," Francis said.

Carter glanced back at Francis, then shook his head. "You are the only person I know who would buy a talking bird that criminals owned."

"Nuns owned him first," I said. "Maybe it will all balance out."

"I'll pray for you," Francis said.

"Thanks," Carter said. "I could use all the prayer I can get with these three around."

"Jason Momoa is the hottest guy ever," Francis said.

Carter raised one eyebrow.

Ida Belle started laughing again. I grinned. "You know how those nuns talk."

"I'm going to leave before I hear something I'm required to take action on," Carter said.

"Make sure he doesn't leave Florida," Francis said.

As soon as Carter shut the door behind him, Ida Belle came up for air. "Don't say I didn't tell you so. That bird and your mouth are a problem waiting to happen."

"When does the dynamite arrive?" Francis asked.

"Thank God he waited for Carter to leave before he came

out with that one," I said. "Make sure that bird doesn't spend any quality time with local law enforcement."

Gertie waved a hand in dismissal. "Stop your worrying. It's just a bird...but maybe I'll turn on *Sunday Revival* kinda loud, and we'll eat our muffins in the breakfast nook with the living room door closed."

"The only good idea you've had today," Ida Belle said and headed for the kitchen.

CHAPTER FIVE

THAT AFTERNOON, we were all sitting in my backyard, drinking sweet tea and looking out over the water. After the Great Bird Reveal, we'd all gone to church where I'd enjoyed one of those naps where your eyes are open but your mind goes blank, then had lunch at Francine's, per our usual Sunday schedule. The only difference was there wasn't a banana pudding run today because there was no banana pudding. Apparently, Francine needed the refrigeration space for Thanksgiving goodies she was offering the entire week. Plenty of people at church and the café were talking about the body in the concrete, but the fact that it was Venus hadn't yet made the rounds.

Ida Belle dropped me off after lunch and I ran through a bunch of chores that I'd been ignoring. By the time Ida Belle and Gertie showed up with a batch of Gertie's homemade caramel brownies, I'd already cleaned the bathrooms, mopped the floors, and done two loads of laundry. I was contemplating giving the refrigerator a good scouring when they knocked on the door, saving me from a life of certain domestic boredom.

"Have you seen Godzilla lately?" Gertie asked as we headed for the backyard.

I shook my head. "No. Thank goodness. I can't have that gator hanging around my yard. Ronald is still trying to figure out a way to sue me over the last time."

My next-door neighbor, Ronald J. Franklin Jr., was an eccentric who wore crazy outfits, didn't like most people, and absolutely hated me. He'd lost a pair of designer pumps to Gertie's "pet" gator and was still mad that a lawyer wouldn't take his case. The fact that he was trespassing in my yard when it happened, Godzilla was a wild animal, and I was a former CIA agent with a former federal prosecutor as my personal attorney prevented anyone with two brain cells from giving Ronald more than a cursory chat. But apparently, Ronald was really passionate about those shoes and was still trying to find someone with nothing to lose.

"I've been out a couple days this past week looking at all his old haunts," Gertie said, "but I can't find him anywhere."

"Maybe he went looking for a girlfriend," I said.

"They don't do that until April," Gertie said.

"He might have found new territory," Ida Belle said. "Or got tired of your cooking."

Gertie sighed. "I guess so. But I miss him."

"I'm sure he's fine," I said. "And he belongs in the bayou eating fish. Not in your house eating chicken casserole. Besides, he'd make a snack out of Francis in a second."

"I suppose you're right," Gertie said. "But he sure was fun."

"Something tells me he'll be back," I said.

"Why do you think that?" Gertie asked.

"Because it's you and he's trouble," I said.

Gertie brightened. "That's a good point."

I looked over at Ida Belle. "You're kinda quiet today. What's up?"

Ida Belle shrugged. "Nothing really."

"She's bored," Gertie said.

I nodded. "I can appreciate that. I mean, the whole turkey run fiasco was rather entertaining but it didn't last long. Do you want to go fishing?"

"Water's too muddy for fishing," Ida Belle said. "We'd just wind up sitting there with no bites. Might as well stay here and not have to bother with loading up all the gear."

While my growing understanding of local fishing said she was right, there was something in her tone that was off. Regardless of what Gertie might think, something was up with Ida Belle besides boredom. But since Ida Belle played things as close to the vest as I did, nothing short of the Jaws of Life or Jesus would be able to pry it out of her until she was ready. So I made a mental note to keep watch—as if I needed a reminder to notice things—and changed the subject.

"Any word on how Percy took the news?" I asked.

"One of the Sinful Ladies is a third cousin," Ida Belle said. "They're not close—Percy's not close to anyone, really—but I gave her the news after lunch and she headed over to see if there was anything she could do. Percy wouldn't even let her in the house. Said he had things to do and he didn't need any help with funeral arrangements. He shut the door before she could even respond."

"Everyone grieves differently?" I suggested.

"I doubt he's grieving so much as he is angry," Gertie said. "He might get around to feeling bad about things later on, but right now, he's probably thinking Venus managed to cause trouble in every aspect of her life, and her death is no different."

Ida Belle nodded. "I imagine Percy figured he'd lost Venus completely when she ran off to New Orleans the first time. He probably reconciled himself to it then. I don't think he ever expected that she was back in Sinful to stay, so he probably never allowed himself to get involved in her life again other than allowing her to stay under his roof."

"You don't think..." I shook my head. "Never mind. I don't even want to go there."

"That Percy took his daughter out?" Ida Belle finished my thought. "I honestly don't know. I wouldn't say that he's ever struck me as the kind of man that has low morals where that sort of thing is concerned. And I've never heard that he had a temper, but Venus managed to bring it out in a lot of people I thought were beyond it."

"Venus brought out the worst side of everyone she came in contact with," Gertie said.

"Besides," Ida Belle said, "even if Percy could have done it, why would he?"

"She robbed him blind when she was in high school," Gertie said. "Hocked anything of value. He kept his tools locked in his truck and finally stopped replacing the television. Didn't get another one until months after she took off."

"That's true enough," Ida Belle said. "But if he was unhappy with her shenanigans, seems like kicking her out would be the easier route. Not like she was a minor anymore."

"I wonder when Carter will get cause of death," I said.

"I haven't heard anything yet through my channels," Ida Belle said. "But given that the body was buried under concrete, and the ME's assistant is covering this weekend, I'm going to guess that everyone is waiting on the ME to come in tomorrow and give his opinion on the matter. Unless, of course, there was a bullet hole through her head or something. That would be easy enough to recognize."

"We would have heard about it already if there was," Gertie said. "The guys who helped get the body out of the ground aren't versed in forensics, but you can bet they all recognize bullet holes."

"True," Ida Belle agreed. "But that's also assuming they had a clear look at the head. I assume parts were probably encased in concrete and couldn't be seen."

"It's just like a Mafia movie," Gertie said. "Except it was a whole body and not just the feet, and the body was in the ground and not the water."

Ida Belle stared. "Yep. Just like a Mafia movie." She looked at me. "You heard anything else from Carter today?"

"Just a short call to say he was working and he'd get in touch when he could. I think there was a break-in at the medical clinic last night, so he's got that to deal with on top of the Venus thing."

Ida Belle's phone rang and she pulled it out of her pocket.

"Hey, Myrtle," she answered.

Gertie and I perked up. Carter tried to be careful about Myrtle overhearing things because he knew it traveled straight to Ida Belle, but the walls in the sheriff's department were thin and the air vents carried sound, and Myrtle had been figuring out ways around Carter for a long time.

"Uh-huh," Ida Belle said. "Is that so? Well, that's interesting. Thanks for the information."

"Well?" Gertie asked as Ida Belle slipped the phone back in her pocket.

"Carter is bringing Percy in for official questioning," Ida Belle said.

"So the ME declared it a murder?" I asked.

"Myrtle doesn't know for sure," Ida Belle said.

"But if he's bringing Percy in for questioning..." Gertie said.

"Regardless of how she died, someone tried to hide the body," Ida Belle said. "That's still a crime. Venus was known to use drugs. She could have OD'd and someone found her and panicked. Decided to hide the body instead of deal with the cops."

"Surely Percy would have called the cops," I said. "He doesn't have anything like that to hide, does he?"

"I don't even know that Percy drinks," Gertie said. "I can't imagine him doing drugs."

Ida Belle frowned. "You're right. If Percy had found Venus that way, he would have called the police."

"Which means things just got interesting," Gertie said, getting excited. "So what are we going to do about it?"

"Nothing," Ida Belle said.

Gertie's face fell. "Why not?"

"Because there's nothing to be done," I said. "It's police business. We don't have a client asking us to poke our nose in and although I'm sure Percy is nice enough, I'm not going to get on Carter's bad side to try to help him out. Besides, getting an official statement from the person who Venus lived with sounds like protocol to me."

"You guys are no fun," Gertie said. "Hey, I've got an idea. I can hire you."

"And what would be the basis for acquiring my services?" I asked.

"Because if we had a case, Ida Belle probably wouldn't be so grumpy," Gertie said.

"While making sure your best friend is satisfied with all avenues of her life is a noble goal," I said, "I don't think Carter will buy it."

"I'm not grumpy," Ida Belle said.

"Did you hear your tone when you said that?" Gertie asked. "And look at your expression. Looks like you've been sucking on a lemon."

"Maybe my feet hurt," Ida Belle said. "Or maybe my underwear's too tight. Or maybe I was hoping we could get through one holiday in peace and quiet before things went south again. Things in this town are starting to worry me."

She rose from her chair and headed for the house. "I'm getting a refill. Yell if you want one."

Both Gertie and I glanced back to watch her walk away, but neither of us yelled for refills. When I heard the back door bang shut, I looked over at Gertie.

"What's up with her?" I asked. "You've known her since the crib. If anyone's going to know, you will."

Gertie frowned. "But I don't, and that concerns me. I agree with you that something's up, but she's not talking and I haven't overheard anything. I did see her talking to Walter on the sidewalk the other day. Things looked a bit tense."

"Any idea why?"

"The last time Ida Belle got really peeved at Walter was when he asked her to marry him again."

"When was that?"

"A couple years ago. He usually makes a run at it every two to three years. I wish she'd just say yes to the poor man. He's got to be miserable on some level, pining over her all these years."

"I think she's afraid marrying him would make him even more miserable."

"I know what she thinks," Gertie said, rather forcefully. She looked over at me and sighed. "She's never come out and said it, but I know she thinks her choices would send Walter into an early heart attack. Or worse, that if she made things legal, he'd think that meant he had a say in those choices."

I nodded.

When I was deliberating whether or not I could have a future with Carter, Ida Belle had confided in me her reasons and they pretty much matched what Gertie had surmised. I didn't necessarily agree with Ida Belle's beliefs in how things would go, but it wasn't my place to try to push a grown woman into doing something she was dead set against. Especially something as personal as marriage.

"Mind you," Gertie said, "I don't agree with her line of thinking. If Walter doesn't know by now that can't no one tell Ida Belle a single thing, he's the dumbest man in Sinful. And I happen to think Walter's pretty sharp. He just doesn't like to let on how much he knows."

"Yeah. But if Ida Belle is convinced, I don't think there's anything that's going to change her mind."

"Got that right," Gertie said. "Lord knows, I've spent more hours than I should have fighting that battle. Faith might be able to move mountains, but it's not shifting that woman's mind."

"Well, how long does it take her to get unpeeved when Walter's asked her before?"

"Couple days. A week or two. It varies. Maybe depending on how hard it is for her to say no. It seems it's getting harder as we've gotten older. Been worse since we've put a couple of friends in the grave. That's kinda why I was hoping we'd have a case to work on. I thought it might redirect her."

"Ha. You want a case to work on because you can't stand not being in the thick of things."

Gertie grinned. "And that. You know me too well."

"I'm getting there. But I'm afraid I can't come up with a viable reason to stick our necks out on this one. You're going to have to make do with an official police investigation and the local gossip train."

Gertie sighed. "Maybe Thanksgiving will perk her up. She really enjoys frying a turkey."

"I'm really looking forward to eating that turkey. I've never had it fried before."

"Once you do, you'll never want a baked one again."

The back door banged again and several seconds later, Ida Belle plopped back down in her chair. She stared at the bayou, completely silent.

"Walter asked me to marry him again," she said finally.

Gertie gave me a knowing look. Bingo. She'd called that one correctly.

"I'll bake him a chocolate cake," Gertie said. "It's his favorite. Might take some of the sting out of the rejection."

Ida Belle looked over at us. "I didn't say no."

CHAPTER SIX

I HADN'T EVEN HAD time to recover from Ida Belle's bombshell statement when Deputy Breaux called out to us. We turned around and saw him walking across the backyard, a worried expression on his face.

"I'm so sorry, Ms. Hebert," he said. "But Carter asked me to bring you down to the sheriff's department."

"For what?" Gertie asked. "I haven't blown anything up in a while, and you can get a search warrant, but you're not going to find any dynamite at my house."

Deputy Breaux looked pained. "It's not the dynamite, ma'am, although I am relieved to hear you're currently low on inventory."

"Then what is this about?" Ida Belle said.

"I'm not allowed to talk about an ongoing investigation," he mumbled, staring at the ground.

"Ongoing?" Ida Belle asked. "The only thing you've got ongoing at the moment is the clinic break-in and Venus Thibodeaux. Gertie doesn't do drugs, thank the Lord. I don't even want to imagine the horror. And surely Carter doesn't think Gertie hauled that poor girl's body into that construction site."

"I'm not sure what he thinks," Deputy Breaux said. "He doesn't give me details, especially when he sends me out to do official business with any of you."

"Smart man," I said.

Ida Belle rose from her chair. "I guess we'd best go see what this is about."

Deputy Breaux's eyes widened. "I'm only supposed to bring Ms. Hebert in."

"You know that's not going to happen," Ida Belle said. "Might as well head back to the sheriff's department. We're right behind you."

Ida Belle strode off for the house. Deputy Breaux looked momentarily confused, but then must have figured that was as good as he was getting. He gave us a nod and headed off.

"I suppose we have to put on shoes," I said.

Gertie sighed. "And a bra. I was really looking forward to keeping my bra off the rest of the day."

"So do it. If Carter drags you into the sheriff's department for some silly crap, why should you care if he has to face you in your 'afternoon off' clothes?"

"What if I have to do a mug shot?"

"Did you kill Venus?" I asked.

"Of course not."

"Then I think you're good."

"I'm still going to put on my bra. You never know when you might run into a hot man who is in need of an equally hot woman."

I stared. "In Sinful? At the sheriff's department?"

"You're right. Maybe just a thicker T-shirt."

"I'm wearing flip-flops and I'm not even going to comb my hair."

"Are you going to put on your bra?"

I shook my head. "The only man I put my bra on for on a Sunday is Jesus."

Gertie grinned. "Rebel."

Carter looked less than thrilled but not surprised when the three of us came walking in behind Deputy Breaux.

"Sorry, sir." Deputy Breaux began his apologies, but Carter waved a hand at him.

"Don't worry about it," Carter said. "They're above your pay grade."

The young deputy looked confused but also relieved as he strolled off to his desk.

Carter looked at Gertie. "I don't suppose there's any chance of questioning you alone."

"What's the point?" Gertie asked. "I'm just going to tell them everything anyway. Heck, I might text them from the interrogation room."

He sighed and pointed down the hall. We followed him back to the room they used for interrogations, conferences, and the occasional team lunch and all took seats on the opposite side of the table from Carter.

He reached for an envelope on the table and pulled a plastic bag out of it. Something gold and shiny glittered inside. He pushed the plastic bag across the table to Gertie.

"Do you recognize that?"

She picked up the plastic bag and her eyes widened. "That's my locket. I've been looking everywhere for this. I thought the clasp must have broken at church. That's the last place I had it on before I realized it was gone."

Then she frowned and looked at Carter. "You made me put on shoes and a thicker T-shirt just to give me back my own jewelry?"

"I think there might be more to it than that," I said. "Or it wouldn't be in an evidence bag. Sort of."

"Evidence?" Gertie said. "This is a sandwich bag."

"Apparently, there was a problem with supply delivery down at the ME's office," Carter said. "They had to improvise."

Gertie's eyes widened. "ME's office? You mean? This was..."

"I'm afraid so," he said.

"But how?" Gertie asked.

"That's what I need to find out from you," Carter said.

"Oh, good grief," Ida Belle said, clearly frustrated. "You can't possibly think Gertie offed the girl and lost her locket when she was shoving her body in a hole. Gertie couldn't even lift Venus. And I want you to think really hard before you say something stupid like 'she could have had help' because I'm in no mood for stupid today."

Carter raised his hands. "I'm not saying any of that. But the fact is Gertie's property was found with Venus's body and I have to figure out why so I can document it."

"Why in the world are you making this so difficult?" I asked. "Obviously, it broke and fell off Gertie's neck and Venus found it. Maybe she was going to return it."

"Doubt it," Ida Belle grumbled.

"The problem with that theory is that the necklace wasn't broken," Carter said. "The clasp is fine and there are no breaks in the chain."

Suddenly, Gertie jumped up from her chair, her face red. "That little witch!"

I grabbed her sleeve and tugged her back into her chair. "Not a good look for this particular line of questioning."

"Sorry, but I'm not apologizing for it, either," Gertie said. "I got a call about an eBay order when we were in Francine's after church and went outside to take it. When I was finishing up, I saw Venus coming up the sidewalk. I hadn't bumped into her yet on her return visit so she stopped and chatted for a minute, which I thought was odd. But it was Sunday and I was feeling charitable. Then she hugged me. That must have been when the witch...er, Venus stole my locket."

"That sounds about right," Ida Belle said.

Carter sighed.

"Look," Ida Belle said. "I know it's the South and we're all 'don't speak ill of the dead,' but the truth is the truth. Venus had a habit of lifting things she could hock and you know it. I don't think any of us believe for a minute that she hightailed it back to Sinful because she had a religious experience and changed her ways."

"If she'd had a religious experience, she would have been in church that Sunday," I said.

"Guys, I'm not disagreeing with anything you're saying," Carter said. "In fact, I'm inclined to agree that it probably happened just as Gertie thinks. I just need to put down the facts for the report."

"You don't think Gertie's going to catch any trouble over this, do you?" I asked. "Because I can get her an attorney."

"No," Carter said. "Let's not call in the big guns unless necessary. This is just something that came up in the course of the investigation and it has to be documented. I don't see it going any further than this. I just want to get all the administrative BS out of the way so I can concentrate on the investigation."

"Do you have cause of death?" I asked, not ready to let go of the potential for this to blow up in our faces.

"Yes," Carter said.

We all stared but Carter was silent.

"Well, at least tell us if Gertie's locket was a witness to a murder," I said.

"You know I can't do that," Carter said.

I slumped back in my chair. "You could if it wasn't homicide."

Ida Belle rose from her chair. "I guess that brings us all up to speed. You have Gertie's statement. Get it typed up and she'll be back to sign it."

Ida Belle exited the room, leaving all of us staring after her.

"Is she all right?" Carter asked.

"Peachy," I said, not about to clue Carter in on the fact that his uncle had sprung the marriage question on Ida Belle again and this time she hadn't said no. Gertie and I hadn't had a chance to get the whole story from Ida Belle yet, and no way was I going to send Carter down an avenue of thought that might be incorrect. Not to mention that unless or until Ida Belle declared that particular bit of information up for public consumption, it would remain in my tight-lipped vault. Not even Carter could get past it.

Gertie had tried to wheedle more out of Ida Belle on the ride to the sheriff's department, but she'd ignored the question, stating that we needed to focus on whatever nonsense Carter was up to now. Then she'd gone into silent mode.

Gertie and I rose from our chairs and Gertie looked over at Carter.

"When can I get my locket back?" she asked.

"Not just yet, I'm afraid," Carter said. "I need to clear up some things first."

"Surely you don't have to hold it until the investigation is over," I said.

"No. But I need to be a little further along with things," he said.

"Please take good care of it," Gertie said. "My mother gave it to me. I retraced my steps for hours looking for it."

"I will put it in the safe," Carter promised.

Gertie nodded and we headed out.

"I'm really sorry about your locket," I said. "Why didn't you tell Ida Belle? I'm sure she would have helped you look."

Gertie shrugged. "She couldn't have done anything that I hadn't already done. I searched every inch of the church and walked my exact route to Francine's. No one turned in a locket to either place, and if someone had found it on the street, they would have asked Walter or Carter about it. Either would have called me immediately."

"She could have had a drink with you and commiserated," I said.

"Guess we don't need to anymore since it's found," Gertie said.

We stepped outside and spotted Ida Belle, already sitting in her SUV waiting on us.

"What are we going to do about her?" I asked, feeling completely out of my element.

"Heck if I know."

"What do you mean you don't know? She's your best friend. How have you handled this sort of thing before?"

"I haven't. She's always said no."

Ida Belle honked the horn and gestured to us to hurry up.

Gertie sighed. "This afternoon just got a lot less peaceful."

No one seemed to be interested in sitting on the lawn any longer, and since the breeze had disappeared and the humidity had moved in, I wasn't about to argue. Ida Belle and Gertie took a seat at my kitchen table and then both of them just perched there, silently. I put the beers I was grabbing back in the refrigerator and reached for the bottle of whiskey I had bought on our last trip to New Orleans. I poured generous amounts into three glasses and sat them all on the table. They didn't even raise an eyebrow. Just lifted the glasses and knocked back the servings.

"I guess I better bring the bottle to the table," I said and got up to grab it off the counter.

I poured another round for the two of them and took a sip of mine. They started on the second round slower than the first, which was a relief as I'd only bought one bottle. But no one seemed eager to talk, and I was practically itching for someone to break the silence.

"Okay," I said finally. "You know I like a little peace and quiet more than most, but this is so uncomfortable I might have to list my house and move."

"I'm sorry," Gertie said. "I'm sitting here stewing over my necklace, even though I know it's a waste of time. I can't change the fact that Venus stole it right off my neck or that it's sitting in a sandwich bag in the sheriff's department."

"If it makes you feel any better, I think both of those things suck," I said.

Gertie gave me a grateful smile. "They do. But I think I'm focusing on them to ignore the real problem."

"And what's that?" I asked.

"That she didn't notice Venus stealing it." Ida Belle finally broke her silence.

"Oh." I slumped back in my chair. I hadn't even thought of that angle but I could totally see why she was stewing over it. I would be too.

"I just hate admitting that I might be slipping," Gertie said. "I know I always joke about being young and living to be two hundred, but things like this just highlight what a far-fetched fantasy I'm pushing."

"You need to give yourself a break," Ida Belle said. "Did you think Venus had turned over a new leaf and was living on the straight and narrow?"

"Of course not," Gertie said.

"And did you really think she was happy to see you and that show of affection was genuine?" Ida Belle asked.

"No," Gertie said. "I thought she was prepping me for something else. Maybe hitting me up for money or asking me for help with a job."

"Exactly," Ida Belle said. "You thought she was working an angle because as long as Venus was conscious, she *was* working an angle. You just didn't clue in that it was an immediate one. You thought she was putting out a marker that she was going to try to call later on."

Gertie brightened a little. "That's exactly right. So maybe I'm not losing it altogether. I just miscalculated her target and the speed she intended to acquire it. That sounds much better than 'she got one over on me because I'm getting old.'"

Ida Belle gave her hand a squeeze. "If age is really a mental state, like some believe, then you're still a teenager. Your body might not have gotten the message, but there's nothing wrong with your mind."

Gertie smiled. "By God, you're right. I don't know what I was thinking. And I'm not sure where you were going with that whole body thing. I'm practically a *Ninja Warrior* contestant."

"And she's back," Ida Belle said.

"Darn tootin'," Gertie said. "So now that things are back in line with me, let's address the elephant in the room. You can't just deliver a statement like 'I didn't say no' and then refuse to talk about it."

I nodded. "I gotta go with Gertie on this one. You watch television with us. You know how we hate a cliff-hanger."

Ida Belle's lips quivered. "I suppose I don't want to be responsible for you two tossing and turning tonight."

"So spill," I said. "Did you set a date?"

"Nothing like that," Ida Belle said. "I didn't say yes. I just didn't say no, either."

"What does that even mean?" Gertie asked.

"It means I told him I'd think about it," Ida Belle said as she rose from the table. "I've got to drop off some spare boat parts to Scooter. You want to leave now, Gertie?"

"No," Gertie said. "I think I'll stick around for a bit longer. Drink some more of Fortune's whiskey and maybe talk her into breaking out those brownies again."

Ida Belle nodded. "Then I guess I'll see you two tomorrow. We're still doing breakfast, right?"

"Nine o'clock at Francine's," I said.

She headed out of the kitchen and Gertie and I stared at each other until we heard the front door close.

"What the heck?" I asked as soon as the door clicked shut.

Gertie shook her head. "I'm as confused as you are."

"You think she might really go for it this time?"

"I can't imagine that she would...not after all these years. But then, Ida Belle would never play with Walter's feelings, either. So if she says she's thinking about it, then that's what she's doing. But I have no guesses as to why now or what the outcome will be."

"Well, if you don't know, there's no way I'm figuring it out."

"Thank goodness no one will be hiring us to solve this mystery."

CARTER HAD INVITED me over for dinner the week before, and despite the fact that he looked as though he'd rather be napping in his hammock than cooking, he did a fine job grilling up some pork chops and baked potatoes. Since he always bought pork chops that looked as if they'd been cut from a dinosaur, both Tiny and I were stuffed by the time we piled the dishes in the sink. Carter carefully avoided any talk of Venus but I could tell that another murder in Sinful was weighing on him. We watched a little television and called it a night fairly early.

After the amount of calories I'd consumed at dinner, I should have been halfway into a food coma by the time I got home, but instead, I was restless. I tried watching television but kept getting up and walking into one room or another, then glancing around, looking for something to do. Unfortunately, I'd been on a cleaning and organizing kick lately and everything was pretty much set. Finally, I plopped down at the kitchen table with my laptop, somewhat concerned that the lack of a load of laundry was now a disappointment.

Maybe I'd do some online shopping. I needed a filing cabinet for when I finally had enough clients to create files. So far, my only detective work conducted as a pro had been when Carter asked me to launch an investigation when he got kicked off a case by the state police. But since that was an unofficial, off-the-books, no-invoice sort of deal, I still didn't have a file for my yet-unobtained cabinet.

Ida Belle had assured me the business would come. People just needed to wrap their minds around me being a former CIA agent and not the librarian they'd thought I was, and then the phone would start ringing. Of course, she'd also informed me that I'd probably get a lot of calls for lost reading glasses, missing cats, and sketchy husbands, but I figured that was par for the course for a place like Sinful. It couldn't all be high crime, and I didn't want it to be. I just wanted puzzles to solve. They didn't need to have a deadly component to occupy my mind.

I located a cool four-drawer that was a good match for my other office furniture and stuck it in my shopping cart. Now I just had to decide on file folders and hanging files. Did I want standard beige folders and green files or did I feel whimsical and thus should order the multicolored ones? Since Gertie had volunteered to help me with any of the administrative sort of stuff, I decided to go with the multicolored and located a set with bright pink, turquoise, purple, green, and a yellow so bright you could probably see it from space.

I was just finishing up my purchase when I heard a noise in my backyard. Noises at night weren't unusual. I did live on a bayou and all manner of critters roamed around at night. But this was different. Something large had brushed against the side of my house. And it was too high up on the wall to be a dog.

My back porch light wasn't on. I'd stopped turning it on a while back when I realized all it did was call to every bug on the bayou and ask them to hang out on my porch. I stepped into a crunch of dead bugs every morning when I'd go outside with my coffee. Or worse. Sometimes the small bugs attracted larger bugs, like huge spiders. Or snakes. Since I wasn't interested in hosting a nightly party on my back porch or walking out to the remains of the night the morning after, I had made the executive decision to leave the backyard cast in darkness.

That meant peeking through the blinds wouldn't yield anything except tipping off whoever was back there that I'd heard them. That was the last thing I wanted to do. I grabbed my nine-millimeter off the kitchen table and hurried out of the kitchen and to my front door. I suppose I could have just opened the back door and yelled at whoever was lurking around, but I didn't like peepers and preferred to scare them into never creeping around my property again. I found that a gun leveled at their forehead tended to do the trick.

I hurried around to the rear of the house and paused at the corner, listening. I heard footsteps going up my porch steps and slipped into the hedges that lined the back wall of the house and crept toward the door. The sliver of moon provided just enough light to cast a dim glow around the shadowy figure standing on my porch.

Six foot two. Two hundred twenty pounds. Probably male. Never going to lurk around my property again.

I crouched at the edge of the porch, then sprang up, leveling my gun at the trespasser.

CHAPTER SEVEN

"THERE'S a gun pointing directly at your chest," I said. "I suggest you don't move."

Normally, I'd go for the headshot. That was sorta my training. But since I wasn't sure I needed to kill anyone, I figured I'd be conservative about things. A red dot on a chest was easily seen by the target and let people know you meant business.

"Whoa!" he said, his hands flying up in the air. "Don't shoot. It's Whiskey. From the Swamp Bar. I just wanted to talk to you."

"Whiskey?" I said.

I stepped out of the bushes and squinted into the dim light. The build was right and the voice sounded familiar. I hit the tactical light on my pistol and lifted it to his face. A very concerned-looking Whiskey held one hand over his eyes and left the other one in the air.

I lowered my gun. I knew Whiskey was capable of being a threat but I couldn't imagine that he had a problem with me.

"Are you crazy?" I asked. "You could have been shot."

"I'm definitely crazy," he said. "Ask most anyone. And I'm starting to see the seriousness of the coulda-been-shot thing."

"What the heck are you doing lurking around my house at 11:00 p.m.?"

"I needed to talk to you but I didn't want to wake you up. I was trying to see if you were still up. I couldn't get away from the bar earlier, but things finally slowed down and I was able to run off the few regulars that were still there and close up early."

"Have you heard of a telephone?" I asked. "It's this cool invention that allows you to talk to people without getting shot."

"Yeah, maybe that would have been a better choice."

I shook my head. "Well, you better come inside before Ronald notices and launches another campaign to get me arrested or figures out some way to sue me for having guests after his bedtime."

Whiskey laughed and followed me around to the front door and then inside. "That dude is a piece of work. You know he came into the Swamp Bar one time."

I came to a dead stop and turned around and stared. "No."

Whiskey nodded. "Swear to God. Came in dripping wet. At first, I thought maybe a storm had come up and got him in the parking lot, but I looked outside and it was still clear as day."

"So...?"

He grinned. "Said he'd heard it was wet T-shirt night, and as he'd never been to a wet T-shirt party, he thought he should go and check it off his bucket list."

"He did not!"

"I couldn't make something like that up. Even when I'm drunk, I'm not that creative."

"And how did he react when you explained what wet T-shirt night really was?"

"He turned white as a sheet, then beet red, then started gasping like he couldn't breathe. I was about to call for the paramedics. I thought the dude was having a heart attack. Then he wags his finger at me, like I'm ten years old or something, and says he'll pray for me."

I grinned and waved him into the kitchen. "Beer?"

"I wouldn't turn one down. It's been a really weird day."

I pulled out a beer for Whiskey and a soda for myself and took a seat across from him. I'd first come into contact with Whiskey during our investigative excursions to the Swamp Bar, but we'd never really had much to say to each other until recently. Of course, sometimes I'd been to the bar in disguise and most of the time, we'd had to run out of there before we had to fight or participate in a gun duel. And then there was the time Gertie stole a boat at the bar and led everyone on a merry chase. Whiskey still didn't know who'd done it, though. Thank goodness.

Given that the limited knowledge I had of him mostly included illegal activities or the propensity for violence, I suppose I should have asked him to make an appointment and come back during daylight. But curiosity had overridden good sense. Whatever had him closing the bar early and lurking outside my windows had to be good. And I wanted to know what it was. Plus, even though Whiskey was a big guy, he wasn't all that fast. I'd taken down bigger.

"So what did you need to talk to me about?" I asked.

"You're one of those PIs, right?"

"Yes."

"I suppose you heard about Venus Thibodeaux."

I nodded.

"Good. I need you to find out who killed her."

I frowned. "Investigating murders is more of a police detective thing."

"Yeah, well, I don't like cops."

"I can appreciate that. But I don't understand why you want me to investigate. What's your interest?"

"Because I don't want it pinned on me."

"Do you have reason to think it might be?"

"You mean aside from Carter dragging me down to the sheriff's department this afternoon and questioning me for a good hour?"

"But he didn't arrest you."

"No. But I think it's coming."

"I know Venus worked at the Swamp Bar and the two of you were, uh, involved."

"Ha. *Involved.* Is that what they call it these days when someone's taking you for a ride?"

"It is if everyone else thought you were dating."

He shook his head. "Yeah, I guess so. Look, Venus was like sugar to a diabetic. You couldn't help but want her, but she was toxic. I should have known better than to get hooked up with her. Hell, the truth is I did know better."

"But you couldn't resist."

He gave me a sheepish look. "Guess not. Stupid, right?"

"Probably. Particularly in light of current circumstances."

"Yeah. I wonder sometimes if Nickel hadn't been in jail when Venus blew back into town, if he could have talked some sense into me. But as usual, he wasn't around when things went sideways. He can't seem to manage more than a few months out at a time before he screws up something and they haul him back to New Orleans for an extended visit."

I frowned, feeling sorry for Whiskey. His situation would be a lot easier if his brother got his life straight. "So why do you think Carter is going to arrest you? Dating someone isn't a crime, even if they're not worth the effort."

"I was one of the last people to see her the night she was

killed. And I might have told her I'd strangle her if I ever saw her again."

"Well, that's unfortunate. Especially if it turns out she was strangled."

"Carter wouldn't say."

"No. I don't expect he would. Why did you threaten her?"

"Caught her stealing from the till, the customers, the stock. Pretty much had her hands in everything. I drew the line when I saw 'em on a customer's pants. And she wasn't looking for his wallet, if you catch my drift."

"Wow. Okay. That's pretty awful. Did anyone overhear your threat?"

"Everyone in the bar."

I sighed. "Maybe next time, you can think about that whole witness thing before you get going."

"That would probably be a good idea."

I wasn't sure what was more disconcerting—that Whiskey was allowing me to point out just how foolish he'd been without even a hint of anger or argument or that he was certain he'd be in the same position again.

"So how are you sure she was killed that night?"

"Because they poured the basketball court the next day."

"Well, that certainly narrows down time of death."

He nodded. "I went by her dad's place a couple days later when I didn't hear anything from her. Still had her final paycheck to issue even though she'd probably lifted five times that from the register. He told me she'd cleared out while he was at work and sent a text saying she was going back to New Orleans."

"And given what you know now, you don't think that's odd?"

"What do you mean?"

"If we assume Percy is telling the truth, then someone let

themself into Percy's house, packed up Venus's things, and sent a text from her phone."

Whiskey's eyes widened. "The killer."

"I can't imagine it would be anyone else."

He whistled. "Now that you lay it out, whoever it was had some seriously big balls. I mean, to stroll in that man's house and take her things out. I know he was at work, but this is Sinful. I can't believe someone didn't see something."

I nodded. That had been the one sticking point that had been bugging me as well. It was possible someone had sneaked in that night and packed up Venus's stuff without waking Percy, but it wasn't overly likely. Packing and toting luggage around made noise. Opening windows and doors made noise. Unless Percy slept like the dead, I found it hard to believe that had been the case. Which left a daytime visit and no witnesses.

In Sinful.

It didn't exactly add up.

"I know you don't like cops," I said, "and I can appreciate that. But you don't really think Carter will arrest you without good reason, do you?"

He shrugged. "Carter's all right. He's always played things fair as far as I can tell. But it's not up to him, is it? Carter gathers information. The DA decides whether or not to file charges. And with my record, how do you think that's going to pan out for me?"

"Maybe not good."

"Exactly. You know my situation. Even if they can't make anything stick, I don't have the money for bail. Not for a murder rap, and that's assuming the judge would even set bail. And if I'm locked up, then so is the bar, which means no money coming in and no one to take care of my pops."

"What about Nickel?" In addition to being Whiskey's brother, Nickel was co-owner of the bar.

"Nickel's doing two months on a probation violation. Again."

I blew out a breath. Whiskey's situation was fairly grim. With his prior record and his threat against Venus the night she disappeared, he was a prime candidate for the DA to target. Whiskey's father had cancer and needed the money and care his son provided. Locking Whiskey up might mean an actual death sentence for his father.

"I got money to pay you," Whiskey said. "I ain't asking for nothing for free."

"It's not about the money," I said.

"You're not worried about pissing Carter off, are you? Because you didn't strike me as the type to care what no one else thought."

"That's fairly accurate. But it's not the reason for my hesitation. I guess I'm afraid to take the case because a lot is riding on it and I might fail."

"Then all we can say is we gave it our best shot. Those two ladies you run around with know most of what goes on in this town and probably suspect a lot of what they don't see outright. And I figure with your background, you won't shy away from trying to corner a killer. That's as good a bet as I can make."

"You promise you won't shoot me if I don't figure out who killed her?"

He smiled. "I know your type. You're like a dog with a bone. If you can't figure it out, then no one's going to. And no way would I pull a gun on you unless I'm a good hundred yards away and your back is turned."

"Okay, then consider yourself a client." I reached across the table and extended my hand and he shook it. "I'll put together a contract for you to sign and figure out a retainer. I can drop by the bar with it tomorrow, if you want."

"Sounds good." He rose from the table. "I'm sorry about the creeping around. Probably not the smartest thing I've ever done given your former profession."

"Probably not the smartest thing to do given that this is Louisiana and most people are armed to the hilt."

He grinned. "That too. I'll see you tomorrow. And thanks for doing this."

"No problem. Oh, and Whiskey? You're not the last person to see Venus that night."

"I'm not?"

I shook my head. "Whoever killed her was."

CHAPTER EIGHT

I JUMPED out of bed the next morning, practically giddy. I even hummed while I was making coffee. Then I felt just a tad guilty because my happiness centered on my new case, which centered on an innocent man potentially being brought up on a murder charge. The guilt, however, was temporary and then I was back to humming.

After Whiskey had left, I'd showered and gone to bed, but I hadn't slept. Instead, I'd rolled around questions and scenarios and wild thoughts for hours before finally drifting off. But the one thing I'd decided I was set on was Whiskey's innocence. Not that I didn't think he was capable of throttling someone to death—especially someone who dipped into the till, his wallet, the bar's inventory, and a customer's pants—but I simply couldn't picture him killing a woman. It was quite sexist of me, but I had a feeling that despite hiring me, Whiskey wasn't exactly the most progressive male in Sinful.

And why would he hire me if he'd done it? There was no way he'd be clever enough to cover it up. His past arrests were a testament to his inability to avoid detection. And those were for relatively minor things like poaching. No way had his IQ jumped up ten points just because his girlfriend went fishing in another man's pants.

On paper, Whiskey looked good for it, but that's where it ended. At least, that's where it ended for me. The DA was a whole other story. I had a feeling that his take would be a lot different from mine, which meant the first order of business was to find another suspect. It might not prevent the DA from filing charges, but it could buy a delay. Any delay allowed us more time to get to the truth.

Once the coffee finished, I took the entire pot into my office, along with a stack of cookies. Breakfast wasn't for two more hours and no way I was going to make it until then. I'd just scarf down the cookies and coffee while drawing up the contract, and then I'd have a jog to work them off before I headed to the café to load up on something that would almost certainly require another round of jogging.

I made it to the café at 8:59, paperwork on my passenger seat and jog complete. I couldn't wait to tell Ida Belle and Gertie that we had a case. They were already inside, occupying our usual table in the back corner. Ally waved at me as I walked in, and then she headed for the kitchen. She knew what we all drank, so the only thing she needed from us was the breakfast order, which varied some depending on café specials and our general mood. I varied mine some based on the amount of exercise I'd done, but as I'd put in three miles this morning, I felt an order of blueberry pancakes was in my immediate future.

Ida Belle and Gertie both greeted me as I sat and I gave them both a once-over. Ida Belle didn't look quite as tense as she'd been the day before, but Gertie looked a wreck. She'd rolled her hair but hadn't made it all the way around picking it out. Two giant rollers remained on the back of her head. She'd put green eye shadow on one eye and blue on the other, which would work fine in a café in New Orleans but stuck out a little in Sinful.

Ida Belle caught my glance and waved a hand. "Don't bother. I've already told her and she refuses to wipe it off."

"Do you have any idea how hard it was to get it on in the first place?" Gertie asked.

"Why is that?" I asked. "You look like you fought a war last night."

"If it was War of the Words, then I did," Gertie said.

"Was Francis feeling chatty?" I asked.

"That bird started quoting Bible verses at midnight. I swear, he knows more of them than I do. And at the end of every one, he does this huge squawking 'amen.' I'd barely manage to doze off, then scramble back up thinking I fell asleep in church."

"Surely he didn't do that all night," I said.

She shook her head. "When he ran out of verses, he started preaching...in Latin. He also knows a ton of hymns. He can't carry a tune though."

I grinned. "Maybe he's just going for the 'make a joyful noise' thing."

"Nothing about a bird singing at 3:00 a.m. is joyful," Gertie said.

"I told you that bird was a bad idea," Ida Belle said.

"Did you cover his cage before you went to bed?" I asked.

"No," Gertie said. "I turned out the lights. It was plenty dark."

"Not dark enough for an animal that belongs in a jungle," I said. "Jungles don't have red lights on alarms and street light trickling through blinds. Trust me, I've been there. It's pitch-black."

Gertie's eyes widened. "You've been in a jungle at night?"

"It was work related," I said.

"Ah," Gertie said. "So tossing a blanket over his cage will keep him from evangelizing all night?"

"I can't make any promises," I said. "But it certainly wouldn't hurt to give it a try."

"I'll get my darkest, heaviest blanket," Gertie said. "And leave it open in the back for air flow."

"Did you see much wildlife when you were on your business trip?" Ida Belle asked.

"A ton," I said. "But when you're alone and on foot, it's a bit scarier than sitting in one of those Hummers and looking at everything through thick glass."

"At least you were armed," Gertie said.

"Yeah, but I was also supposed to be silent," I said. "Shooting before you're supposed to tends to draw attention. I walked right up on a den of tigers one night. Thank goodness, they'd just finished devouring something huge. I think they were all half asleep and too lazy to move."

"Wow," Gertie said. "That's so cool. I mean, in a could-have-gone-horribly-wrong sort of way. You never told us you'd been anywhere but the Middle East."

"Because she's not supposed to tell us anything at all," Ida Belle said.

"It was just the one trip," I said. "Sometimes odd allegiances are formed among certain people. A road trip can offer up a two-for-one."

Ally slid coffee in front of all of us and gave us a huge smile. "It's great to see you ladies this morning. Gertie, I'm sorry about your turkey getting away. I wish I could have seen it but we were short at the café and I couldn't ask off."

"It worked out much better for the turkey," Gertie said. "He didn't have to face Ida Belle."

Ally's smile faded. "Probably also good because that whole

other thing wouldn't have come to light if you hadn't pushed over that basketball goal."

"I assume Venus is the big topic of the morning," Ida Belle said.

Ally nodded. "People aren't talking about much else."

"And what are they saying?" I asked.

"That Venus was bound to come to a bad end with the choices she was making," Ally said. "That there's no shortage of people that she ripped off, lied to, or otherwise put in the red."

"And since the leopard doesn't change its spots," Ida Belle said, "I'm sure she took her show to New Orleans and collected a number there as well."

Ally's eyes widened. "I hadn't even thought about that. Maybe someone followed her here. Maybe it's not...you know."

I nodded. We got it. Ally didn't want the killer to be a local.

"Well, ladies," Ally said, forcing a smile again. "The special today is a four-cheese quiche. Until they're gone."

Ida Belle raised an eyebrow. "Fancy."

Ally blushed a bit. "It was my idea. I've been playing around with them some. I mean, if I ever get my bakery going, I figure it's a good idea to offer something with a little protein in it. People can't live off muffins and croissants alone."

"Speak for yourself," Gertie said.

"I'll try the quiche," I said.

"I figured you'd go for the blueberry pancakes with all that jogging you did this morning," Ida Belle said. "Saw you pass my house three times."

I grinned. "I'm getting those too."

"I'll try the quiche as well," Gertie said. "And a slice of banana nut bread."

"I'll have biscuits and gravy," Ida Belle said.

Ally took the orders down, flashed us a final smile, and hurried back to the kitchen.

Ida Belle looked over at me as I dumped sugar and cream into my coffee. Might as well live it up.

"You look peppy this morning," Ida Belle said. "I guess you got a full eight hours."

"Not even close," I said. "I had a late-night visitor and then I couldn't sleep."

Gertie grinned. "I don't think sleep is the point of a booty call."

"It wasn't Carter," I said.

Gertie's eyes widened. "You had another guy sniffing around?"

"In a manner of speaking," I said. "And he was interested in my services but only in a business capacity."

I told them about Whiskey's visit.

Gertie was practically bouncing in her seat before I finished. If she'd been capable of doing cartwheels, I'm pretty sure she would have done a round right there in the middle of the café.

"We have a case," she said gleefully.

Ida Belle had perked up a little at the introduction of a case, but she looked a bit more reserved about the prospect than Gertie.

"You think it was a good idea to take the job?" I asked her.

"If you're asking me if I think Whiskey killed Venus, then the answer no," Ida Belle said.

"Why not?" Gertie said. "He's capable. I believe he's capable, anyway."

"I have no doubt that he's capable," Ida Belle said. "But if Whiskey had done it, he'd have weighted the body and dumped it in the bayou. He wouldn't have left it at a construction site, hoping no one poked around in the dirt before pouring the concrete."

"That's a really good point," I said. "I think most people around here would know that a bayou dump is the way to go."

"So you think it's someone from New Orleans," Gertie said.

"Or someone who didn't have access to a boat," I said. "Or didn't have the physical ability to haul a body around that way."

"Or someone who didn't have the time to do things right," Ida Belle said. "The construction site could have been the easy and most efficient option, even though the risk of discovery was greater."

"So maybe someone who would have been missed," I said. "Especially as it was the middle of the night."

Gertie sighed. "That puts us right back to everyone as a suspect."

"Except Whiskey," Ida Belle said. "He had the time, the knowledge, and the physical ability to do it right and I have no doubt that if he ever does kill someone, that's exactly how he'll handle it."

"So we all agree he's good as a client?" I asked.

They both nodded and Ida Belle frowned.

"Hiring you might have been the smartest thing he's done in years," Ida Belle said. "When the DA gets a look at him on paper, he's going to salivate."

"Yeah, I figured," I said. "On paper, he's the perfect fit."

"Carter won't let them railroad the wrong man," Gertie said.

"Carter only has so much control," Ida Belle said. "Carter investigates, but the DA is the one who pulls the trigger."

"He does seem to have an itchy trigger finger," Gertie said. "So what's our first step?"

"Find another suspect," I said. "Or several suspects. We need to create enough doubt that the DA can't focus on Whiskey without a good defense attorney presenting other viable options."

"Where do we start?" Gertie asked.

"We need to create a profile for Venus," I said. "Which I see as two parts. The first is figuring out everything she was up to in Sinful. The second part is finding out why she came back."

Gertie clapped. "Road trip!"

"Sinful first," I said. "Then we'll tackle New Orleans."

"What do you need from us?" Ida Belle asked.

"A list of people to start with," I said. "Anyone that Venus had dealings with after she came back. And anyone who knew her reasonably well. I need insight as to what made her tick so we can figure out what kind of scams she might have been running."

Ida Belle nodded. "She wasn't what you'd call close to people, and it's going to be harder to get some of them to talk straight now that she's dead. But we can probably get a few to offer up the ugly truth. I suppose we have to start with Percy."

"Taking into account opportunity, he's the first potential suspect on my list," I said. "And given the situation with Gertie's locket, I don't figure we'll have to dig too deep to come up with motive."

"You don't really think he'd kill his own daughter for hocking his stereo equipment or something, do you?" Gertie asked.

"Sometimes it's not the last thing that a person did," I said. "It's the culmination of all the crap they've done. The stereo, or whatever, is simply the final straw."

Ida Belle nodded. "Given the choice of body placement, this doesn't strike me as a premeditated sort of thing. Seems more like something done in a rage and then the killer had to scramble to cover it up."

"I agree," I said. "Which is both good and bad. Good in that it shoves the door to the suspect list wide open. Bad in that narrowing down that list to people that a defense attorney could make a doubt stance on is going to take a lot of legwork."

"My legs needed work anyway," Gertie said.

"I've got to drop off the paperwork to Whiskey after breakfast," I said. "Maybe you two can put your heads together and tap into your sources and put together a list of people to start looking at."

"And I'll pull out a casserole and get it ready for a visit with Percy," Gertie said.

I lifted my coffee mug in the air. "To our first official case."

Gertie nodded. "Hopefully, our client won't go to prison."

"Maybe you should put that on the business cards," Ida Belle said drily.

"If we do, we should leave out the 'hopefully,'" Gertie said.

"There might be a legal problem with that if we fail to deliver," Ida Belle said.

"Please," Gertie said. "We always deliver."

"Speaking of delivery," Ida Belle said, "when are you going to deliver the news of your client to Carter?"

I grimaced. "I guess I should do that before I head over to the Swamp Bar, right?"

"Carter needs to put on his big-boy panties," Gertie said. "This is bound to happen again."

"Are you volunteering to speak to him about his undergarments?" Ida Belle asked.

"Heck no," Gertie said. "The only woman that needs to speak to a man about his personals in the woman he's sharing a bed with."

Ida Belle looked at me and grinned. "Looks like the panty discussion is all on you."

"And I'm really looking forward to it," I said as I rolled my eyes. "This time and every time in the future."

"It will get easier," Gertie said.

"You think so?" I asked.

Gertie shook her head. "No. Not really."

IT WAS AROUND 11:00 a.m. when I walked into the Swamp Bar. A couple of early adopters were already in place at the bar, throwing back beer and snacking on ribs, the lunch special for the day. Whiskey was stocking the bar for the night and gave me a nod as I walked in.

"I have some business with this lady," Whiskey said to the men at the bar. "Anyone walks off without paying better not come back. I won't be gone long."

The men all turned around and gave me the once-over. One of them chuckled.

"Ain't saying much about yourself if your business with her ain't gonna take long," the man said.

Whiskey gave him a dirty look. "It ain't that kind of business, and since you're going to be a smart-ass today, no discount on your lunch."

"Ah, Whiskey," the man complained. "I was just razzing you."

Whiskey waved a hand in dismissal as he walked away, motioning me toward a door at the rear of the bar. I followed him down a hallway and into a room that must serve as his office, if you considered a sheet of plywood on crates a desk. He pointed at a folding metal chair and I perched on it, hoping it wasn't too rusty to hold.

I pulled out the paperwork and slid it across the plywood. "The first thing is the contract. It's a basic representation contract. Details the scope of my work, my hourly rate, and the retainer I'll collect from you today."

Whiskey surprised me by reading every line of the contract and asking for clarification on a couple of points. Then he nodded and signed it. As he pushed the papers back across the desk along with a check for the retainer, he smiled.

"You weren't expecting those kinds of questions from someone like me," he said.

"Maybe not," I said, not wanting to just blurt out a resounding "no."

"People underestimate me a lot. But I spent enough time on the wrong side of the law and the right side of this business to figure I needed to get savvy on legal matters."

"Makes sense. Listen, if you don't mind, I'd like to keep our business relationship on the down low. I will have a better chance getting information out of people if they don't know I'm working for you. As soon as things become official, some people clam up."

"And some won't like the idea of helping out a guy accused of murder. I get it. So what do you do first?"

"I find more suspects so I can create reasonable doubt. That gets the legal side covered. Then if you want me to keep going, I poke harder at the suspects to narrow them down."

"And find the killer."

"That's the hope. But I need you to understand the scope of this and the potential cost. Based on my somewhat limited knowledge, I'm already aware that Venus created a lot of hard feelings. That gives me a long list of people to look into."

"I imagine it does. But I figure what I spend with you would still be a sight cheaper than a murder defense."

"That's true. Can I ask you a personal question?"

He shrugged. "I'm your client now so that means you can't repeat anything, right?"

"Why Venus? Based on the things I've heard, everyone she came in contact with was a mark. What was the draw? You said yourself that you should have known better."

He sat back in his chair and scrunched his brow. "You ask good questions. And it's one I've pondered time and time again. I don't like being made a fool of, especially in front of a crowd at my bar."

"I imagine not."

He shook his head. "It's hard to explain, but for starters, Venus was beautiful. I don't mean your basic looker. It was everything—the blond hair, the big blue eyes, the big, er... hooters. She had the face of an angel and the body of a devil. And when she set her sights on you, she could make you feel like you were the most important, smartest, hottest guy on earth."

"So she knew how to work the ego, and the angelic looks helped mask her true personality."

"Yeah. But it wasn't just that. It was that injured-innocence thing she had going. You know—mother abandoned her, father didn't really want nothing to do with her. She had a way of making you believe that everyone had let her down and that she was counting on you to be the one person who changed her mind about the human race."

"White-knight syndrome."

"Sounds silly when it's summed up in a couple words, but I suppose you're right. I guess some of us men have earned those labels women slap on us."

"Sounds to me like you were taken in by a pro. And given the embarrassment of it all, not to mention the potential murder rap, my guess is you won't make that mistake again."

He grinned. "I wouldn't bet on that. If a woman like you looked my way, I'd probably be a fool all over again."

"I don't have that skill set. I haven't even managed a moment of whimsy where Carter is concerned, much less a complete abdication of common sense."

"Carter is no fool. Never was. And he's the only cop I trust to do things straight. But ultimately, he ain't calling the shots." He frowned. "Bet that pisses him off sometimes."

"More than you know. Carter's not a fan of stupid, and it shows up a lot in our legal system."

"Well, I hope taking me on don't cause you two no problems. But I couldn't just sit here and pray for the best. Ain't the way I was raised."

I nodded. "Speaking of which, did Venus ever tell you anything about her time in New Orleans?"

He shook his head. "I poked around there a bit, but she was tight-lipped on the subject. I do know she found her momma. Let that one slip one night when she was drunk. But she caught herself quick enough, even with all the alcohol she'd consumed. Her tone said it all though. I don't think it was a Hallmark reunion."

"Hallmark? Really?"

"My grandma used to watch those movies all the time. Sometimes a grandson just has to go with it. But I'd appreciate it if you didn't let on to that kind of thing with other people."

I rose from my chair. "Don't worry. Your sometimes-a-nice-guy secret is safe with me."

"You were CIA. If you can't keep a secret, nobody can."

CHAPTER NINE

According to Ally, via the local café gossip chain, the job Percy was currently working had closed up shop the entire week, so we figured we stood a good chance of catching him at home. After breakfast, Ida Belle and Gertie had headed to Gertie's house to prep a casserole and I was supposed to meet them there when I was done with Whiskey. I pulled up a bit after noon. Perfect timing for a food delivery.

The front door wasn't locked so I let myself in.

"Take care of him, Shorty," Francis said. "No body."

I shook my head, wondering how many crimes were saved in that bird's recall. I headed toward the kitchen and he started singing "Jesus Loves Me."

"That's a new one," Gertie said. "So far this morning, he's come out with two hymns, one questionable attempt at rap, and three Elvis renditions."

At the word "Elvis," Francis stopped singing and a second later said, "Thank you very much."

"I'm more concerned about what Shorty did with the body," I said. "Elvis songs never killed anyone."

"That you know of," Ida Belle said. "How did it go with Whiskey?"

"Good. He's an interesting guy. And sharper than I thought."

I gave them a rundown of our interaction. When I was finished, Gertie nodded.

"Whiskey was always a smart one," Gertie said. "Got decent grades in school without really trying. I always wondered what he could have managed if he'd had more push in that direction. But his daddy is an old-school Cajun. He made a living off the bayou until he opened the Swamp Bar, and he intended his sons to carry on the family tradition."

"There's worse things than a viable business in a town like Sinful," Ida Belle said.

"It certainly seems to work for him," I said. "I can't really picture him in a suit and sitting in a glass office. What do you think about his take on Venus?"

"Accurate," Ida Belle said. "We saw a ton of people fall for her act over the years."

Gertie nodded. "Heck, I fell for it myself."

"What were you going to do?" Ida Belle said. "Punch her in the face for trying to hug you? Wrestle her in the middle of the sidewalk?"

"I guess not," Gertie said. "But you can bet I'll be a lot more careful about that locket from now on. As soon as Carter turns it loose, I'm getting two security clasps put on it to go with the original. I don't hug anyone long enough to get three clasps undone."

"There's four clasps on your bra," I said. "You'd hug a hot guy long enough to get that undone."

"Don't encourage her," Ida Belle said.

I grinned. "So, we hit up Percy first. Did you two put together a list of potentials?"

Ida Belle nodded. "I'm afraid it's a pretty long list. Between the men Venus took advantage of and the women they were supposed to be involved with at the time, she managed to spread quite a lot of animosity."

"Boy, isn't that the truth," Gertie said. "And we figured we probably shouldn't limit it only to the trouble she caused on her most recent visit, so we went back to when she lived here before. We put those people on the bottom of the list, but we figured they still warranted a look."

"Sure," I said. "She wasn't here very long the last time before that concrete thing happened. It's entirely possible that someone she hacked off before didn't take kindly to her return. You guys ready?"

Gertie pointed to a casserole dish on the counter. "It's still warm."

"Then let's go have a chat with the seemingly unaffected father," I said.

We headed out to Ida Belle's SUV and took a short drive to Percy's house. It was on the outer edge of the neighborhood, near the park and at the end of the street. I scanned the surroundings, assessing the difficulty of getting in and out of the house unseen. Given that the house backed up to the woods, it wouldn't have been impossible.

Ida Belle noticed my gaze and nodded. "You're thinking someone could have come in from the back without being seen."

"Yeah," Gertie said, "But then they'd have to tote luggage through the woods. Not like they could park one street over or something. And it's a good half mile through the woods to anywhere you could park a car and not be visible from a house."

"You're assuming they took the luggage away," I said. "They could have just buried it in the woods."

"That's smart," Ida Belle said. "Couldn't just leave it sitting out, because it's likely to be found, but it wouldn't take a lot to bury some clothes. Not like an animal is going to come digging them up."

"The houses on each side have a view of the backyard, though," Gertie said. "And since none of them have fences, it would still be a risk."

"Who are the neighbors?" I asked. "Retired? Mothers at home with children?"

"The house on the right is owned by a retired couple," Ida Belle said. "They travel a lot so there's a chance they weren't home when this went down. The one on the left is a young couple. No kids. The husband works for an oil company. The wife is a seamstress—upholstery mostly. So it's possible she was at a client's house that day."

"There's also the car to consider," I said. "It was gone as well. I'm assuming Percy wouldn't have thought anything of Venus not coming home overnight."

"I'm sure not, given her habits with men," Ida Belle said.

"So that means the car was probably removed from wherever Venus was last," I said.

"Which could have been where she was murdered," Gertie said.

"Which also means that car has to be somewhere," I said.

"It's a lot harder to hide a car than a suitcase," Ida Belle said.

I nodded. "Let's go see what Percy can tell us."

We knocked on the door and waited a bit but heard nothing inside. Percy's truck was in the driveway, so it was likely he was home but hoping to avoid visitors. Gertie wasn't having any of that. She knocked again. Louder this time. Several seconds later, the door swung open and a tired-looking man looked at us.

Midforties but looks every bit of fifty. Five foot eleven. One hundred eighty-five pounds. Nice tone in his forearms. Probably from the welding. The rest of his body is softer. No threat unless he was holding a blowtorch.

"Hello, Percy," Gertie said, and held up the casserole. "We wanted to bring you this and see if there was anything we could do."

I could tell Percy would rather have a root canal than invite us inside, but Southern manners won out and he stood by and motioned us in.

"I appreciate the food," he said as he took the casserole from Gertie.

We followed him to the back of the house and he sat the casserole on the kitchen counter.

"I just made some tea, if you want a glass," he said.

"That would be great," Ida Belle said, and took that as an invitation to sit.

We all sat at the kitchen table and Percy served everyone a round of tea, still so warm it quickly melted the ice. Percy sat down and gave me a curious look.

"I'm sorry," Ida Belle said, noticing his expression. "This is our friend, Fortune Redding. She bought Marge Boudreaux's old place."

Percy studied me a little harder. "The spook? Don't look like I imagined."

"That gave me an advantage," I said.

"I suppose it did," he said.

"We're really sorry about Venus," Gertie said. "I know you two had your troubles, but those things don't matter anymore."

"That's what people say," Percy said. "The truth is, I lost my daughter years ago. And that's assuming I ever had her to begin with. Just like her mother, I'm afraid."

"Still, it's got to be hard," Gertie said.

Percy's jaw flexed. "What's hard is hearing the gossip about all the people she stole from or scammed and the men she ran around with who was supposed to be involved with others. She never cared about anyone but herself and her wants. And she was willing to do anything to get them. Did you know she got kicked out of kindergarten? She was biting the other kids for the toys. Had so many complaints the principal said they just couldn't let her stay. She had to mature before she could come back. I'm not sure how you mature someone out of being mean."

"I didn't realize," Gertie said.

"Guess I should be happy only the one made it, given how she turned out," Percy said.

"What do you mean?" Ida Belle asked.

"Starlight was carrying twins," Percy said. "That's why she had to be in the hospital for so long. Both were born small but Venus's sister was a lot smaller. The doctors said Venus had been taking up all the nutrients and the other baby hadn't gotten enough. She was in the hospital for a couple weeks. They tried to save her but couldn't."

"I never knew that," Gertie said.

Percy shrugged. "Not the sort of thing there's any use talking about. Can't nobody change it and all it does is make people sad."

"I'm really sorry," Ida Belle said. "Is there anything we can do to help? Perhaps with arrangements...assuming the police have let you know when you're able to."

"I already made the arrangements," Percy said. "She'll be cremated. I'm not having a service. Don't see the point as no one would come anyway except to speculate and gossip. No sense obligating people to show up and pretend they care just for my sake."

It was a sad statement but I had a feeling he'd probably nailed it.

"Do the police have any idea what happened?" Ida Belle asked.

Percy shrugged. "Didn't let on to me if they did. Had a ton of questions though. Not that I was any help. The truth is I don't know what Venus did when she was out of my sight 'cept what I heard from the whisperings of others. I have no idea what she was up to in New Orleans, but I figure it was no good. And I couldn't begin to guess the things that ran through her mind."

He rose from the table. "Anyway, if it's all the same, I'd like to get to work in my garage. I appreciate you stopping by and I'm sure the food will go down good for supper. But I'm just not feeling much up to company."

"Of course," Ida Belle said, and we all rose and headed to the door.

Percy swung it open and when he saw the woman standing on his porch, the blood drained from his face.

"Starlight," he said, his voice barely a whisper.

Midforties but easily looks ten years older. Five foot four. A hundred fifty pounds, a lot of it boobs. Too much makeup. Too much hair. Just too much all around. Only a threat to Percy, based on his reaction.

Gertie sucked in a breath and even Ida Belle's eyes widened. This was a twist neither one of them had seen coming.

"What are you doing here?" Percy asked. The color flooded back into his face and shifted from white to red.

Starlight looked momentarily confused. "Why, I'm here about our baby, of course."

"You don't have a baby," he said. "You abandoned her, remember? Gave up rights."

"Jesus," Starlight said. "Are you still holding a grudge about all that? It was years ago."

"Believe it or not," Percy said, "there's some things you can't sweep under the rug. I suggest you get off my property before I call the sheriff and have you picked up for trespassing. And don't even think about sniffing around. If I have to load my shotgun, no one's going to be happy with the outcome."

Starlight's head moved back as if she'd been slapped. Clearly, she wasn't used to men who didn't roll over and cater to her. Despite the wear, she was still an attractive woman. And my guess was she knew how to pick her targets well. But the look on her face said she'd made a gross miscalculation this time.

"It doesn't have to be that way," she said.

"Yeah," Percy said. "I think it does."

He stood back and gestured to us to walk out. Starlight gave him one final glance, apparently cluing in to the fact that he wasn't joking, then spun around and headed toward a late-model Mustang parked at the curb. We hurried out and headed down the walk.

"This isn't the last you'll hear from me," Starlight said without looking back. "I want my share of my daughter's things."

Percy slammed the door so hard the porch shook. Starlight got into her car and pulled away from the curb, tires squealing. We headed to Ida Belle's SUV and climbed inside, none of us saying a word. Finally, Ida Belle looked over at us.

"Things just got very interesting," she said.

CHAPTER TEN

We followed Starlight into downtown. Not because we were trying to follow her, per se, but simply because the shortest distance between Percy's house and Main Street was the direction she was going. She didn't stop anywhere, but instead kept driving through downtown and toward the highway.

"You think she's going back to New Orleans?" I asked.

"Something tells me no," Gertie said.

"I agree," Ida Belle said. "She didn't drive all the way out here just to razz Percy for a minute, then turn around and leave. Starlight always had an angle. And you can bet that if she's darkening Sinful's doorstep, she has one now. She's probably holed up at the motel."

Ida Belle pulled up in front of the sheriff's department and parked next to Carter's truck. I looked over at her, somewhat confused.

"You said you needed to pick up a food order at the General Store," Ida Belle said. "And I figured while we were here, we should probably let Carter know that Starlight is back."

"Oh, right," I said. "Yeah, I don't want him to get surprised by that one and then find out I knew."

Ida Belle nodded. "And I figure while you're doling out that information, you can go ahead and tell him that you've taken on Whiskey as a client."

"How do you know I didn't already?" I asked.

"Because you were entirely too pleasant when you got to Gertie's, and there's no way you had that conversation with Carter and were still smiling."

I sighed. "Fine. I didn't stop before I went to the Swamp Bar because I figured there was a chance Whiskey had slept on it and changed his mind. I called dispatch on my way back, but they said Carter was out on police business. I didn't figure waiting around was an efficient use of my time, especially as I had no idea how long said police business would take, so I headed to Gertie's and figured I'd tell him later."

Ida Belle stared at me, one eyebrow raised. "That was a whole lot of talking."

I threw my hands in the air. "Fine! I was happy Carter wasn't available. But it's not like I was going to try to keep it a secret. You know, for someone who doesn't want any input into her own personal life, you have an awful lot to say about mine."

"That's true," Gertie said.

Ida Belle shot her a dirty look. "You're one to talk. You're always butting in."

"Which I've already learned to accept and ignore," I said. "But you're a different story."

Ida Belle stared silently at the sidewalk. Finally, she shook her head and said, "Maybe I just don't want you in my position when you're my age. This kind of conflict with professions is bound to happen over and over again. You both need to figure out how to handle it like it's any other part of your regular life, because once people get comfortable with the idea that you're really good at what you do and you're here to stay, you're going to be busy, and a whole lot of it might cross police lines."

"I hate to admit she's right," Gertie said. "Especially since she usurped my position as the nosy friend, but I have to agree."

I slumped in my seat. "I really hope this doesn't put a damper on dinner. I have two awesome rib eyes in that grocery order and nobody grills a steak like Carter."

"I give up," Ida Belle said. "I'm trying to help smooth the path for your relationship future and your biggest concern is rib eyes."

"Steak is serious business," Gertie said.

I nodded. "But your point is taken. However, I'd like to state that I still think my policy is going to be, I don't speak to Carter about my clients until I have a contract. One, because anyone is subject to change their mind, and two, because I want confidentiality to be firmly in place."

"I think that's entirely reasonable," Ida Belle said.

We headed into the sheriff's department and went through our standard Southern greetings with Gavin, the young and fairly new daytime dispatcher, and then asked to speak to Carter. Gavin had a brief phone conversation, then waved us back.

I started down the hall, then realized Ida Belle and Gertie hadn't moved. I looked back at them.

"You first," Ida Belle said. "Then holler for us."

I headed for Carter's office and he looked up and smiled at me when I walked in. I gave him a quick kiss before sitting. He looked tired and I felt bad that I was about to cause him more grief, but it couldn't be helped. This was my new life. And Ida Belle was right. Our paths were bound to cross more often as my business picked up.

"I need to tell you something," I said.

He looked over at me and frowned, my tone letting him know that what I was about to say probably wasn't going to be well received.

"I have a new client," I said.

"That's great...isn't it?"

"I think so. But I'm not so sure you're going to be as excited about it. My client is Whiskey."

He stared at me for a moment, then sat back in his chair. "Can I ask why he hired you?"

"Because he's afraid he'll be railroaded for Venus's murder. Given his record and the fact that he threatened her in a bar full of people the night she was killed, he figures the DA might want to move forward."

"You know I'm not going to settle for maybe. I won't stop investigating until I know for certain who did this."

"I know that, but I don't have the same confidence in the DA. And neither does Whiskey."

Carter blew out a breath. "I wish I could say you're both wrong..."

"But you can't. And Whiskey doesn't have the money for bail on a murder rap, assuming he even got it. If he's locked up for any length of time, the bar income dries up, since Nickel's back in jail."

"Then there's no one to take care of his father," Carter finished. "I know all of that. And I don't like it, but I can't gloss over the facts to keep the DA from making a move on him."

"I don't expect you to, and neither does Whiskey. But he wants someone working solely for him—preparing an argument for the defense, in case it comes to that."

Carter nodded. "I'm not going to say that I'm thrilled you're going to put yourself on the trail of a killer, but I think

Whiskey is playing this smart."

I stared. "You're not mad?"

He gave me a small smile. "There's no future in it. You are who you are and you're going to do what comes naturally to you and what gets your blood racing. I might not have known that when I started pursuing you, but I was really clear on it when I decided not to stop my pursuit. You can't change who you are and neither can I. And to be honest, I don't want to. So I'm going to ask you to be careful because there is a killer out there, and he thought he got away with it."

"He'll be on the defense."

"Or worse. Panicked."

"Do you think Whiskey did it?"

"I think he's capable given the right circumstances. But no. I don't think he did it."

"Good," I said. If Carter didn't believe Whiskey was involved, then he wouldn't be pushing him at the DA unless he had no other choice. He'd be following the forensics, trying to track down the real killer. Our task was a little more broad, at least for now. We needed to find two or more potential suspects. Enough to create doubt.

But if we happened to find the killer, I wasn't going to be sad about it.

"Thank you for being so cool about this," I said.

He frowned. "Were you worried that I wouldn't be?"

"No. Well, maybe a little. And I have rib eyes for pickup at the General Store. I really wanted dinner to go well."

Carter perked up. "From that butcher in New Orleans?"

"That's the one."

He rose from his chair and extended his hand, pulling me up from my seat. Then he gathered me in his arms and kissed me soundly. "I love you, Fortune Redding. I'm not going to say that I won't worry or that you won't ever make me mad, but nothing you do is going to keep me from wanting you."

"Good. Because there's one more thing, and this one is probably going to frustrate you a little but I swear, it's not on me."

He released me and stared. "Since you led with Whiskey being your new client, I'm not sure I want to know."

I opened his office door and yelled for Ida Belle and Gertie.

He went back to his chair and dropped into it, probably figuring if I was calling in the Troublesome Twosome, it couldn't be good. They headed in and Carter gave them a half-hearted hello while they each took a seat. Ida Belle glanced over at me and I gave her a tiny nod, letting her know the air was clear in the relationship games.

"We know you're busy," Ida Belle said, "so we won't take much of your time. But we figured you needed to be warned."

"I'm almost afraid to ask," Carter said.

"We were at Percy's earlier," Ida Belle said. "Doing the whole Southern Baptist someone-died routine."

"And pumping him for information for your new case," Carter said.

"Yes, but we would have taken over a casserole and offered to help with arrangements whether we had a case or not," Gertie said. "Certain manners are not optional."

His lower lip quivered. "You're right. So what is so disconcerting that you felt you had to tell me about it?"

"When we were leaving, Starlight showed up," Ida Belle said.

CHAPTER ELEVEN

CARTER IMMEDIATELY STRAIGHTENED, his expression one of both surprise and dismay. "You're kidding me."

"I wish we were," I said. "I didn't like her."

"You're not the right sex or foolish enough to like her," Carter said. "What did she want?"

"Said she wanted half of her daughter's things," Gertie said. "Which makes no sense because Venus didn't have anything to speak of."

Carter frowned. "How did Percy take it?"

"As expected," Ida Belle said. "He turned white as a ghost when he saw her standing there, then got mad as a hornet and told her to get off his property or he'd have her arrested for trespassing. Told her if she came lurking around, he'd load his shotgun."

"*That* is trouble I don't need," Carter said.

"We were behind her as she drove away," Ida Belle said. "She headed through downtown and toward the highway, but that doesn't mean she's headed back to New Orleans."

"No," Carter agreed. "I don't imagine she is. If Starlight showed up on Percy's doorstep, then she had a reason. And since her reason is usually money, I'm a little at a loss as to what her angle is."

"Me too," Gertie said. "She's certainly not getting anything out of Percy."

Carter rubbed his jaw and I could tell he was trying to figure out what Starlight could be getting at and coming up as short as we had.

Finally, he shook his head. "Well, I don't know what to make of it, but thank you for warning me. The last thing this town needs is Starlight to descend on it again."

"Looks like she's not going to give us a choice," Ida Belle said. "Anyway, we've all got work to do, so we'll get out of here. If I hear any gossip on that end, I'll let you know."

"I appreciate it," he said.

We all rose and I gave him a quick kiss before leaving.

"Starlight showing up bothers me," he said. "Makes me think there's something going on that we aren't seeing. The kind of thing that surfaces and bites you in the butt. Please be careful."

I nodded. "You too."

We headed out of the sheriff's department and climbed into Ida Belle's SUV but instead of starting the vehicle, they both stared at me.

"Well?" Gertie asked. "How did it go with Carter?"

"Oh," I said, now understanding the anticipatory expressions. "Sorry, I was back in case mode."

"Good," Ida Belle said. "That means the discussion went well."

"Very well," I said. "I'm afraid we didn't give Carter enough credit. He was cool about the whole thing. I mean, he gave me the whole 'be careful' routine, but that's normal given that it's a murder."

"Even in Sinful, a missing cat can become something it

never should," Gertie said. "Lately, it seems we're geared for the more dramatic side of things."

"And then there's your purse," I said.

"My purse isn't dramatic," Gertie said. "It's practical."

"That purse is a cross between a horror movie and a postapocalyptic story," Ida Belle said. "I don't suppose he felt so generous that he gave you cause of death?"

"I don't think Carter will ever feel that generous," I said. "But I think we have to assume it wasn't basic drugs or the death might be deemed accidental and the crime would be hiding the body."

"That still leaves a bunch of options," Gertie said. "Poison, gun, strangling, suffocating, a conk on the head..."

"I'm going to do a preliminary rule-out on gunshot and poisoning," I said.

"Why those two?" Gertie asked.

"Gunshot because neither Whiskey nor Percy mentioned Carter asking them about the weapons they owned. Also because he hasn't issued a search warrant for Percy's house or the Swamp Bar. So it makes me think it was a hands-on kind of deal."

"Smart," Ida Belle said. "You're really thinking like a pro."

"I've been doing a lot of studying," I said. "And watching all those forensic shows. The other thing with poisoning is that it's a premeditated sort of crime. And the way the body was dumped doesn't say planning to me."

Ida Belle nodded. "It was a good spur-of-the-moment option, but it was a lot riskier than doing a bayou dump."

"Exactly," I said. "Plus, the killer not only had to dispose of the body but get rid of the car, which I figure he did that night. Then he came back the next day when Percy was at work and got rid of her things."

"The chances of us finding them if they're buried in the woods behind Percy's house are slim to none," Gertie said.

"I agree," I said. "And I don't think finding them would tell us anything anyway. If Venus had something of value to the killer—blackmail notes, or something else to that effect—the killer would have destroyed them."

"So what now?" Ida Belle said. "Do you want to start running down the interview list?"

"I suppose we should," I said. "But there's something I keep coming back around to. And I know it's one of those needle-in-a-haystack things, but I can't stop thinking about it."

"What's that?" Gertie asked.

"The car," I said. "Where is her car? The killer had to take it to make it appear as if Venus really left, so where is it? If it had just been abandoned somewhere publicly, it would have been reported by now and Carter would have been asking questions then."

"We assume that maybe it was used to transport the body and then dumped somewhere that it hasn't been found, right?" Ida Belle said.

"But it could be anywhere," Gertie said. "The killer could have hightailed it to New Orleans and sold it for scrap metal or to illegals for cash. For all we know, it could be out of the country."

I shook my head. "I don't think so. Whoever killed Venus was back the next day packing up her things. I doubt you'll find an Uber in the middle of the night ready to haul you from the city to Sinful."

"Maybe they had an accomplice," Gertie said. "Someone who followed them into the city and gave them a ride back."

"That's possible," I said. "But it doesn't feel right. If we leave out premeditation and also eliminate gunshot, then the remaining options fall more under crime-of-passion sort of things."

Gertie sighed. "You know what all that speculation means, don't you?"

"What?" I asked.

"That it's highly unlikely some stranger from Venus's past in New Orleans hiked down here and did it. What are the odds that they'd know about the construction site and where Percy's house is? What his work schedule was? How to get to it from the woods in the back?"

"I agree that a local is a better bet," I said. "And I'm thinking if we find the car, that might lend even more to that train of thought."

"Someone commits a crime of passion and has such a short amount of time to get it covered up, they are bound to have made a mistake or two," Ida Belle said.

"Doesn't look like it so far," Gertie said. "If that turkey hadn't gotten away, the body would have never been found. It's not like anyone from Sinful was going to go looking for Venus. And even if they did, she wasn't exactly the kind of girl to take on a lease or any other daily living stuff that made her easy to track down."

"I agree that someone was very clever," I said. "And that's something we have to take into account while we're investigating, both during the interviews and watching our back."

"So...the car," Ida Belle said.

I nodded. "I know it sounds like looking for the proverbial needle in the haystack, but it has to be someone near Sinful. Whoever dumped it had to walk back from the dumping site. I don't figure they went any farther than they absolutely had to. So any ideas?"

"It's probably not sitting under some branches in the woods," Gertie said. "All sorts of hunting seasons opened up the last few months. Hunters will have been across every square inch of woods around here. If anyone had seen it, they'd have reported it."

"Has to be in the bayou," Ida Belle said. "It's the only place people aren't going to get in for a closer look. Boat hits something solid, you just assume it's a submerged tree or piece of a broken wharf...that sort of thing. With all the lack of maintenance and hurricanes, there's a ton of stuff shifting under that water. You don't stop to take a closer look."

"Okay," I said. "So where can someone get a car into the bayou where it's deep enough to sink under the water and won't be an obstruction? It's not like he could have sent it down a boat ramp. That would have been caught."

"Sure," Ida Belle said. "A boat ramp's the only place people worry about clearing submerged items. The problem is finding a place where you can get close enough to the bayou to send a car into it. Most roads end well before the bayou begins and the trees are usually too thick to fit a car between."

"What about a camp?" I asked. "Some of the camps are accessible by cars. Is there one with enough clearance to drive around behind the cabin and into the bayou? And with water deep enough to get rid of a car?"

Gertie and Ida Belle stared at each other, as if they were sending data between two computers. Finally, Gertie nodded.

"There's several that meet the driving criteria part," she said, "but we'd have to check on the depth of the water. The Swamp Bar is one of them, of course."

"But if we accept that Whiskey didn't do it then it wouldn't be there," I said.

"Unless someone wanted to frame him," Gertie said.

"That's a risky proposition," I said. "There's always people in and out of that bar. And I'm not sure Whiskey leaves much except to fish."

Ida Belle nodded. "It's definitely risky, but if we're going to be thorough, we have to check it out."

"Okay. You said there's a couple other spots?" I said.

"I can think of four more," Ida Belle said. "Two that have a bit of an overhang. Would be easy to put a board on the accelerator and send a car off it."

"I know the two she's got in mind," Gertie said. "Water's fairly deep past those overhangs."

"Good," I said. "Then we'll start with those. Who owns them?"

"One of them belongs to Pastor Don," Ida Belle said.

"And the other?" I asked.

Ida Belle and Gertie exchanged looks.

"The other belongs to Nickel," Gertie said.

I sighed. No matter how I tossed things, they came back around to all fingers pointing at Whiskey.

"We'll start there," I said.

THIRTY MINUTES LATER, we were loading my airboat. I'm not sure if I was excited that we might find the car or worried that we might find the car. Locating Venus's vehicle at Nickel's camp was no different from finding it at the Swamp Bar. I had pulled out my new toy at the house and Ida Belle had been so excited that for a minute she looked as if she were going to bounce like Gertie. It was a handheld underwater metal detector. The kind the SEALs used, and if there was a quarter in the bayou, it would let us know.

"But the bayous are loaded with trash," Gertie said. "It's going to pick up every beer can from here to Mexico."

"I can set the tolerance so we only get large, dense items," I said. "We'll still pick up submerged boats and other larger structures that might be there, but it will ignore the smaller items."

"And what then?" Gertie asked. "You're not going to jump in like you did that one time. Remember how that turned out."

"I remember," I said. The last time I'd thought it was a good idea to take a dip in pursuit of evidence, an alligator had decided that pursuit of me was a good idea. It had put an end to my ideas of swimming in the local waters but did have me thinking about putting in a pool.

"I have an underwater camera as well," I said. "But if the water's too muddy, we're not going to be able to make out much."

"Maybe we'll get lucky and it will be clear," Ida Belle said. "That's assuming we find anything in the first place."

I nodded. "I know interviewing people would probably be a better use of our time, but I just can't shake this thought."

"If it's got a hold of you then that's what we need to pursue," Ida Belle said. "You've got good instincts. We need to trust them. I'm not saying they'll always be right, but we're not the police. We can afford to make mistakes."

"Except with alligators," I said. "Which is why no one is going in the water."

"Why did you look at me when you said that?" Gertie asked. "I have no intention of going in."

"You rarely do," Ida Belle said. "But then, there you are."

"That last fall off the pier wasn't my fault," Gertie said. "Those boards were rotted."

"You intended to go into the water in Florida," I said. "And ended up topless and facing a murder charge."

"Good point," Ida Belle said.

"That was an extreme situation," Gertie said. "I'm telling you, I'm not even going to get near the edge of the boat except to get in. Well, and out."

Ida Belle didn't look convinced. I figured it was the "out" part that she was sketchy on, but it was as good as we were getting.

"Let's worry about things if they happen," I said. "I know that sounds odd coming from someone who used to have to time even her breathing on the job, but this is a new day and a new occupation. Sometimes you just have to play it by ear."

Ida Belle nodded and secured the equipment in the storage bench. Gertie climbed in and onto her padded seat in the bottom of the boat in front of the bench, I took the passenger's seat, and Ida Belle took over the driver's chair. Technically, it was my boat, but Ida Belle was a better driver and more importantly, she knew where we were going. Work was all about efficiency, especially when you were charging your client by the hour.

We set off down the bayou until we hit the lake, then Ida Belle skimmed across the southern edge until she located the channel she was looking for. She made a hard right, the airboat gliding across the surface as if it were glass, then set off down a fairly wide bayou. The terrain on the side went from marsh grass closest to the lake, to marsh grass and a couple of scraggly trees, then eventually to cypress trees lining both sides of the bank.

I couldn't help but smile. The sun was out, the bayou was smooth, I had on shorts, T-shirt, and tennis shoes, and I was getting paid to do this. It was a far cry from my previous working conditions.

Gertie pointed at a glint of metal in the distance and as we approached, I could see the sun reflecting off the tin roof of a camp that was located on an overhang that sat about eight feet above the bayou. A steep, narrow path led from the overhang down to a small dock on the bayou. Ida Belle slowed the boat to a crawl and we approached the dock.

"This is Nickel's place," Ida Belle said. "It's a little more remote on the driving side of things than Pastor Don's, so I figured we'd start here first. The road to Pastor Don's has a couple of permanent houses on it. This one doesn't."

I nodded. The killer had less chance of being seen on the route to Nickel's, which made it the better choice. People in Sinful didn't keep banker's hours. You never knew who might be wandering around during the night. Not to mention that the sound of an approaching car on a road with no through traffic was the sort of thing that got people out of bed to take a look.

Gertie opened up the storage bench as Ida Belle killed the engine and I jumped down from my seat to get the radar ready. I'd already adjusted the settings at my house, so it was really just a matter of putting the strap in place and firing it up.

"Where should I look?" I asked.

Ida Belle pointed up to an area of the overhang about thirty feet away from the dock.

"The road dead-ends right in front of the camp," she said. "But he cleared a larger area in order to haul the water tank off to the side. You could easily fit a car through the opening, even with the water tank in place."

Gertie grabbed a long cane pole and stuck it in the water, directing the boat toward the area Ida Belle had indicated. Fortunately, the tide was barely moving, so that made things easier. When we were within ten feet of the spot Ida Belle had indicated, I turned on the radar and leaned over the side of the boat and waited for the magic to happen. The screen was mostly a blurry gray, but if something large and solid appeared, it would register as darker black and should have more clarity of shape than the smaller debris that the radar was picking up.

We moved along for a good ten feet when I caught the edge of something on my screen.

"Wait," I said. "Stop here and move us out by a couple feet."

Gertie dug the pole into the water and directed us back a bit, then she went to give it another shove and the pole dropped straight down, sending her plunging into the bottom of the boat. I managed to grab the pole and Gertie popped back up.

"Got deep," she said. "I didn't hit bottom, even falling."

Ida Belle consulted the depth finder. "Look like a good twenty foot drop here. Probably only six feet or so before."

"I have something," I said, staring at the large black mass on my screen. "It's big and boxy."

Ida Belle came over to look and nodded. "Doesn't look like the shape of a boat. No narrowing at either end. Could still be a shrimping barge, though."

"Let's see if we can find out," I said, and grabbed the underwater camera. "Do you think you can get me close to the back end using paddles?"

"Tide's not going out yet," Ida Belle said, "so it shouldn't be a problem."

She and Gertie each grabbed an oar and took opposite sides of the boat, directing it per my instructions. When the radar indicated I was at the back of the structure nearest the overhang, I dropped the camera in the water and let it sink. Ida Belle tossed the anchor and I heard it splash into the bayou behind me.

I watched the screen, trying to locate the structure in the murky water, but so far, I'd only managed to spot the occasional fish that swam right up to the camera to inspect it, probably attracted by the lights. Still too high, I thought, and lowered the camera more. When I was about ten feet down, I stopped and moved it a bit from left to right. Then I caught sight of something lighter-colored in the distance.

"Pull the anchor and move us forward maybe two feet," I said.

I watched the screen as we moved forward until the lighter-colored object finally came into focus.

Bingo. It was a license plate.

CHAPTER TWELVE

I CAPTURED a screenshot of the license plate and pulled out my phone.

"Carter," I said when he answered. "We found an abandoned car. Can you run the plate?"

I gave him the plate number and waited. A couple minutes later, I heard him curse.

"Where are you?" he asked.

"Who does the car belong to?" I asked.

He didn't answer.

"Here's how this works," I said. "You tell me who the car is registered to and I'll tell you where to find it. I mean, you could probably find it on your own, but with everything else on your plate and all..."

Ida Belle gave me a thumbs-up.

He sighed. "The car belongs to Venus."

Jackpot.

Ida Belle motioned for me to hand her the phone.

"You're going to need a strong wench," she said to Carter. "And a barge large enough to haul a car." She gave him the coordinates of where to find the car.

He was still swearing when she handed the phone back to me, grinning.

"Tell me you did not get in the water," he said.

"Not even a finger," I said. "Even Gertie has managed to stay topside."

"Good. That's good," he said, and I could tell he was relieved. "It's going to take some time for me to put that kind of equipment and men together. The car's not going anywhere, so you guys clear out before someone sees you."

I knew exactly what his worry was. Now that Venus's body had surfaced, the killer might worry that the car would be found as well. It was highly unlikely that any forensic evidence would be present after being underwater this long. But with all the news reports about cold cases being solved by new technology and then the blatant exaggeration and misinformation bandied around social media, the killer might have different thoughts on the subject.

I glanced up at the overhang and saw a flash of blue. It was gone so quickly that the average person would have dismissed it as a chance of light or their eyes playing tricks on them. But I knew better. I was trained to observe and record everything. Something blue was moving on the overhang, and since I wasn't aware of any blue animals, I could only assume it was a person.

The tide had started to go out during my phone call to Carter and the boat had drifted within five feet of the dock. Before Ida Belle and Gertie could ask me what I was doing, I climbed into the driver's seat and jumped out of the boat. I heard the gasp behind me but I didn't have time to explain. I took the small dock in two strides then scrambled up the narrow steps to the top of the overhang.

I didn't see anything behind the camp, so I ran around, scanning the woods as I ran. When I got to the front, I heard a vehicle start up in the distance and peel out in the gravel. I sprinted up the road, but when I broke free of the thick trees, it had already disappeared around a bend about a quarter mile away, leaving only dust to let me know it had passed that way.

I turned around and hurried back to the boat before Ida Belle and Gertie attempted to follow me. They'd pulled the boat right up to the dock in my absence and Ida Belle was on the dock, preparing to head up the steps when I called out for her to wait. She looked up and I could see the relief on her face when she caught sight of me.

"Thank goodness," Gertie said as I followed Ida Belle back into the boat. "We didn't know what to think. Why did you take off like that?"

"I saw something move in the woods above us," I said.

Gertie's eyes widened. "And you think it was the killer?"

"It wasn't Nickel," I said. "So unless anyone else had good reason to be out here and even better reason to run when I chased them, then yeah, it's possible."

"Could have been kids looking for a place to party," Ida Belle said.

"Or someone who heard Nickel was locked up and was looking for something to steal," Gertie said. "There's been a rash of break-ins lately."

My shoulders relaxed a bit. "Yeah. I suppose you're right. Either of those are probably just as logical as what I was thinking."

Ida Belle glanced up at the overhang and frowned. "But your initial thought isn't completely far-fetched. Now that the body has been found, I suppose the killer is panicking."

"But coming here is stupid," Gertie said. "Even if the car had somehow surfaced, what were they going to do about it? And honestly, what difference does it make if it's found now? Carter already has the body."

"Maybe there's something inside that could point to them," Ida Belle said.

"Like what?" Gertie asked.

"A piece of clothing, jewelry, a pen," I suggested. "Something that could have fallen when they were in the car and they didn't realize was gone until afterward."

Gertie stared into the water and shook her head. "How scared does someone have to be to consider diving in there and trying to find a tiny object in a car that's been submerged for months?"

"Pretty scared, I'd think," Ida Belle said. "If it was the killer up there, then that lends more support to our crime-of-passion theory."

"And by someone who wouldn't stand out as the obvious choice," I said.

"So someone who wasn't planning to kill someone, did," Gertie said. "Then they rushed to hide it and did a pretty good job until my turkey caper uncovered it. Now they're thinking they didn't do such a good job covering things up as they thought and they came to make sure the car was still unexposed."

"Which makes them panicked and dangerous," Ida Belle said. "If it was the killer, and he saw us down here, then he'll know exactly what we were doing."

"He won't know who we're working for," Gertie said.

"It will get around eventually," I said. "There were a couple guys in the Swamp Bar when I was there earlier. You know how things make the rounds here."

"So what now?" Gertie asked.

"I give Carter another call," I said, "and let him know that someone has to sit on this car until he can get it up. You're armed, right?"

Ida Belle pulled a .45 from her backpack, a compact nine-millimeter from her ankle and a knife the size of the Mississippi River from her back. I didn't even want to think about how she sat with that thing back there.

Gertie opened her purse and smiled. "Let's see, I've got—"

"No!" Ida Belle and I both spoke at once.

"It's probably better if I just get a 'yes' and not an inventory," I said. "Definitely better if Carter doesn't know."

"Okay, but you guys are missing out on some cool stuff," Gertie said. "I found this former prepper online who was selling off everything."

"Why is he no longer a prepper?" Ida Belle asked.

"His mother told him he couldn't have all that stuff in the house anymore," Gertie said.

"How old was he?" I asked.

"Thirty-two," Gertie said.

"His mother needed to tell him he couldn't have *himself* in her house anymore," Ida Belle said.

"That's pretty much what happened," Gertie said. "She said he had to cut his hair, get a job, and pay rent. He figured since he's been on a run of bad luck that if things go down, it will be while he's at work. Therefore, there's no point in prepping anymore."

"So where did he get the money for the prepper stuff?" Ida Belle asked.

Gertie shrugged. "I don't know. I guess his allowance."

Ida Belle sighed. "What has happened to our society?"

"That question is as loaded as Gertie's handbag," I said. "You don't have any preppers in Sinful?"

"In a manner of speaking, probably half the population is sitting on six months of food and a pile of ammunition equal to that of a small military reserve," Ida Belle said. "But they don't consider it prepping for anything. They consider that normal living."

"So in case of an apocalyptic situation, Sinful might be the last town standing," I said. "There's an interesting thought. Or frightening, depending on which side of things you're looking from."

I shook my head of thoughts that would lead down long, scary paths and studied the terrain. "I think the best position for us to take is up on the embankment. We have a clear view of anyone approaching from the bayou, and that way no one can flank us from above."

Ida Belle nodded and stepped onto the dock. She eyeballed the narrow steps leading up the embankment and glanced back at Gertie.

"Maybe one of us should stay with the boat," she said.

"I know what you're trying to do," Gertie said. "And it won't work. I'm not staying down here by myself, being all bored. If we'd brought some fishing equipment, then that would be different. Besides, I can go up those steps same as you two."

Except that I was pretty sure she couldn't. The steps were nothing more than narrow dirt carvings into the hard part of the embankment. They were two feet wide at the most and had no rail at all. One missed step and you were falling off the embankment and into the bayou. Given that Gertie had a sense of balance that sometimes fled the building and her glasses were completely out of date, I didn't hold out much hope that she could make it to the top without issue.

"Grab the rope from the bench," I said. "I'll go up first and secure it to something solid. You guys can wrap it around your waist and that way if anyone slips, they'll have rope burns but won't go for a dip."

"You mean *I* can secure it around *my* waist," Gertie said. "You never think I can do anything."

"This is not about what I think you can do or can't do," I

said. "This is about me running a business and you working for me. I'm liable. If something happens and I didn't take proper precautions, I could have my license pulled."

Gertie grumbled some more but bent over to retrieve the rope from the bench.

"Good one," Ida Belle whispered.

I headed up the steps with the rope and Gertie's purse, which was so heavy it had me thinking about the contents, something I try not to do. I wrapped the rope around the trunk of a cypress tree near the back of the house. That way as Gertie went up the steps, I could take up the slack. So if she slipped, it wasn't that far to fall. I tossed the rope down to Ida Belle and she pulled a flotation belt around Gertie's chest and under her arms, then secured the rope through it.

"Good idea," I said. At least the vest would prevent damage from the rope in case of a slip.

"I feel ridiculous," Gertie said.

"State agencies don't care about ridiculous," Ida Belle said. "They only care about liability. We have to do some things differently now that we're official."

"You're telling me you're going to wear this contraption when it's your turn?" Gertie asked.

"Absolutely," Ida Belle said.

"Fine," Gertie grumbled, and headed for the steps.

"Take it nice and slow," I said. "You'll need to turn your feet out a bit like a duck for some of the really shallow ones."

Gertie started up the steps, taking things slowly and walking like a duck when needed. I took up the slack as she went, making sure I had a bit of tension on the rope at all times but not enough to throw her off balance.

She was halfway up when things went all Gertie.

I saw her foot slip as soon as she stepped up. The dirt must have been a little loose. She grabbed for the embankment, but there wasn't anything there except a wall of dirt. She teetered for a second, then pitched off the side of the steps. I dug in my heels, bracing myself for the yank that I knew was coming, but my tennis shoes were no match for the loose, dry dirt. I slid almost to the edge of the steps before I whirled around, wrapping the rope around my waist then dropping to the ground to prevent myself from being pulled over.

I peered over the ledge and saw Gertie swinging back and forth alongside the embankment, just inches from the water. When she got close to the dock, Ida Belle tried to grab her, but she was just out of reach. In usual fashion, instead of being terrified that I was the only thing keeping her from dropping into the abyss, Gertie was having a grand time, waving her hands and hooting as though she was on a ride at an amusement park.

"She's dangling just above the water line," Ida Belle yelled. "Get her up before a gator thinks she's bait."

I managed to turn around in the dirt, then positioned my feet against a tree and pushed. At the same time, I rolled over again, pulling the rope around me in another loop in order to lift Gertie high enough that the gators couldn't reach her. I did another push and roll and felt the rope tighten around my waist so hard that I was afraid I was going to lose my lunch. What the heck were women thinking wearing corsets? One medium-sized rope around me and I thought I was dying.

I took a deep breath and closed my eyes, preparing for another round.

"I see you're following instructions, as usual." Carter's voice sounded above me.

I looked up and grimaced. "You want to help me get her back up or would you prefer her odds in the bayou?"

Carter's eyes widened and he rushed to the ledge to peer over, cursing when he saw Gertie swinging back and forth. He grabbed the rope and pulled it enough to get me back from the ledge, then looked over again.

"We can't pull her up," he said. "She'll come up under the lip of the embankment."

I tried to get up but there was too much tension on the rope. So instead, I rolled myself out of it as Carter stared down at me, shaking his head. As the rope came loose from my waist, I grabbed it with my hands and sat up.

"Stop pulling!" Ida Belle yelled. "That life jacket was intended to float an adult body, not dangle one like a parachute. It's going to tear if you pull on it much more. I'll position the boat underneath her and you can lower her in."

I managed to get myself into a standing position and looked up at Carter, who was shaking his head.

"We were trying to help," I said. "And then Gertie Gertie'd."

"And you're well aware of her propensity to do so."

"Which is why I had her harnessed. Having her walk up those steps without a harness would have turned out much worse."

"Why were you walking up the steps at all?" he asked. "I told you to get out of here."

"Yeah, well, that warning came about a minute too late. When I got off the phone with you, I saw something moving up on the embankment. I ran up but they got away in a car. I heard it tear out of here but didn't get close enough to see it."

Carter glanced at the camp, a worried expression on his face. "No idea on the vehicle?"

"Nothing with a big engine," I said. "Didn't have that depth of sound. But beyond that, I can't tell you anything else. Did you pass anyone on your way here?"

"Not on the road to the camp. I was headed up the

highway when I got your call, which is why I got here so quickly." He blew out a breath. "Apparently, not quickly enough."

"Anyway, the lurker is the reason we didn't leave. I was afraid there might be something in the car—something they dropped maybe—and they'd have a chance to retrieve it if no one was here. The best vantage point for guarding and for our own safety was atop the embankment."

He nodded. "I appreciate you taking ownership, but I don't want you putting yourself at risk for things that are my responsibility."

"Do you really think the odds were in the killer's favor? Gertie brought her purse."

"Maybe I was worried about the killer."

"Probably a better use of time."

"Hey!" Ida Belle yelled. "Stop your jawing and give me some slack before Gertie pulls an armpit muscle."

I rose and repositioned my grip on the rope. Carter stood close to the edge of the embankment with me behind and we let it out a little at a time until finally, we heard Gertie plunk down into the boat. Then there was a big splash.

"She missed!" Ida Belle yelled. "Man overboard!"

Carter and I immediately dug in our heels and pulled the rope again, then moved forward to look over the edge. Gertie had taken a full dip into the bayou and was wet from head to toe. The tide was moving the boat and Ida Belle had a hold of Gertie, struggling to get her into the boat or the boat underneath her—whichever way you wanted to look at it.

"It's like fishing, except with people as bait," Carter said.

Finally, Ida Belle managed to maneuver Gertie over the boat and Carter and I released the line completely, dropping her into the bottom of the boat with a thud.

"Perfect!" Ida Belle shouted, and Carter tossed the rope to Ida Belle. We both looked over to see Gertie pulling herself up from the bottom of the boat, then wrestling to get the life preserver off her.

"Perfect? Are you kidding me?" Gertie groused. "My perm is shot. That water is way too cold for swimming, and I'm going to have a bruise on my butt the size of Texas."

"Stop your complaining," Ida Belle said. "Your butt's not even that big. Arizona maybe."

"You say the nicest things," Gertie said.

I grinned. "Did you find someone to lift the car?"

"Yeah. One of the smaller drilling companies agreed to help me out. It's going to be pricey, but they've got the equipment to do it right and fast. If I tried to cobble together some locals to give it a go, I couldn't be certain of the outcome."

And he wasn't about to call in the state for assistance. He didn't say it, but I heard it anyway. "Cool. So how soon will they be here?"

"They're mostly shut down for the holiday, so no equipment is out. They said give them an hour or so to get some guys in and then they'd be on their way."

"So they're coming today. That's great."

He nodded. "With any luck, we'll get it up before dark."

"I don't suppose you need some help keeping watch."

"If I tell you no, will you leave quietly?"

"I'm not sure we can do quietly. We keep trying but something always prevents it. And I can't guarantee you we won't sit at the end of the bayou to cover you, unless you've got backup coming. Two can play the 'you need to watch your back' game."

"Fine. Stick around, but Gertie is staying down there."

I looked over the embankment as Ida Belle secured the boat to the dock.

"The equipment to lift the car is on its way," I called down.

"Carter says we can stay as long as Gertie doesn't try to come up the steps again."

"Why would I want to come up the steps?" Gertie said. "The car is down here. This is a front-row seat. Just toss my purse down."

"No way," I said. "For all I know you have something in there that will explode on impact."

Gertie scrunched her brow. "No. Wait. Yeah, maybe keep it up there."

Carter gave me a pained look.

"I need to get out of these wet clothes or I'm going to get sick," Gertie said. "I can dry the clothes and myself out here on the dock."

Carter's expression shifted from pain to one of utter dismay.

"You are not going to put your naked butt on display for God and everyone to view," Ida Belle said.

"God sees it every time I shower," Gertie said. "And there's nobody else here to catch a glimpse except you guys and you've already been down that road."

"Which is exactly why we don't want to travel it again," Ida Belle said.

"Fine," Gertie said. "Fortune, open up my purse and toss me down my red bikini. Don't let Carter see into the side pocket or the middle one. You know what, just move away from him while you look. And don't send down the blue bikini. It crawls up my butt."

I didn't even want to think about why Gertie had a bikini in her purse, much less two. But it spared Ida Belle the bare butt portion of the afternoon, although I was betting that Ida Belle wouldn't consider herself spared anything.

I finally located the red bikini and tossed the scraps over

the side. Ida Belle handed them to Gertie, then turned her back to her.

"Let me know when you're dressed again," Ida Belle said.

"You mean decent again?" Gertie asked, and I saw her grin.

"There's nothing decent about any of this," Ida Belle said.

I stepped back from the edge, not wanting to spectate on the disrobing events any more than Ida Belle. Carter had fled a good ten feet away and kept glancing at Gertie's purse, clearly trying to decide if the law of professional ethics required him to search it.

"How do you want to handle guard duty?" I asked.

"I'll stay down here with Gertie," Ida Belle called out. "You two cover land. I've got water."

I looked at Carter. "You have to admit, we're better backup than Deputy Breaux."

"If someone needs to be shot, sure," he said. "But we kinda like to maintain that as a last resort."

"You've also got Gertie in a bikini," Ida Belle said. "That's a deterrent if I ever saw one."

"I know your back is turned," Gertie said, "so I'm telling you that I'm giving you the finger."

"I can do other things besides shoot people," I argued. "I found the car, didn't I?"

"Yeah. You want to run me through how that happened?"

I explained my thought process involving the car and finished with Ida Belle and Gertie providing me with a list of places you could set one off into the bayou to disappear.

"We started here because it's Nickel's place," I finished.

Carter raised one eyebrow. "I thought your client was innocent."

"I believe he is, but if you were the killer and you had the option to point the police in someone else's direction when you ditched the car, wouldn't you hedge your bets?"

He was silent for several seconds, then sighed.

"I'm sorry it's a local," I said, knowing exactly what the sigh was about.

He nodded. "Me too. This town has had enough problems lately. I was really hoping things were going to calm down. But I'm starting to wonder if trouble is just here to stay."

"In all fairness, some of the trouble had been here for years."

"That's true enough, but it doesn't make me feel any better about it. This used to be a town of simple people. Honest people. Get up early. Go to work. Eat dinner with your family. Fish on the weekends. And it was all a smoke screen."

"Not all of it. I think the majority of people are as you described. At least the ones I've met. But the people who deviated from the norm also grew up here. They know how to blend with the average folk."

He reached out and gave my hand a squeeze. "I know you're right. Even small societies within societies have always had their issues and scandals. I guess when I was overseas, Sinful looked like Mayberry. I suppose I'm still trying to reconcile myself to reality."

"Compared to the Middle East, Chicago is Mayberry. People who've never been to war can't begin to conceptualize what it's really like."

"Are you trying to cheer me up by telling me another murder is no big deal?"

"Murder is always a big deal. But in the big scheme of things, we're still as close to a slice of Mayberry as we're getting. I mean, if you wave a magic wand and make Mayberry the strangest place on earth."

He was silent again for a while, then finally nodded. "Let's go see if there's any evidence left where that car went off the embankment."

CHAPTER THIRTEEN

IT TOOK two hours for the oil field guys to show up with the equipment to lift the car, and another hour-plus to get the car up on the small barge. Lucky for everyone involved, Gertie's clothes had dried and she was back to looking the way a senior lady boating in November should look. Although I had to agree with her on the perm. Her hair was going to need a serious fix.

The actual acquisition of the car was uneventful and I found myself somewhat disappointed when it was all over. I'm not sure what I'd expected, but once the barge started pulling away, I couldn't help but feel a bit let down.

"You did good work," Ida Belle said, cluing in on my mood. "The car itself was never the point of this exercise. Proving your theory was. And proving your theory eliminates the need to investigate what Venus had been up to in New Orleans."

"Yes and no," I said. "The location of the car pretty much guarantees the killer is a local, but something sent Venus back to Sinful. I'd still like to know what. Especially since Starlight showed up expecting some sort of payout. She knows something. A woman like that doesn't appear unless there's something in it for her."

Ida Belle frowned. "That's true. Lord knows, we were no particular friends of Starlight. No one was, really. But I suppose she lost a daughter same as Percy. It wouldn't be good manners to offer Percy help but not Starlight."

I smiled. "You think she's at the motel?"

Gertie nodded. "If Starlight thinks there's something here to be had, then she's still hanging around. We'll track her down and get what we can out of her."

"I don't think a casserole is going to get her lips moving," I said.

"No. But a nice bottle of wine might," Ida Belle said. "And I've been holding a good one for a special occasion."

"I don't know that I would call this special," I said. "Or that I'd give up good wine for Starlight."

Ida Belle shrugged. "You can reimburse me. Business expense and all."

"Hey," Gertie said. "If she gets reimbursed for wine, then I want reimbursement for explosives."

"Really?" I said. "And how would you like me to categorize that on my tax return—in the illegal equipment category?"

"I suppose that might stand out in an audit," Gertie said.

Ida Belle shook her head. "Sun's starting to set. Let's get out of here before it gets completely dark. I need a hot shower, a good dinner, and cool sheets. I suppose your steak dinner with Carter is delayed?"

I nodded. "He's on car duty for the duration. But I've got some chicken we can throw on the grill if you want."

"No need," Gertie said. "I made enchiladas, tamales, and two Bundt cakes last night."

We stared.

"I couldn't sleep with that bird chattering, so I cooked.

Turns out good for the two of you. Everyone grab a shower, then we'll meet up at my house for dinner. You're on your own for cool sheets."

I STOOD in the shower until I used every ounce of hot water, which wasn't nearly as long as I thought it would be. I'd have to ask about getting a second hot water heater. Was that even possible? Or maybe one of those tankless ones where you never ran out of hot water? I'd never been a homeowner before, so these were questions that had never come up. Now I found myself humming happily as I dried off, thinking about all the completely normal things I was responsible for.

It was a far cry from my previous life, and I was loving every minute of it.

I brushed my wet hair and left it alone. I didn't feel like taking the time to dry it, especially since I was starving, so I pulled on some clothes, grabbed my keys, and headed out to Gertie's. I didn't figure on seeing Carter tonight. He had the car to deal with and that would take a while. And since his day had been even longer than mine, he'd probably want a hot shower, food, and bed. He'd probably start going over every inch of the car the next day with the forensics team, so he'd need to be back at it early.

Gertie's foray into Mexican food was the stuff dreams were made of. At least, the kind of dreams you had after you spent a day trying to hunt down a killer. I ate way too much, but that was expected. I probably should have stopped at the second piece of pound cake or maybe the sixth enchilada, but my willpower had clocked out for the night.

Once we were essentially immobile, we shifted the plates to one side and I grabbed my laptop from my backpack. Ida

Belle pulled out a notebook that she and Gertie had been using to make the list of suspects, and we were ready to work. I had already started a document with notes on the case and took a few minutes to add some about locating the car and our visit with Percy.

"All right," I said when I was done. "Let's talk suspects. I know Starlight is on the must-see list for tomorrow."

Ida Belle nodded. "I've already verified through my sources that she's at the motel. Paid for a single night but didn't give a checkout date."

I made a note in the document, not even bothering to ask Ida Belle how she'd come about the information. The Sinful Ladies always had a niece or nephew or fifth cousin or friend of their banker or doctor or whoever that worked somewhere and could filter information. It was a big advantage to me. Like having my own local information network, but the off-grid kind.

"Okay, who's next?" I said.

"They're not suspects, necessarily, but I think we should start with the two girls Venus was friends with before she left town," Gertie said. "I don't think they were close or anything. Not sure Venus was even capable of a real friendship, but I'm guessing they'd have a take on her that went further than most."

"Probably so," Ida Belle agreed. "Girls are just young women, and unless a woman is silly, she notices things. They probably know more about Venus than what she put out to be seen."

"Sounds good," I said. "Names and background?"

"First one is Melanie Breaux," Gertie said. "She was the nice girl I mentioned before. The one that Venus took up for when she got picked on. She married a local boy. He works road construction—night shift. Currently on the highway job just out of Sinful. Melanie is a part-time teller at the bank."

I typed as Gertie talked, then looked up when I finished.

"Second one is Haylee Wills," Gertie said.

"*Not* a nice girl," Ida Belle said. "Haylee and Venus were cut from the same cloth. Her parents spent more time in jail than at home and Haylee worked hard at following their path. Had more juvenile arrests than Gertie has dynamite."

"Probably true," Gertie agreed. "Haylee seemed to straighten out a bit later on, but as far as I know, she still lives the wild life compared to regular Sinful. Works as a tattoo artist, rides a crotch rocket, probably still into the wrong kind of man. Since her cousin moved away, I haven't gotten updates. Her mother and father both split some time before. I have no idea where they are."

"Cool," I said. "Two completely different personality types might yield a decent picture. What about people who had a grudge?"

Ida Belle turned the notebook around and I looked at the list of names that went all the way to the bottom of the page.

"There's more," she said.

I flipped the page over and saw more names covering half a page. "There's at least forty names here."

"I'm afraid so," Ida Belle said. "Started with around sixty, but we managed to narrow it down some by eliminating those without opportunity."

"Eliminated them how?" I asked.

"They weren't here," Gertie said. "Either on a trip, or visiting a sick relative, or in the hospital themselves, or injured so that they couldn't go running around digging holes and burying bodies."

"And you're sure we can eliminate them?" I asked. "Someone could have claimed to be gone and doubled back."

Ida Belle nodded. "We only took people off the list who were gone, hospitalized, or injured before Venus disappeared. Since it doesn't appear as if it was planned, we figure none of them were setting up an alibi."

"Okay," I said. "So are there any on the list you like for it more than others?"

"Bart Lagasse would be one of my top five," Gertie said. "Venus dated him in high school. Of course, he thought it was a relationship. The feeling was not mutual. He caught her with other boys but never could shake the habit. His stereo equipment went missing from his bedroom the night she took off for New Orleans. I don't think it's a stretch to assume Venus took it."

"What is Bart up to now?" I asked.

"Handyman and maintenance sort of stuff," Ida Belle said. "When he can keep a job. He's got a temper. Always has. Tends to tell people what he thinks, which usually isn't much. Doesn't work so well when you're telling the boss. Definitely doesn't work well when you follow it up with a right cross. That's how he got fired the last time."

"Sounds like a lovely guy," I said. I made a note to be dressed for a fistfight when we cornered Bart. "Did he hook up with Venus when she made her return trip?"

"The rumor is he was making another play for her when she took up with Whiskey," Gertie said. "That backed him off. He's a hothead, but he's not going toe to toe with Whiskey. Especially not over someone like Venus. There's no future in it."

"Got it," I said. "Who else?"

"Dean Allard is the top of my list," Ida Belle said. "Local fisherman and regular at the Swamp Bar. Rumor has it that he spent some quality time with Venus when she first returned. When he didn't fork over enough cash, she told his wife, who promptly left him and filed for child support for their six kids. He couldn't make rent anymore on their house. Last I heard, he moved back in with his mother, who makes the proverbial cat lady seem sane."

"Ouch," I said. "I can see why he might be holding a grudge."

They continued down their list, giving me their picks and why, but no one seemed as good a bet as the top two. Finally, I saved the file and closed my laptop.

"This is great," I said.

"Now we just need to figure out which one of them is the killer," Gertie said.

"Remember, all we have here is the information you guys could round up through your channels," I said. "It's entirely possible that Venus made enemies you haven't heard about. That's why I want to talk to the girlfriends first. They might be able to put us on to one over the other or add someone we didn't know about to the list."

Ida Belle nodded. "That's smart. And you're right. Venus was certainly capable of making a new and bigger enemy whose misfortune hasn't made it our way. I imagine most go to great lengths to keep people from finding out they were made a fool."

"Definitely," I said. "We'll hit the girlfriends first and then try Starlight. Then we'll move on to the guys. Maybe we'll luck out and some of them will be off work this week."

I shoved my laptop into my backpack, preparing to wrap things up and head home for some much-needed sleep. Then someone knocked on Gertie's front door.

"Hide the drugs!" Francis yelled.

I checked my watch and glanced at Gertie and Ida Belle. Almost 10:00 p.m. Much too late for a social call. We hurried into the living room and Gertie peered through the peephole.

"It's Carter," she said, and pulled open the door.

He stepped inside, looking like a running year of bad weather.

"Run!" Francis said. "It's 5-0."

Carter shook his head. "Are you supposed to run before or after you hide the drugs?"

"Depending on what you have, maybe run *with* the drugs," Gertie said.

"What's up?" I asked. "You don't look so good."

"It's been a long day, and things are going from bad to worse," he said.

"Did you find something in the car?" Ida Belle asked.

"Yeah," he said. "I did a preliminary search for evidence and found a pocketknife on the floorboard. It had 'Whiskey' engraved on the handle."

Crap!

"That doesn't mean Whiskey did it," Gertie said. "Venus probably stole the knife. She didn't seem to be able to help herself. If something was there and her fingers could reach it, she took it."

"I know," Carter said. "But I've got to record my findings, and when the DA reads the case file..."

He didn't have to finish the sentence. Whiskey had threatened Venus and she was killed the same night. She'd cheated on him and stolen from him and played him for a fool. His knife was in her car and that car had been dumped into the bayou at his brother's camp. Everything pointed to Whiskey and that's exactly how the DA was going to see it.

"I'm sorry," Carter said. "I know Whiskey's situation with his father and the last thing I want is for him to go up on charges for a crime he didn't commit. But my hands are tied. I have to report the facts as they arise."

"No one is blaming you," Ida Belle said. "That's the job

you're entrusted with and you have to do it correctly. You won't do any of us a bit of good if you get yourself fired, least of all Whiskey. Another deputy would stop looking now, figuring his work was done. We know you won't stop digging until you have the truth."

"I just hope I find the truth before it's too late for Whiskey and his father," Carter said.

I put my arms around him and gave him a squeeze. I knew he felt horrible about the situation and had probably spent a while trying to figure a way out of it before he'd come over here and broken the bad news to us.

"I appreciate you letting us know," I said. "When will the DA have the updated file for review?"

"I can stall a little," Carter said. "Wait until the forensic team is done, at least, but after that I have to get everything in. The fact that it's a holiday week might help or hurt, depending on the DA's mood. Everyone is trying to lighten their load before Thanksgiving. This isn't the biggest thing the DA has on his desk at the moment, but it's still murder. He's not going to let it slide for very long."

"So worst case, we have a couple days," I said.

"There's something else," he said. "And I shouldn't be telling you this, so I'm trusting you not to repeat it. Not even to Whiskey. I'll question him about the knife, but this other thing is something I'm holding back."

I stared at him, intrigued. "What is it?"

"I found Venus's suitcases in the trunk of the car...packed with her belongings."

DESPITE BEING EXHAUSTED and the enormous amount of carbs I'd consumed, it took me forever to fall asleep. And then when I did, it wasn't restful at all. I dreamed all night of submerged cars and suitcases packed with pocketknives. Once I even dreamed of a suitcase with Francis in it. He was praying the entire time, then burst into a rendition of "I Saw the Light" when I opened it.

I finally gave up around 6:00 a.m. and shuffled into the kitchen for coffee, briefly considering snorting some of the grounds right out of the can. Merlin was awake and demanding breakfast, so I got him fixed up while I waited for the coffee to brew. Then I poured a thermos full and headed outside to my lawn chair.

As I sipped and watched the water roll by, I worked through everything we knew about the case. I'd been riding on a bit of a high yesterday when I found the car, thinking I was getting good at this detective stuff. Then Carter had blown a hole in my well-constructed theory and I was faced with revisiting everything all over again.

Ida Belle, Gertie, and I had discussed things briefly after Carter left Gertie's house the night before, but none of us were firing on all cylinders given the hour and the fact that we all needed to sleep. I'd been restless ever since Gertie had unearthed the body and I imagined Ida Belle had been as well, even though she didn't let much get through her calm demeanor. Gertie had lost at least one night to the noisy bird, and I wondered if putting a blanket over his cage last night had helped any. If it hadn't, Lord only knew what Gertie had cooked up. We might have enough food to feed all of Sinful before she got that bird sleeping right.

Then there was the whole other issue—the one that had nothing to do with murder. I could tell Ida Belle's energy level was down some and I figured that a lot of her thoughts were on Walter's proposal. Neither Gertie nor I had broached the subject again, figuring all we'd get was a butt-chewing for our effort, at best. At worst, she *was* armed. But I couldn't stop wondering why she was thinking about it now. Why, after all these years, did she not hand out the automatic "no" that she always had on tap? Whatever she was wrestling with had to be big because Ida Belle didn't do drama. And she didn't usually take much time to make up her mind about things. She was a woman who knew what she wanted, did it, and gave no excuses or explanations for her decisions.

I took another sip of coffee and blew out a breath. While the inner workings of Ida Belle's heart and mind were an interesting puzzle to tackle, I had a more pressing issue on my plate. If we didn't find a better alternative than Whiskey, I had no doubt Carter was going to have to arrest him. And based on his record and the evidence, bail was either going to be a big nope or so high he couldn't swing it. I could only hope that the holiday delayed any action from the DA rather than prompting him to fill up jail cells before he bowed out of the office for a long weekend.

The suitcases.

Such common, uninteresting objects and yet in this case, they were the most fascinating thing I'd heard about in weeks. Even without access to the ME's report, we knew the window of time in which Venus had been killed. Whiskey kicked her out of the bar around 11:00 p.m. The cement workers showed up to start on the basketball court the next morning at 8:00 a.m., but the sun was up a bit before.

Venus's car had been with her that night at the Swamp Bar and her belongings were gone the next day. Percy had been at home that night, and no matter how heavy someone sleeps, they couldn't have failed to hear someone enter their home and start packing suitcases. And even if he'd thought it was Venus moving around and had ignored it, would the killer have been so brazen as to attempt it in the first place?

I couldn't imagine that was the case, because it meant the killer had to stash the car that night, return the next day and pack up Venus's belongings, then drag them through the woods to the nearest side street and get them to the car for disposal. Hauling the luggage through the woods wasn't a quick or easy job and it increased the chances of being seen. Or what if he was stopped on a traffic violation, had an arrest warrant—which was fairly common in Sinful—and got caught with Venus's belongings in his vehicle?

And then there were the additional issues with the car. Since it couldn't have been ditched that night, that meant more chances of it being discovered. Even if the killer had stashed it at Nickel's place, there was still a chance someone would see it before the killer got back with the luggage. Ida Belle and Gertie had already pointed out that kids would break into vacant camps to have parties or sexy time with girlfriends, and there was always the possibility of someone thinking they could find something to steal.

Quite frankly, someone might have shown up just to use his dock for fishing. Ida Belle had already verified through Myrtle that Nickel hadn't been released from jail until a week after Venus was killed. My limited experience with boats had taught me that they were broken at least half the time, so someone could have figured that since Nickel wasn't there to police his dock, it was open for business. Not to mention that any number of locals with boats that were operable could have been out fishing and seen the car go over the embankment during the day.

For that matter, why put the luggage in the car at all? Why not ditch the car that night and bury the luggage in the woods as I'd suggested to begin with?

I sighed. It didn't make sense. Which meant I was going to have to go back to the beginning and try to figure out a different scenario, because the current one no longer worked. Not in a plausible way.

"I thought you might be up." Carter's voice sounded behind me.

I turned around and saw him walking up with a thermos of coffee. I held mine up.

"Great minds," I said.

"More like not enough sleep."

"That too."

"You make any sense of things yet?" he asked.

"Not even. Every scenario I come up with that fits makes the killer either one of the dumbest people on the planet or the most arrogant."

"Criminals are usually one or the other. That's why they get caught."

"I get that, but there's got to be limits. Given the method of disposal, I don't think Venus's murder was planned, but someone was clever enough to make it appear as if she'd gone back to New Orleans. Someone who knew no one in Sinful would go looking for her. Then they, what? Get away with hiding the body but risk it all on packing up her clothes in the trunk of her car before sending it off that embankment? Why not get rid of the car that night and the luggage the next day? Why hold the car waiting for the luggage and take all the risk that someone would find it or see them sending it over that embankment?"

Carter shook his head. "I haven't come up with anything reasonable either. Not even reasonable on the side of idiotic."

"We're missing something."

"We're missing a lot of something, but that's the way investigations go. You pick up a piece here and there and hope when you've collected all you can find that you have enough to form a picture. There's always holes, but if you have a good enough basis, you can fill them in."

"This case has a hole you could drive a shrimp boat through."

He nodded and frowned. I knew he was in his usual slump that he got into when a major crime happened in his town, but he seemed even more concerned than he had been the night before.

"Is something else wrong?" I asked.

"Did you know Walter asked Ida Belle to marry him again?"

I nodded. "Ida Belle was snippier than usual and Gertie and I finally got it out of her." I didn't elaborate on Ida Belle's out-of-the-ordinary response because I wasn't sure what Carter knew, and it wasn't my place to tell him Ida Belle's personal business.

Carter stared at the bayou and shook his head. "I don't know why he does it. All these years and he still keeps trying. And every time, she breaks his heart a little more. He ought to know better by now, but he's spent his life pining for a woman who doesn't want him."

He sounded a tad angry and a tiny bit bitter, but I couldn't blame him. Walter was his uncle and had stepped in as a father figure after Carter's dad passed.

"I don't think it's that simple," I said quietly.

He looked down at me and sighed. "I know that. Ida Belle isn't cruel and even if she had a reason to be, it would never be directed at Walter. I guess I just wish he'd figured out how to move on years ago."

"I know you don't get it, and I'm not about to say I understand it either. Hell, I'm a complete beginner at the relationship thing. But maybe in the big scheme of things, they're both where they have always needed to be. It might not be enough for us, but it must be for them or they wouldn't still be doing this dance."

He leaned over and brushed my lips with his. "You're right. It wouldn't be enough for me. But I get what you're saying. I'll call you before I bring Whiskey in for questioning."

"Thanks."

As he walked away, I rose from my chair and headed inside. I needed a good breakfast and an influx of ideas. I figured a trip to Francine's would cover one of them.

CHAPTER FOURTEEN

IDA BELLE and Gertie walked into the café about ten minutes after I arrived. Ida Belle appeared alert and rested and I wondered how the heck she managed to sleep with all the things she had going on. Even Gertie looked a bit better, but in comparison to the morning before, that wasn't saying a lot.

Ally popped over and took our order, but she didn't have time to chat as the café was busy and she had food up in the window.

"Did the blanket over the cage work?" I asked when Ally headed off.

"It did," Gertie said. "Well, until about 5:00 a.m. when he started doing morning prayers."

"He must have picked up on the nun's schedule," I said.

"It's a wonder the criminals didn't shoot him," Ida Belle said.

"They probably kept him in the back room of some seedy bar where they did all their business," Gertie said.

"You've been watching Mafia movies again," Ida Belle said. "Not all criminal enterprises own a bar."

"I'm pretty sure it's required," Gertie said. "You know, some sort of code."

"And what happens if you don't comply?" Ida Belle asked.

"You're forced to pay retail for your drinks and find your cheap women on the street corner?" I suggested.

"Despite the levity intended, you do make a somewhat viable point," Ida Belle said.

"If only I had everything else figured out," I said.

"I take it you didn't have an investigative epiphany last night?" Ida Belle asked.

"Oh," Gertie said. "I wonder what that would look like."

"She'd probably leap out of bed and shoot a hole in the roof," Ida Belle said.

"I've actually already done that," I said. "Not together, but separately."

Gertie waved a hand in dismissal. "If you haven't shot a hole in your house, you shouldn't even be allowed to live in this town."

Ida Belle looked over at me. "Good news. You're safe from eviction."

I grinned. "Glad I won't have to pack and run but unfortunately, there was no leaping and shooting as part of my nighttime program. I'm as confused this morning as I was last night. Heck, maybe even more so since I've had longer to think about it."

Ida Belle nodded. "I will admit, I can usually come up with some sort of viable explanation for things that seem completely odd—Gertie is my best friend, after all—but this one has me stumped."

"And as someone who regularly comes up with those completely odd lines of thinking, I don't have a clue either," Gertie said.

"Carter stopped by on his way to work this morning," I

said. "He's as clueless as we are. Which is why we need to stop concentrating on the why and focus on the who."

Ida Belle nodded. "I agree. After breakfast, we'll see if Melanie is at home. She usually works afternoons at the bank so we might be able to catch her this morning."

"Then we can head up the highway and see if Haylee is at work," Gertie said. "We couldn't run down a home address for her."

"So we're visiting a tattoo parlor?" I asked. "Yippee. What could possibly go wrong there?"

Ida Belle pointed at Gertie. "*No one* is getting a tattoo."

"Not even a little one?" Gertie asked. "I've been thinking—"

"No you haven't," Ida Belle said. "Look around this dining room. You see what happens to tattoos once skin sags. Your skin's already there. Anything you do will look like a blob."

"Maybe I was thinking of getting a blob," Gertie said.

"Well, you're not doing it today and certainly not at any place that employs Haylee," Ida Belle said. "If you insist on that madness, then you need to make a trip to New Orleans and go to a place that actually cares about health code."

"Probably a good idea," Gertie said. "I suppose I shouldn't do it on the clock anyway." She looked over at me and I shook my head.

"There is no way I'm calling a tattoo a business expense," I said.

Ally stepped up with our breakfast and grinned. "Maybe you could get a trademark for your business and make everyone get a tattoo," she said.

"You're not helping," Ida Belle said.

"Wasn't trying to," Ally said as she put plates on the table.

"Any gossip?" I asked.

Ally shook her head. "Not since they identified the body. I

mean, there's low talking about who might have done it, but mostly people think someone followed her from New Orleans. The ones who don't have landed on Whiskey, since he was seeing her and they had that big fight the night she was killed."

"What do you think?" I asked. Ally was young and had grown up in Sinful. Because of her age, she sometimes had a different perspective than Ida Belle and Gertie.

"I honestly don't know," she said. "I'd love to think it was a stranger but I think it's the coward's way out. The truth is, Venus created plenty of hard feelings here in Sinful. No use looking elsewhere until you've gone through all of them."

"So you're leaning toward Whiskey?" I asked. As far as I knew, no one was aware that Whiskey was my client except Ida Belle, Gertie, and Carter. I wanted to get Ally's unbiased opinion.

"You know, I don't think so," Ally said. "I mean, just the sight of him scares me a little, and I have no doubt he could have throttled her with those big hands of his. But even though most wouldn't believe it, Whiskey's smart. The CPA I've been talking to about my bakery concept does the books for the bar. He said I should talk to Whiskey sometime about inventory methods and identifying and catering to a customer base. Said Whiskey was one of the sharpest clients he had for squeezing every ounce of profit out of a business."

"That's fascinating," Ida Belle said.

Ally nodded. "Goes to show you can't tell by looking at a person. So anyway, I figured if he's that smart, he's not going to throw it all away on someone like Venus. Besides, he's got his daddy to look after, and he does a real fine job there. I visit him a couple times a month to drop off meals from Francine and Whiskey is really taking good care of him."

"He was always a good son," Gertie said.

Ally frowned. "There was one thing I overheard this

morning that I didn't like. Dorothy was in here earlier with Aunt Celia. She said that earlier this year, Percy had a complete meltdown in the bank, accusing the manager of stealing from his safe-deposit box. Her implication was that he was unstable and given how Venus was always stealing from him, maybe he finally made sure she couldn't anymore."

"That's a particularly insidious piece of gossip," Ida Belle said.

Ally nodded. "I hope people don't start thinking Percy did this. I mean, I suppose he could have, but I just don't think so. But then, I can't picture him going off on the bank manager either." She sighed. "I guess you just never know."

"Probably true," I said.

"Well, I better go grab some food," Ally said. "I'll bring you guys a coffee refill on my way back."

"Seems no one of consequence and good common sense likes Whiskey for this," Ida Belle said.

"Since the DA has no common sense, I guess that lets him out of that line of thinking," Gertie said.

"Can't really blame him," I said. "On paper, Whiskey looks like a great option. And the evidence is pointing his direction."

"On the surface, sure," Ida Belle said. "But it's all circumstantial."

"Not sure a jury would get a look at Whiskey and think so," Gertie said.

"We're trying to prevent it from getting to that point," I said. "So let's dig in and get moving. What do you think about that bank story about Percy?"

Ida Belle and Gertie glanced at each other, clearly unhappy.

"I don't like it," Ida Belle said. "For several reasons. The first being that I don't want to think Percy did it. The second that even if he didn't, Dorothy and Celia are going to spread that bit of nastiness through Sinful faster than the speed of light. You know how things go here. It could make things hard on Percy."

"Then I guess we best hurry," I said.

We made quick work of breakfast, said goodbye to Ally, and headed for my house first to drop off my Jeep. Then we drove over to Melanie's house with a batch of cookies that Gertie said would serve as a "friend" condolence sort of offering. Melanie's car was in the driveway, which was a good sign. We knocked on the door and a couple minutes later, a young woman opened the door.

Twenties. Five feet four. One hundred ten pounds. Plain hair. Plain face. Plain clothes. Would be great undercover as this woman could pass on a street completely unnoticed. Threat level zero.

She gave us a polite smile but looked a little confused. "Hello, ladies. How can I help you?"

Gertie displayed the cookies and I held in a grin. Living in Sinful, I'd discovered that the quickest and easiest way to gain access to a house when you weren't expected and not necessarily wanted was to present food. Apparently, some law more important than even the Ten Commandments made denying people with food the right to enter a form of blasphemy.

"I brought you some cookies, dear," Gertie said. "We thought you might be upset, given the things that have happened."

"Oh, of course." She stepped back and waved us inside. "I just made another pot of coffee. Jeff poured most of the first one in his thermos before he headed out. I barely got a half cup and that wasn't going to cut it. I'm allowed a full cup a day and I intend to get it."

Gertie brightened. "You're pregnant? I hadn't heard."

Melanie blushed. "We've been keeping it quiet for now. With all the trouble we've had getting pregnant and the miscarriage earlier this year, I didn't want to get my hopes up.

I'm three months along. We're going to tell Jeff's parents at Christmas, so if you'd keep it secret for now, I'd appreciate it."

"Of course," Gertie said and gave her a hug. "Congratulations. I know how much it means to you and Jeff to have a family."

A flicker of something, maybe grief, flashed on Melanie's face, but it disappeared quickly. "Thank you. You ladies come on back and we'll have some coffee and sample those cookies. I've had an awful sweet tooth ever since I got pregnant."

"You're not still riding that bicycle, are you?" Ida Belle asked.

"No," Melanie said. "I'm being extra, extra careful. I got rid of it back in the spring. The only exercise I get now is walking and yoga."

We stepped into a pretty little kitchen, with light blue walls and white cabinets. Fresh-cut flowers were on the breakfast table and herbs grew in pots in a window above the sink. The room was small, as was the rest of the house, but I could tell care had been taken with its decoration and upkeep. I found the result charming and I rarely found anything charming. Perhaps this was where plain Melanie showed her true colors.

"I love your kitchen," I said.

"Ha." Ida Belle laughed. "Coming from her, that's high praise. She probably doesn't even know how to turn on the stove."

"I heat up casseroles," I said.

Gertie patted my hand. "That's the oven."

Melanie smiled and served us all coffee, then set a tray of sweetener and cream in the middle of the table. "You must be Fortune," she said. "We've never formally met although I've seen you in town a couple times. And, of course, I've heard all the gossip but that's probably not polite to say."

I waved a hand in dismissal. "I'm sure everything you've heard is true or at least almost."

Melanie nodded and took a seat. "You're going to do well here with that attitude. Can't stop folks from talking."

"Not unless you shoot them," Gertie said. "And that's been frowned on for a while now. How are you doing, Melanie? I know you and Venus were close. I hope this hasn't upset you too much, especially in light of your baby news."

Melanie shrugged. "It's shocking, of course. Would be if it was anyone...you know, a murder and all right here in Sinful. But I guess if I'm being honest, I'm more shocked than surprised. If that makes any sense."

Ida Belle nodded. "Given the way Venus chose to live, it does. I think most people feel like you do. They're just not going to say."

"And I know I shouldn't either," Melanie said. "Shouldn't speak ill of the dead and all, but you ladies know the people here better than most, so I know you won't judge me for dwelling in reality."

"Not even a little," Gertie said. "Had you spent much time with Venus when she returned? I know you were close in high school but wasn't sure if you'd kept in touch after she left."

Melanie shook her head. "She told me she was leaving back then. Said she couldn't take it here anymore. She called this town the Walking Dead. Said everyone just moved through the motions like zombies and nothing ever happened. Venus was always looking for something to happen. She wasn't satisfied with regular living."

Gertie nodded. "Even when she was a kid, normal things didn't sit right with her."

"They didn't," Melanie agreed. "She wanted thrills and excitement, and unless you find breaking a fishing record or a fight at the Swamp Bar exciting, there's not much of that here.

I think that's why she caused so much trouble. She thought New Orleans would have everything she was looking for."

"And did it?" I asked.

"I have no idea," Melanie said. "I only heard from her once. Said she'd found a job and a man at a biker bar. That was about a week after she left. Never heard a word again until she knocked on my door in May, telling me she was back."

"You never tried to contact her?" I asked.

"Of course I did," Melanie said. "But her cell phone account was canceled and I didn't know the name of the bar or the man. I tried searching online but couldn't come up with anything. I figured she was putting Sinful in her rearview mirror and me along with it."

"Not much else you could have done," Ida Belle said. "Without access to databases like the police have, it's hard to find someone that doesn't want to be found. And Venus wasn't exactly the type to set up on Facebook or Twitter."

Melanie laughed. "No. Definitely not." She sobered. "I guess she didn't find whatever she was looking for since she came back."

"Did she ever say why she came back?" Gertie asked.

"No," Melanie said. "I asked but all she would tell me was she was getting ready to make a big change in her life and she needed to step back for a bit and get things in order."

"You think she had trouble in New Orleans?" Ida Belle asked.

"I think trouble stuck to Venus like bayou mud," Melanie said. "I'm sure there was something going on. Something bad enough to send her back to her daddy's house. But she never let on what it was."

"I wonder if she was planning on staying," Gertie said.

"I don't think so," Melanie said. "At least, I never got that impression. I guess I figured she was lying low here until whatever trouble she had in New Orleans blew over. Then she'd disappear again. That's why I didn't think anything of it when I heard she was gone again."

"I suppose she left trouble in New Orleans only to find more here," I said. "People are saying she took up with Whiskey. He's a little old and a little rough for a young woman, at least in my opinion."

Melanie frowned. "Yeah, I heard about their fight the night she disappeared again. I don't really know Whiskey but I understand he's a rough sort."

"I suppose that was her type," I said.

"The rough type of man or someone else's man," Melanie said. "I'm sorry. I probably shouldn't have said that."

"That's okay," Gertie said. "I think everyone knows how Venus did people. But men still have a choice, and women need to remember that."

"I know you're right," Melanie said. "But I saw it happen a couple times in high school and it was almost like they were drugged. Just lost all sense of anything. I never understood it, but then I suppose I don't have the wiring to."

"More like a plumbing thing," Ida Belle said.

Melanie smiled. "Have you been to see Percy? I keep meaning to go but I have to be honest, I don't know what to say. Percy was never an easy man to talk to. And given that he and Venus didn't really get on well..."

"We saw him yesterday," Gertie said. "He's as stoic as usual. Which could mean anything, really. You don't often see an emotion sneak out of him—bad or good."

"That's true enough," Melanie said.

"Although we did hear a rumor that Percy got sideways with the bank manager," Ida Belle said. "Any truth to that?"

Melanie frowned and shook her head. "I haven't heard

anything like that and certainly didn't see it. I suppose anything's possible..."

"I guess you heard that Starlight is back in town," Gertie said.

Melanie's eyes widened. "No! What in the world could she want?"

"We ran into her at Percy's," Ida Belle said. "Most unpleasant for everyone. She told Percy she was there for her share of Venus's assets."

"What assets?" Melanie asked. "Besides that rusted-out car of hers, all she had was some cheap clothes and costume jewelry. If she got her hands on anything of value, it went right to the pawnshop."

"We have no idea what Starlight was wanting," Gertie said. "Percy tossed her out on her ear. It's probably the first time I've ever seen him mad but can't say that I blame him."

"Oh my God, how horrible," Melanie said. "There hasn't even been a service yet and that awful woman is demanding money...or whatever. I simply don't understand people."

"That's because you have a proper set of values," Gertie said. "But people who don't seem to sleep well at night no matter the things they do. Makes things harder for the rest of us trying to do things right."

"It does," Melanie said. "Ladies, I'm so glad you stopped by, but I need to get ready for work. I've got to be in a little early to cover for one of the tellers with a doctor's appointment."

We all rose and Melanie followed us to the door. "Thank you so much for checking on me and for the cookies," she said.

We headed out and climbed into Ida Belle's SUV and she pulled away.

"Time to talk tattoos?" she asked.

I nodded.

CHAPTER FIFTEEN

"So you guys know Melanie," I said as Ida Belle pulled away. "Did you get anything from that conversation?"

"Not really," Gertie said. "No more than we already knew."

"She seemed rather matter-of-fact," I said.

Ida Belle shrugged. "If Melanie and Venus had been close then I would have expected a little more in the way of grief, but what I got from that conversation is that they didn't hang out when Venus came back. They never did have anything in common, but they were definitely in different places in their lives as adults."

Gertie nodded. "Venus was never the marry-and-kids sort of girl, and that's all Melanie's really cared about ever since her parents died in a car crash back a few years ago. If Melanie launched into a talk about decorating the nursery or how Jeff won't put the seat down, Venus would have checked out in two seconds flat."

"I agree," Ida Belle said. "Their relationship, if one could call it that, worked in high school because they both got something out of it. Melanie got protection from the bullies and Venus got hero worship and the bulk of Melanie's allowance.

But Melanie didn't have anything to offer Venus anymore. She could get money easier off of men and she was well past the age that hero worship would give her a boost."

"You think this tattoo girl is going to know any more than Melanie?" I asked.

"If Venus hooked up with her when she returned, maybe," Ida Belle said. "Haylee was always more interested in trouble than walking the straight and narrow, but she wasn't one to necessarily instigate it."

"So Venus created the trouble and Haylee was happy to be along for the ride," I said.

"Exactly," Ida Belle said.

"Well, let's hope Venus and Haylee got together over tattoos and shots and traded war stories," I said. "Then at least we might know what Venus was up to while she was in New Orleans, which could point us to what kind of trouble she might have been in when she returned to Sinful."

"You think she was dealing drugs or something?" Gertie said.

"I don't know," I said. "I suppose working at the Swamp Bar would be the perfect place to set up shop if she was, but I can't imagine Whiskey allowing that to happen."

"Unless she was so good at it he didn't know," Gertie said.

"She couldn't keep her hands off other men's pants right there in front of Whiskey," Ida Belle said. "How in the world could she have managed to deal drugs and keep it off-radar?"

"Yeah," Gertie agreed. "I'm sure someone would have talked and it would have gotten back to Whiskey. But there's other things she could have been using the Swamp Bar for. Blackmail, for one. Plenty of men in there taking up with loose women when they're supposed to be home with their wives."

"I'm sure she wouldn't have been above it," Ida Belle said. "Especially if she thought there was any money to be had. And blackmail is definitely the kind of thing that might prompt someone to kill you on the spot."

I nodded. "It's a really good thought. The only part I don't like is where it extends our suspect list to everyone misbehaving at the Swamp Bar. There aren't enough detectives in Louisiana to cover that ground."

"Someone has to know something," Gertie said. "Nothing stays a secret here forever."

"I'm hoping Haylee knows something," I said. "But my money is on Starlight. The question is, can we get it out of her?"

"Not unless she wants to give it," Ida Belle said. "Let me take the lead when we talk to her. I know the way her mind works. She'll only give up something she considers valuable if we have something to offer in return."

"Our turnoff is coming up," Gertie said.

"Did you call ahead?" Ida Belle asked.

Gertie nodded. "Haylee's working today."

"Hopefully, they won't be very busy and we can pull her away for a chat," I said.

Ida Belle located the tattoo parlor at the end of a seedy-looking strip center just off the highway. A pizza place, a Laundromat, and two bail bonds places occupied the other spots. There were no cars parked in front of the parlor, so our odds were looking good.

We headed inside and spotted a young guy sitting in a bean bag and reading a car magazine. He took one look at us and raised one eyebrow, which I found impressive given the amount of hardware he had stuck through it. And that was nothing compared to the rest of his face.

Midtwenties. Five feet ten. A hundred fifty pounds without the hardware. Add another ten with it. Only a threat to those with good taste.

His head was shaved and he had a giant spiderweb tattooed across one side of his scalp that stretched onto his face. A spider was dangling from his chin, trying to climb up. I could only assume it was hindered by his tongue, which he couldn't seem to get all the way into his mouth, probably due to the enormous stud piercing through the tip.

"You girls interested in some work?" he asked.

"No!" We all put our hands up and responded at once. I held in a grin. Apparently not even Gertie wanted a piece of this action.

"We're looking for Haylee," Ida Belle said. "Is she here today?"

He nodded and yelled. A couple seconds later, a young woman came through a door at the back of the room.

Early twenties. Five foot three. One hundred five pounds. More tattoos than clothing. Threat level nil unless she kicks you. Her tennis shoes had spikes around them.

If it weren't for the short, jet-black hair, the dark makeup, and the assortment of bands with studs, she would have looked like a young teen. Even with the hair, makeup, and tattoos, Haylee was still a really pretty girl. If one didn't take into account the scowl on her face.

"These people want to see you," Tongue Stud said.

She stared at the three of us, her expression part confusion, part disinterest. Then her eyes widened and she smiled. "Ms. Hebert?"

Gertie smiled and nodded.

"Sorry about the dirty look," Haylee said. "I didn't recognize you at first. Of course, I never expected to see you someplace like this so it threw me. Don't tell me you're here for a tattoo?"

"Not this time," Gertie said, "although I've been thinking on it a bit." She waved a hand at Ida Belle and me. "You remember Ida Belle, right? And this is our friend Fortune. She's fairly new to Sinful. We were hoping to talk to you if you have some time."

Her expression shifted to openly curious but I didn't spot any wariness in her at all. She was either unafraid of what the conversation might bring or figured she could get out of it if she decided it wasn't to her liking.

"Sure," she said. "I was just eating my lunch. We can talk in the break room if that's all right."

We nodded and followed her to a tiny room at the back of the building. It had a cabinet and counter alongside a refrigerator and a table with four chairs that barely fit in the corner. We inched around the table and squeezed into seats. Haylee grabbed a sandwich and took a bite.

"You been working here long?" Gertie asked.

"About a year," Haylee said as she chewed.

"You were always good at art," Gertie said. "I remember you carried around that notebook, always sketching."

She nodded. "Worked at a place in New Orleans right after high school. That's where I learned how to use the equipment. Like you said, the drawing was always there. It was just a matter of learning to put it to skin."

"Why didn't you stay in New Orleans?" I asked. "Seems like there would be more opportunity there."

"And more competition," Haylee said. "New Orleans collects artists like a bum collects cans. I just want to put cool things on people and not worry about rent. I'm not good at playing the big-city game."

"I never see you around Sinful," Gertie said.

"Don't live there," Haylee said. "My grandfather had a place about ten miles up the highway. Left it to me when he died, so no rent. It's small, but that means less to clean and the utilities are low. It's perfect for me."

She cocked her head to the side and looked at us. "I don't figure you came out here to ask me about my job and living arrangements, so what's this about?"

I glanced over at Gertie, who gave me a slight nod. That was the indication that I should proceed in a straightforward manner, which pleased me because straightforward was what I did best. And so far, it seemed that Haylee preferred straightforward as well but in a noncombative way. I had expected her to be surlier and far less pleasant, so this was a welcome surprise.

"We'd like to talk to you about Venus Thibodeaux," I said. "I assume you heard about her death?"

"Probably about two seconds after the body came out of the ground," Haylee said. "Hard to keep a secret around here."

"I don't know," I said. "Someone had a pretty good one until that bulldozer got loose."

Haylee leaned back in her chair and studied me for a moment. "You're the one I heard about, aren't you? CIA? Why would the CIA care about Venus?"

"Former CIA," I said and pulled out a business card to set on the table. "I'm a private investigator now."

Her eyes widened. "In Sinful? That's a bit of a step down, isn't it?"

"Yeah, well, Washington, DC, collects agents like a bum collects cans and I don't like the game either. Hard to walk the streets there without wanting to shoot a politician."

She laughed. "I like you. You look like a Barbie doll but I bet you can kick some serious butt."

"Very serious," Gertie said.

"So how does that PI thing work?" Haylee asked. "Someone hired you to investigate Venus's death? I'm having a hard time imagining who would care."

"Someone who didn't do it and might be accused of it," I said.

"Oh, I didn't think of that," Haylee said. "Yeah, I can see where that would worry people. It's bad enough to get rolled by Venus when she was alive, but I'm sure no one wants her getting one over on them in death, too. Although if she can see all this crap going on right now, she's probably tickled."

"Sounds like you didn't think much of her choices," I said.

"I'm not going to be a hypocrite or anything," Haylee said. "Back in high school, I spent most days angry at the world. My dad was a mean son of a bitch. Some people like to start the day off with coffee. He liked to start the day off hitting someone. My mom took off when I was fifteen, so that only left me."

I held in a sigh. It made sense that Haylee had taken up with Venus in high school. Both of them abandoned by their mothers and looking to work out their anger.

"I'm so sorry," Gertie said. "I didn't realize."

"No one did," Haylee said. "He was smart about it. Never put marks where people would see them. Mostly gut punches and mid-back. Some days, it was all I could do to walk normal so people wouldn't notice something was up."

I clenched my teeth, trying to block the mental image of a child with a battered body forcing herself to move normally so no one would know she was hurt.

"Why didn't you tell someone?" Ida Belle asked.

Haylee shook her head. "And go into one of those group homes? No way. You know the kind of stuff that goes on in those places. My dad had a mean streak a mile long, but he didn't do none of that other stuff. I figured I could dodge him best I could until I turned eighteen, then I'd get out."

"I'm sorry you had to go through that," Ida Belle said.

"Is your father still alive?" I asked.

She studied me for a couple seconds, then shook her head. "You asking in a former professional capacity? There's rumors, you know. About what kind of work you did for the government."

"And if I was?" I asked.

"You're about three years too late," Haylee said. "He drank himself to death. And while I appreciate the inquiry, it wouldn't have been necessary regardless. When I was in New Orleans, I met a woman...a counselor at a church. She used to bring me cinnamon rolls and chat with me every week." She paused for several seconds, and her eyes misted up. "Anyway, she got my head right, you know? I made my peace with things. She died of cancer a year later. Sucks. People like that get taken out young and people like my father get to live so long."

She was silent again, then finally shook her head. "Anyway, you wanted to know about Venus. And Lord knows, I don't want to see someone get railroaded over that one. So what do you want to know? I'm not sure how this works, exactly."

"Let's start with the most recent stuff," I said, not wanting to send her back to high school unless I had to. "Did you see Venus when she returned to Sinful this past spring?"

Haylee nodded. "She came sniffing around. Didn't stay long, though. No angle for her to work. No money to give her. Nothing for her to steal. No man for her to sleep with. No drugs. Heck, I don't even drink anymore."

"Wow," I said. "Those are the only reasons she'd come around? That's fairly awful."

Haylee shrugged. "That's the truth. I got up to a lot of stupid things with Venus in high school, some of them illegal. But I'm not that person anymore. I may not look like the hermit who prefers watching Netflix to partying, but I don't care what people think, either. Venus never took an interest in someone unless it benefited her, and everyone who got involved with her paid for it."

"Did you look her up when you were in New Orleans?" I asked.

"No," Haylee said. "At least, not intentionally. I mean, I tried to get a hold of her after she blew out of town. I was still a mess back then so I didn't realize it was probably the best thing that could have happened to me. At least I managed to scrape together the rest of senior year and graduate. But her old phone number was turned off shortly after she left and she never contacted me with a new way to reach her."

"But you did find her?"

"Didn't mean to," Haylee said. "I was out barhopping with some of the artists. This was before I got my crap together. One of the artists hauled us to a biker bar and Venus was there, hugged up on some guy who was old enough to be her father, but that was no surprise. She always said the older ones had bigger wallets to clean out."

"And probably fell for her crap faster," Ida Belle said.

"She always knew how to pick 'em," Haylee said. "In high school, she'd set her eye on some guy and I'd think 'no way is he going to take that risk,' but she got them every time. Except one."

"Who was that genius?" I asked.

"Jeff Breaux," Haylee said.

"Melanie's husband?" I asked.

"I figured they'd end up married," Haylee said. "Jeff was as big an outcast as Melanie. Couldn't even look at a girl when talking, not even to say hello. And when he did talk to one, his entire face turned so red and blotchy it looked like he'd come down with a case of poison ivy."

"Why in the world would Venus be interested in someone like Jeff?" I asked.

Haylee shrugged. "Because he belonged to Melanie? Venus didn't place much value in things unless someone else wanted them. Or maybe she didn't like that Jeff had stolen some of her thunder. When Melanie didn't have anyone but Venus, then Venus got her to do anything she wanted. Once Jeff came along, Melanie didn't need Venus as much."

"Does Melanie know that Venus made a play for Jeff?" Gertie asked.

"No idea," Haylee said. "She wouldn't have heard it from Venus, that's for sure. She wouldn't dare open her mouth about a guy telling her no. I suppose Jeff might have told her, but I doubt it. He wouldn't have wanted the problems it would bring on either end of things."

"Then how did you find out about it?" Ida Belle asked.

"I heard it happen," Haylee said. "It was raining outside, so I sneaked behind the bleachers in the gym to light up a cigarette. The door opened and I looked through the crack and saw Venus pulling Jeff into the gym. She got all close to him and tried to lay one on him."

Haylee grinned. "I'll never forget it. He looked at her like she was radioactive. Shoved her away and told her not to ever touch him. Then he hightailed it out of there like he was on fire. If she'd had a gun, I have no doubt Venus would have shot him."

"Guess Jeff was the smart one," I said.

"Smart. Scared," Haylee said. "Not sure how much of each, but either way, Venus didn't get her man that time. I always figured him blowing her off like that would just make her work harder, and that might have been the case, but she left for New Orleans shortly after."

"So what happened when you saw Venus in the biker bar?" I asked.

"She spotted me and ran over, hugging me like I was her

long-lost sister," Haylee said. "Don't get me wrong, I was happy to see her at the time. I mean, we weren't exactly close, not in any real way. But at least after all that time, I knew she was all right."

"And did you hang out after that?" Gertie asked. "Was it totally like *Sons of Anarchy*?"

"I wouldn't know," Haylee said. "She invited me back to the bar and I went once, but I didn't get a good vibe from it. For starters, it was clear Venus was trying to set me up with one of the guys. When I told her I was gay, she looked so shocked you'd have thought I slapped her."

"I'm guessing you weren't 'out' in high school," I said.

"I didn't know what I was in high school," Haylee said. "Actually, that's probably not true. I think I've always known, but it wasn't something workable then, you know? Not in high school. Not with my father. It would have been more conflict to deal with and for what? It wasn't like I was planning on staying. Besides, I had enough to deal with dodging my father and all the do-gooders who would have stepped in if they'd caught wind of what was going on."

She looked over at Ida Belle and Gertie. "No offense."

"So how did Venus handle that news?" I asked.

"She tried to play it off as cool but I could tell she was anxious to get me out of there. I figured she'd made some promises she wasn't going to be able to keep. Anyway, I only saw her once again after that but she didn't see me. It was down in the Ninth Ward. Rough area. I had met my friend by then and was helping her haul some canned goods to a food bank. Venus was in a parking lot across the street."

Haylee frowned.

"You think she was up to something?" I asked.

"Venus was always up to something," Haylee said. "But yeah, at the time, I thought it looked like a drug drop."

"She was buying drugs?" Ida Belle asked.

Haylee shook her head. "No. She was giving the guy a box of something and collected a duffel bag. She pulled a stack of wrapped cash out of it and flipped through the bills. Then she shoved the whole thing in her car and took off."

"Sounds like she was playing middleman for a supplier," I said.

"There were rumors about that gang she ran with," Haylee said. "I figure most of them were probably true. But I never heard of anything going down with them and the cops. 'Course I didn't stick around long after that, so who knows what could have happened after I left."

"Do you remember the name of the bar?" I asked. There was no way I was sticking so much as a foot inside the place, but I wanted to see what I could run down on the bikers who owned it.

"Bad Voodoo," Haylee said. "Seventh Ward."

"Did Venus ever mention her mother to you when you ran into her in New Orleans?" I asked.

"She didn't have to," Haylee said. "Starlight was in the bar that night. She was the old lady of one of the top guys."

"I guess that answers the question of whether Venus found her mother in New Orleans," Gertie said.

"I would say it was a mistake to go looking," Haylee said. "But then, sounds like Venus didn't fall too far from that tree, based on the things I've heard about her mother. They probably had quite the scam going with the whole mother-daughter thing."

"Starlight turned up at Percy's house yesterday," Gertie said.

Haylee's eyes widened. "Seriously? How'd that go over?"

"About as good as you'd expect," Ida Belle said.

Haylee shook her head. "What in the world could she possibly want?"

"Maybe she's here to pay her respects," I suggested, to see what Haylee's reaction would be. It was what I expected.

She snorted. "Yeah, because she's mother of the year. If Starlight is here, it's not to shed a tear or commiserate with Percy. He'd probably just as soon shoot her as look at her."

"There was a threat along those lines," I said. "Starlight claimed she was here for her half of her daughter's assets. Do you have any idea what she was talking about?"

Haylee shook her head, looking as confused as we were. "Venus never had anything of value to speak of. If she managed to put something together, she never told me about it, but then I only saw her the once when she came back."

"Can you think of anyone who would want her dead?" I asked. "Not just want her dead, but able to go through with actually doing it?"

Haylee pursed her lips. "That's the key, right? I don't think anyone's going to be too upset that Venus is gone. And assuming she stayed true to form, there's probably a handful of married guys who let out a big breath of relief over it. But I can't imagine anyone who would actually go through with killing her. Unless maybe it was about something that she got up to in New Orleans."

"Anything is possible," I said.

"There was this one guy in high school—Bart Lagasse," Haylee said. "He was really hung up on Venus and she pretty much wiped him out before she jetted. He had a real mean streak. Backhanded Venus a time or two. I never knew why she stuck with him."

"He hit her?" Gertie said.

Haylee nodded. "She tried to play it off as she fell or whatever, but I wasn't buying it. I saw him go all psycho on a guy at a bonfire party one night. It's like his whole face changed and he wasn't the same person. Creeped me out. Still does if I think too hard on it."

"We'll definitely check him out," I said.

"Be careful," she said quietly.

I handed her one of my cards. "If you can think of anything else that might help, or if you hear any gossip that we might be interested in, please give me a call."

She picked up the card and stared at it, nodding.

"I really appreciate you talking to us," I said as I rose.

Gertie stood up and surprised Haylee by leaning over and giving her a hug. "I'm proud of you, honey. You've really gotten your life together. If you ever need anything, you just give me a call."

"Thanks, Ms. Hebert," Haylee said and sniffed. "You were always nice to me. I never forgot it."

"You never really know what's going on with a person," Gertie said. "Sometimes it's best to give them the benefit of the doubt."

"Not with Venus," Haylee said. "Give her an inch, she'd take everything."

CHAPTER SIXTEEN

As we headed back to the highway, I made a few notes on my phone. Ida Belle waited until I was done and then looked over at me.

"I think it's time to have a chat with Bart Lagasse," I said.

"Before Starlight?" Ida Belle asked.

"No," I said. "Starlight first since we're already near the motel. Then Bart. Any idea where to find him?"

"Maybe at the docks," Ida Belle said. "He picks up some day labor gigs there on the shrimp boats when he's in between other work. And he stays more in between than actual work."

"Sounds good," I said. "So what was your take on Haylee?"

"Shock and awe," Gertie said. "I mean, I looked at her and thought 'here we go.' But she's really gotten her life together."

Ida Belle nodded. "She does appear to have a level head on her shoulders. She certainly wasn't thinking straight when she was younger, but after hearing about her home situation, that all makes sense. I can't believe we didn't know."

"Sounds like she went to a lot of trouble to make sure no one knew," I said. "Can't blame her, really, given the horror stories you hear about foster care. The devil you know and all."

My cell phone rang and I checked it. "It's Carter."

Gertie and Ida Belle gave each other nervous glances as I answered.

"I'm sorry," he started out, and I clenched the phone.

"What happened?" I asked.

"Someone made a complaint about the lag time at the DA's office. He worked all weekend and called me for updates about an hour ago. I just heard back. I've been instructed to arrest Whiskey."

"Crap!" I yelled.

"I did everything I could do to stall him, but he wasn't having any of it. He wants someone attached to that body before he sits down for Thanksgiving dinner."

"Whiskey won't get into court this week," I said. "Not with the holiday."

"I'm afraid he's going to spend some time behind bars. Look, I'm on my way now to make the arrest. I just wanted to let you know. And I'd appreciate it if you don't talk to Whiskey until I've got him in jail. I wouldn't put it past him to take a long boat ride if he knew I was coming."

We disconnected and I blew out a breath. "I don't suppose I have to fill in the blanks, do I?" I asked.

"No," Ida Belle said, her expression grim. "It was fairly clear."

Gertie sighed. "Our ticking time clock just became a ticking time bomb."

"What are we going to do?" Ida Belle asked.

"Everything we'd planned to do before, except now we're looking for the murderer, not just a suspect," I said. "And we need to do it all a lot faster."

Ida Belle floored her SUV and we leaped forward, throwing Gertie, who had been leaning through the middle of the front seats, tumbling backward on the rear bench.

"She didn't mean right this very second," Gertie grumbled as she righted herself.

"Every second counts," Ida Belle said. "Fasten your seat belts."

I had already buckled in as soon as I'd taken my seat. I knew better than to go freestyle with Ida Belle driving. Gertie grumbled some more but I heard her belt click into place, just in time for Ida Belle to make a hard right on the service road. We were pulling into the motel parking lot in about half the time it should have taken to get there. A couple of people saw the SUV sliding into the entrance and scrambled for the sidewalk.

Ida Belle wasn't remotely fazed. She slid to a stop in a slot near the entrance and we headed to the front desk. A sleepy-looking young man stared at us for a couple seconds, then blinked twice and yawned.

Midtwenties. Five foot eleven. One hundred sixty pounds. No threat at all, especially with the hangover he's sporting.

"Sorry," he said. "Late night and all. You ladies need a room or something?"

"Something," Ida Belle said.

He scrunched his brow. "Huh?"

"We need to talk to one of your guests," I said. "Starlight Thibodeaux."

He tapped on the keyboard, then shook his head. "No one here by that name."

"Midfifties," Gertie said. "Big hair, too much makeup. Looks like a hooker for a biker gang. If you checked her in, she hit on you."

"Oh, her." He nodded. "Yeah, she's staying here. Told me her name was Jane Smith."

"And you believed her?" I asked.

He shrugged. "She paid cash so it doesn't really matter to me. Got four Jane Smiths staying here at the moment."

"I don't suppose you can recall which room belongs to the Jane Smith we'd like to talk to?" I asked.

"Probably, but I'm not supposed to give out room numbers," he said.

"Do we look dangerous?" I asked.

He stared at us for a couple seconds, as if it were a trick question. "I guess not, but that's not in the handbook."

"Is this in the handbook?" I asked and handed him a twenty.

He grabbed the cash and stuffed it in his pocket. "Room 118. Ground floor around back."

We headed out and Ida Belle opened the SUV. "I figure we should probably drive around," she said. "It will save time walking."

Gertie hopped in and buckled her seat belt. "And we might have to make a getaway."

"Why in the world would we have to make a getaway?" I asked.

"Because we often do," Gertie said. "And lots of times, it wasn't something we saw coming."

I couldn't really argue with that statement, so I clicked my seat belt on and Ida Belle launched around the hotel in a blur of metal and rubber. It was like riding a roller coaster on a flat surface. There was a space in front of Starlight's room so Ida Belle backed in and declared that she'd leave the doors unlocked. I appreciated the caution but really hoped none of it would be necessary.

"I don't see Starlight's car," I said as Ida Belle knocked on the door.

"She's probably out scamming someone," Ida Belle said.

Gertie shook her head. "Women like Starlight work after

dark when they get to a certain age. Dim light hides a lot of years. I'm thinking of switching all the light bulbs in my house to that sundown look."

"Do you also plan on never stepping outside in the sunlight again?" Ida Belle asked. "There's no hiding from sunlight."

"Nonsense," Gertie said. "There's giant sunglasses and floppy hats."

"You mean Celia's look?" I asked, unable to help myself.

Gertie grimaced. "Never mind."

Ida Belle knocked again, but we didn't hear any movement inside that indicated Starlight was in residence, and with her car missing as well, it wasn't likely she was there. We were about to leave when the door to the room next to Starlight's popped open and a middle-aged man stepped out. He paused as he saw us standing there.

"You looking for the woman staying in that room?" he asked.

We nodded.

"She left a couple hours ago," he said. "I went up front to fetch a cup of coffee and a paper and saw her talking to some guy over by her car. Looked intense."

"How so?" Ida Belle asked.

He shrugged. "They looked angry and stiff. He was pointing a finger at her and she kept shaking her head. Then he left and she jumped in her car and took off herself."

"What did he look like?" I asked.

"Big dude. Over six feet tall and stout. Long gray hair and beard. The hair was in a braid. Lots of tattoos. Black leather jacket. Took off on a Harley."

"And you haven't seen her since?" I asked.

He shook his head. "She hasn't been back. I've been working in my room and had the curtains open. Even if I didn't, this place is constructed like crap. I can hear every time she opens and closes the door."

"She have any other visitors?" I asked.

"Not that I've seen," the man said. "Sorry, but I've got a meeting to run to. I hope you find your friend. When you do, you might want to chat with her about the company she's keeping. Looks like she's playing with fire."

I thanked him and he headed off toward a truck, giving us a backward wave as he went.

"What do you make of that?" I asked.

"Sounds like Starlight might be in a pinch with her biker friends," Ida Belle said.

"You think it has something to do with Venus?" Gertie asked.

I shrugged. "No way to know yet. But Starlight is definitely up to something." I checked the room door. "This lock would take me about five seconds to pick."

"That's breaking and entering," Ida Belle said.

"Technically, I wouldn't have to break anything," I said. "She wouldn't even know we were here."

"What if she comes back while we're inside?" Ida Belle said. "The only window is the one next to the front door."

"True," I said. "But there's only one entrance into the hotel parking lot. Gertie, head around front and watch the entrance. There's a breezeway two rooms up that you can use. If you see Starlight's car turn in, call and we'll get the heck out."

"Why do I have to stand up front and watch for the car?" Gertie said. "I want to not break and enter too."

"Because we might have to run," I said. "We don't just have to get out of the room. We have to get far enough away that Starlight can't recognize us. And we can't leave Ida Belle's SUV parked close, either, because she might recognize it from Percy's house."

"Fine," Gertie said. "I'm a little sore from chasing that turkey anyway."

She set off for the front of the motel and Ida Belle moved her SUV to the back of the parking lot behind a panel van. By the time Ida Belle got back, Gertie texted me that she was around the building and the entrance was clear.

We donned latex gloves and I made such quick work of the door with a credit card that Ida Belle shook her head in dismay. We stepped inside and closed the door behind us. The shades were drawn, making the aging room so dark we couldn't see. I felt around on the wall and found the light switch. The dim lighting wasn't much better but at least we wouldn't trip over anything.

"Not much of a housekeeper," I said. I thought I was messy, but Starlight had managed to make a motel room she'd occupied for a day look as though she'd been hosting frat parties for a month. Every flat surface contained a beer can. The bed was unmade and clothes were scattered across it and the floor. Bras hung from the knobs of the dresser. The sink in the bathroom had a layer of makeup dust on it so thick it would probably take a sandblaster to get it off.

"You know," Ida Belle said as she lifted a corset to get a look at what was on the desk underneath it, "there are times when these gloves serve a much bigger purpose than not leaving prints."

I kicked a pair of panties off a box on the floor and grimaced. "Definitely."

I flipped back the covers of the bed and frowned. "Here's something I didn't expect," I said as I lifted an iPad. "I didn't take Starlight for the tech type."

I pressed the button to wake it up and was surprised to see no password was required.

"Guess she's not the tech type," Ida Belle said. "I think you've discovered her main use for the tablet."

A video of hot naked men filled the screen, the Play button just waiting for someone to press it. "Gross," I said, and flipped to the main screen. "Let's see if she has this linked to her phone."

I accessed messages and smiled. "Bingo."

Ida Belle leaned in and we scrolled through the messages until we found a number assigned to someone called Catfish.

"Bet that's her biker dude," Ida Belle said. "Doesn't look like she ever deletes anything either."

"First, I'll go back to May, when Venus arrived in Sinful," I said, and scanned the messages until I found what we were looking for.

Catfish: Did you find that little bitch?

Starlight: The Florida motel was a dead end. No one here has seen her.

Catfish: Then look somewhere else.

Starlight: Do you know how many motels are in Miami?

Catfish: Do you think I give a shit? She's a problem and I don't have to remind you that she's YOUR problem.

Starlight: Don't you think if she had anything, she would have already asked for money?

Catfish: I'm not waiting around to find out. Find her now. So I can make her disappear for real.

"Well, that's direct enough," Ida Belle said.

"Why Miami, I wonder?"

"To lead them in the wrong direction? The last place Starlight would assume Venus would go is back to Sinful, but it certainly wouldn't hurt to hedge her bets."

I scrolled through more messages. "Looks like Starlight struck out in Miami and got called back to New Orleans. Look!" I pointed to a message from May. "She found her!"

Starlight: Got a call from an old friend. Said she's working at a bar in Sinful.

Catfish: Thought you said she wouldn't go there.

Starlight: Never figured she would.

Catfish: Get there now and make sure.

Starlight: And if she is?

Catfish: I'll take it from there.

I scrolled through the rest of the posts, but there was nothing that made reference to Venus or Sinful. I flipped over to location history and scanned the dates.

"She was here," I said. "Two days before Venus was killed. Would Starlight know about Nickel's camp?"

"Rumor has it she took a tumble with him for a bit. Wouldn't surprise me if they used the camp."

"What did Venus have that was worth killing her over?" I asked. "It was clear in these messages that Catfish wanted her dead."

"Drugs? Weapons? Who knows?"

My cell phone rang and we both gave a start.

Gertie!

"She just turned in the parking lot and she's hauling booty," Gertie said. "Get the heck out of there."

I tossed the iPad back on the bed and flung the covers over it, then bolted out the door behind Ida Belle, who'd already taken off. I paused only long enough to turn the cheap doorknob lock and pull the door shut behind me, then I sprinted for the back of the parking lot where Ida Belle had secured her SUV. When we climbed inside the vehicle, I saw Starlight entering her room.

"At least she'll never notice we were there," Ida Belle said. "Not with that mess. Do you still want to talk to her?"

I shook my head. "No. She'll just tell more lies. We know more than we would have ever gotten out of her. She wouldn't buy the Southern sympathy requirement like Percy so no use tipping our hand."

Ida Belle nodded and pulled away. As she began to round the end of the motel, I glanced into the passenger-side mirror and saw Starlight rush out of her motel room and jump in her car.

"Crap!" I yelled. "She's coming! Get out of here before she sees your vehicle."

Ida Belle punched the gas and we slid out of the corner and shot off into the front parking lot. I managed to dial Gertie during the mad dash and yelled "Hide" before Ida Belle slammed on the brakes behind two huge pickup trucks. My phone flew out of my hand and hit the dashboard.

"Where's Gertie?" I asked as I straightened myself out.

"There!" Ida Belle pointed. "Running from the entry."

Gertie must have headed for the entry to wait on us, but unfortunately, it offered no place to hide. No pretty brick columns. No trees. Not even a skinny bush. So now, she was running for the front of the motel. I looked over to the right and saw Starlight's car rounding the corner of the building. Gertie must have seen it too. A man who'd exited the office climbed into his car, and a second later, Gertie opened the passenger door and dived inside. Starlight went flying by and squealed out of the parking lot, leaving a cloud of dust in her wake.

"She jumped in the car with a strange man," Ida Belle said, incredulous.

"She improvised," I said.

"That guy could be a serial killer," Ida Belle said. "Oh my God! He's pulling away!"

CHAPTER SEVENTEEN

"HOLY CRAP!" I yelled as the car pulled out of the parking space and took off toward the rear of the motel. Ida Belle put her SUV in Reverse and floored it, launching me forward into the dash. I pushed myself back in my seat and pulled out my pistol as she made the turn backward out of the row of cars, then put the SUV in Drive and punched it again.

We rounded the corner of the motel and I pointed at the car disappearing around the back row. "There!"

Ida Belle whirled around the corner, took off for the other car, passed it completely, then did a sliding stop right in front of it. I jumped out and ran to the front of the car, my pistol trained on the guy inside. Gertie climbed out of the vehicle, looking more than a little stressed.

"Are you crazy?" she yelled at the driver.

I motioned for him to exit the vehicle and he slowly climbed out, his hands over his head.

Fiftyish. Five foot seven. A hundred eighty pounds. A lot of scar tissue. Might have wet himself.

"Are you cops?" he asked, his voice cracking. "I swear I didn't do nothing wrong."

"You took off with this woman in your car," I said, lowering my pistol.

"I didn't take anyone off my car," he said. "She was *in* it."

"He thought I was propositioning him," Gertie said. "Just because I jumped in his car and then knelt down on the floorboard."

I raised one eyebrow.

"She's not a hooker," I said to the guy.

"So she's not a looker," he said. "I'm not that picky. Is that a crime?"

"Is something wrong with your hearing?" I asked and pointed to my ears.

His eyes widened. "Oh. Yeah, I'm probably getting some of this wrong. I can't hear well out of my left ear and none out of my right. I'm a dynamite technician."

"Really?" Gertie perked up. "I should get your number."

"A shed full of lumber?" he asked, looking confused.

"Never mind!" I yelled. "You can go!"

He looked back and forth between us, the bewildered look firmly in place, but must have finally decided it was no longer worth the effort. Shaking his head, he climbed into his car and drove away.

"Good God, woman," Ida Belle said. "One day, you're going to give me a heart attack. And I don't mean one of those couch-recovery kinds where everyone has to wait on you and you give up beer and bacon. I mean the straight-to-the-grave kind."

Gertie waved a hand in dismissal. "You exaggerate."

"What if he'd left the parking lot?" Ida Belle asked. "Headed for the highway?"

"He'd have had to be in a Learjet to outrun your SUV," Gertie said. "Combine that with Fortune's shooting ability and I have a feeling he wouldn't have gotten far."

"I give up!" Ida Belle threw her hands in the air and climbed back into her vehicle.

"We should probably get out of here," I said to Gertie. "Before someone calls the police about our parking lot car chase, complete with my holding that guy at gunpoint."

We hopped into the SUV and Ida Belle took off, as ready as I was to be rid of the motel. I heard the click of Gertie's seat belt and smiled. At least she was learning. If my reaction time hadn't been so good, I might have gotten a bruise or two when I hit the dashboard. As it was, I'd had a split second to get my arms up and brace myself for impact.

"Well, don't keep me hanging," Gertie said. "If I don't get to do the fun stuff, the least you can do is fill me in on it right away."

"You were just kidnapped by a strange guy in a sketchy motel parking lot," Ida Belle said. "How much more fun stuff do you require in a day?"

"That wasn't fun," Gertie said. "It was a little creepy actually."

"A little?" Ida Belle asked.

"Let's move on," I said. "It's not the first time someone has mistaken Gertie for a hooker and probably won't be the last."

"That's true," Gertie agreed.

I gave Gertie a rundown of what we'd learned and she shook her head.

"Can't say it surprises me that Starlight would side with a man over her own daughter," Gertie said. "Also can't say I'm surprised that Venus would be foolish enough to get sideways with a motorcycle gang. She never knew when to stop pushing."

"But the weird part is, why is Starlight here now?" I asked. "If she or Catfish or both killed Venus because of something she took from them, they would have taken it back when they packed her luggage."

Ida Belle frowned. "You're right. That doesn't make sense. Unless what they were looking for wasn't there. Maybe that's why Starlight is here now insisting on her half of Venus's belongings. She thinks they missed something."

"I'm sure that's possible," I said. "Especially since they would have been hurrying to pack up and get out of Percy's house. But still, why would they think Percy would find whatever it is now? And if he did find money or guns or drugs or whatever else they might be looking for, wouldn't he turn them over to the police?"

"Maybe not money," Gertie said. "I think Percy is honest, in general, but if he found a cash stash that he believed belonged to Venus, he might feel justified in keeping it for all the trouble. Plus, he would have figured it was ill-gotten gains, so not like the police would return it to whoever she scammed, even if he turned it in."

Ida Belle nodded. "I have to agree with Gertie on that one. If Percy found a pile of cash and thought it would just sit in an evidence warehouse somewhere, he might not be inclined to go the legal route."

"But if it's something as simple as cash, why the big rush now?" Gertie said. "And if they'd been poking around Sinful all this time, someone would have noticed."

"I don't think they're here for money," I said. "It's not worth risking exposure to a murder investigation. And Starlight hasn't been here except for back in May, just before Venus was killed, and now."

"But now that Venus's body has been discovered," Ida Belle said, "there will be an official investigation. So now they're trying to find whatever it was that they didn't find back then."

Gertie shook her head. "Starlight is seriously delusional if she thought Percy was going to let her go through his house like she had a warrant."

"Or desperate," I said. "None of this has felt very organized, but we know for sure Catfish wanted Venus dead. And he and Starlight doing the deed would also explain why the body wasn't dumped in the bayou. No boat access, and I'm guessing Starlight wasn't the fishing kind, so she wouldn't be able to find her way around the bayous at night. Besides, there's always the risk that things dumped in the bayou will surface, even if in pieces."

Since my first day in Sinful had started off with my inherited dog pulling a piece of a murdered man out of the bayou, I had a firm grasp on just how possible that scenario was.

"No," Ida Belle agreed. "They wouldn't have risked something neither of them were familiar with, especially at night. That's how you wind up crab bait. But like Carter said, the construction was visible to anyone who drove by during the day. With the forms in place and the rebar half done, anyone would have known the slab would be poured soon."

"Why not just haul the body and the car away from Sinful?" Gertie asked.

"Because driving around in a car you don't own—and my guess is that wasn't properly registered—with a dead body in the trunk is just asking for trouble," Ida Belle said.

I nodded. "All it would take is a traffic stop for a broken taillamp or expired registration and the gig would be up. They'd have no registration, no insurance card, nothing to prove they had any right to be in the vehicle."

"I get it," Gertie said. "Cops would have assumed it was stolen."

I stared out the windshield, contemplating the even bigger question of the moment. Unfortunately, an easy answer wasn't forthcoming on that one either. Finally, I blew out a breath and Ida Belle looked over at me.

"Trying to figure out how to tell Carter?" she asked.

"Sometimes I'm convinced we're sharing the same mind," I said.

"Just a similar way of thinking," Ida Belle said.

"I hadn't thought about the Carter angle," Gertie said. "But we have to tell him. I mean, if Whiskey was in the clear for longer, then maybe we could run down this Catfish and figure out what he was looking for, but with Whiskey being arrested..."

"Carter can get information a lot faster than we can," I said. "I know. And I'm going to tell him. I'm just trying to figure out the best way to phrase it."

"I'd go with direct," Ida Belle said. "If he's focused on a little B and E after hearing what those texts said, then maybe he needs to hang up his badge."

"I suppose the things we get up to don't surprise him," I said. "But I got the impression he was thinking I'd turn over a new leaf—maybe a legal one—when I became official."

"Legal is overrated," Gertie said.

"Says the woman who probably has a stick of dynamite in her purse," Ida Belle said.

"Two," Gertie said. "You should always carry backup."

"You've got enough backup in that purse to arm a small country," Ida Belle said.

"We'll leave that tidbit out when we talk to Carter," I said. "He's perfectly happy with suspecting things where Gertie's purse is concerned. Not so much with having actual facts."

"That goes for two of us," Ida Belle said.

I slumped back in my seat. "No use putting it off. Maybe Carter will let me talk to Whiskey while we're there. I need to see about getting him an attorney."

We pulled into town and Ida Belle parked in front of the sheriff's department. We headed inside and saw Myrtle manning the front desk.

"You're clocked in early," Gertie said.

Myrtle rolled her eyes. "Carter finally issued that new guy a pistol, on a probationary deputy basis. First thing the fool did was shoot a hole in his pants and his truck seat. So instead of getting more help, which we desperately need, we've got one less because Carter had no choice but to suspend him for a week."

"Deputy Breaux should send him a Bundt cake for making him look like Robocop," Ida Belle said.

"Lord, isn't that the truth," Myrtle said. "Deputy Breaux is no Carter and not likely to ever be, but he's reliable and trustworthy, and he doesn't go shooting his gun off all willy-nilly. You guys here to see Carter or Whiskey?"

"Carter first," I said. "And then I'm hoping he'll let me see Whiskey so I can help sort out his legal needs."

She nodded and picked up the phone to dial Carter. "It's a real shame that Carter had to lock him up. That boy is a little wild, but he's no killer."

Myrtle informed Carter we were there, then hung up and waved us back. We headed to the office and I rolled the upcoming conversation through my mind. Not a single scenario I imagined was lacking in the yelling department. Since none of us seemed in a hurry to get there, we trudged in and took our time sitting.

Carter took one look at us and narrowed his eyes. "Might as well spit it out."

"We really have to work on our straight faces," Gertie said.

"We went to the motel, figuring that's where Starlight might be holed up," I said.

"What did you think you were going to get out of her?" Carter asked. "Starlight can't open her mouth without lying."

"That's true enough," Ida Belle said. "But sometimes the lies people tell let you know more than they think."

"So what lie do you think is relevant?" he asked.

"We didn't actually speak to her," I said. "She wasn't there. And the guy in the room next to her said he'd seen her arguing with a biker-looking dude earlier, then she took off. So we figured we might take a look around."

"You broke into her room!" Carter glared at us.

"Actually," I said, "there was no breaking required because the locks are really old and—"

He held up a hand. "Skip it. Do I have to tell you how much trouble you could get in? What if someone had seen you? What if something illegal is going on with Starlight and your fingerprints are now in her room?"

"Oh, we wore latex gloves," Ida Belle said. "We always carry them."

Carter closed his eyes and rubbed his forehead, as if trying to stall an oncoming headache. "What did you find?"

I recounted the texts and he managed to listen without interrupting or swearing. When I finished, he frowned and drummed his fingers on the desk.

"That's bad," he said finally. "I mean, good for me in that it's a really solid lead and it might be enough to keep a grand jury from indicting Whiskey. The only problem is I have no way to present that information without access to Starlight's phone or iPad, and I don't have a good enough reason for a warrant to get them."

"We were thinking if you could run down who this Catfish is, that might give you some ammunition," I said. "And maybe if you talk to the desk clerk at the motel, he might remember

Starlight being there in May, which would be suspicious enough, right?"

"When you talk to the clerk, tell him it's the Jane Smith that hit on him," Gertie said.

Carter grimaced, then stared out the window for a bit. Finally, he nodded. "That might be enough. I'll see what I can find out. In the meantime, you three stay out of locked rooms that you do not have permission to enter."

"Technically, I wasn't in there," Gertie said.

"Playing lookout still makes you an accessory," Carter said.

Gertie looked over at me. "We're going to have to discuss my role in this business. If I'm going down for the same crimes as the two of you then I shouldn't be left out of all the fun parts."

"You were kidnapped by a man who thought you were a hooker," Ida Belle said. "That was your fun part."

Carter held up his hands. "I really don't want to know any more of this."

"I don't suppose I could have a word with Whiskey while we're here?" I asked, changing the subject. "I want to get him some legal help if I can."

"He's already made some phone calls," Carter said, "but since it's only Myrtle and me here, you can talk to him. Just make it quick in case anyone else shows up."

"How long are you keeping him here?" I asked.

"Until the state police can arrange a transfer," he said. Then he nodded at Ida Belle and Gertie. "You two wait up front. I don't want to have to explain why the three of you are talking to my suspect if the state police show up unannounced."

"Won't you have to explain her?" Gertie asked.

Carter grinned. "No. I'll just lock her in the next cell and tell them she's a suspect on a B and E."

"Nice," Ida Belle said.

I followed Carter back to the jail cells.

Whiskey was the only one in residence at the moment. I could tell by his expression that he was totally stressed, which was completely understandable, but he looked a tiny bit relieved when he saw me. I clenched my hands a little, hoping I did not screw this up and let him down.

"I'll be right outside the door," Carter said as he unlocked the cell next to Whiskey. "If the state police show up, you know what to do."

I nodded and he left the cells, closing the door behind him.

"You going to play criminal if someone shows up?" Whiskey asked.

"That's the plan."

"Carter's an okay dude, isn't he?"

"I think so. He didn't want to arrest you."

Whiskey nodded. "I got that. I mean, he had to do everything all official-like, and like I said before, I know it's the DA's call, not his. But he didn't look too happy about it."

"No one likes to see the wrong guy go down for a crime, especially murder," I said. "Because that means the real killer is still walking around."

"No one except the killer, you mean."

"That's a given."

"Have you found out anything? I don't want to pressure you or anything but the situation kinda went from critical to dire."

"Yeah, I get that. And to answer your question, yes. We found out that Venus was running with a motorcycle gang in New Orleans that her mother was involved with. Venus did something to make one of the leaders mad and he wanted her taken care of. Starlight was in Sinful right before Venus was killed."

"Wow! I mean, I know Venus didn't get on with her mother but you really think she killed her own daughter?"

"More likely she tracked her down and someone else did the deed."

"Did you tell Carter this?"

I nodded.

"Then why the heck am I still in here?"

"Because I didn't exactly come by that information through legal channels, which means Carter can't acquire it to take to the DA. Not without doing some other legwork first."

Whiskey stared at me for a moment. "So you're saying throwing you in a cell wouldn't be stretching the truth?"

"I might have done a bit of B and E. Well, E mostly as the lock didn't require breaking to get inside."

Whiskey smiled. "I knew I hired the right person. So Carter's going to figure out a way to get the evidence, right?"

"Yes, but it won't happen right away. Neither will a bail hearing, I'm afraid. And the holiday is going to delay that. I know an attorney. Do you want me to call him?"

"No thanks. I already have a guy. He handled Nickel's defense."

"Nickel went to jail."

"And got half the time he should have. The big difference is Nickel did everything they accused him of. But I do have a favor to ask. I'm afraid it's a big one."

"Sure. Whatever you need," I said, figuring he was going to ask us to look in on his father until he could do it again himself or make other arrangements.

"I need you to run the bar."

"What? No! I don't know anything about running a bar."

"Nothing to it. You give people a drink same as you did me the other night in your kitchen. Only difference is you take money for it. I don't run tabs or take credit cards. Just good old-fashioned cash. You can cancel food service for the time being. The regulars will understand and anyone new won't know the difference."

A million reasons why this was the worst idea known to man ran through my mind. "But it's the Swamp Bar. There's bar fights and all kinds of other issues besides serving drinks. Surely you know people better suited to helping you out?"

"Better suited for what—robbing me blind? If I let any of my regulars open the place up, drinks will be free and the cash register will be empty at the end of the night. And as soon as that first guy gets a free drink, he'll call everyone he knows and have them all down there. My stock wouldn't last two days."

He blew out a breath. "Look, I know it's not your thing. But I don't have anyone else to ask. Not that I'd trust. I talked to my cousin Ronnie over in Alabama. He's trying to work something out but he can't get here right away. And I can't afford to have the bar closed or I'll be choosing between my defense or taking care of my pops."

"If Ronnie can get here within a couple days, wouldn't that work?"

"Not really. Do you know how much profit I make on a holiday week?"

I shook my head. Bar profits were not on my list of things to know.

"I can net two thousand a night."

"Holy crap! That's a lot of profit."

"Ten times what I make on a weeknight in a regular week. Most people cut way back on hours. Rigs send people home. A holiday week like Thanksgiving is one of the biggest profit weeks for the bar during the year. For the waitstaff, too. Most of them use Thanksgiving tips to buy their Christmas gifts."

I sighed. "Now you're just trying to make me feel too guilty to say no."

"Is it working? Seriously, everything I just told you is true. If that bar isn't open this week, it puts a serious crimp in my future deposits. Most of Pops's treatments aren't covered by insurance. Big surprise there, so I've been covering them myself. It's worn down my savings to a concerning level. I need the Thanksgiving money, especially now."

My shoulders slumped. The situation was worse than I'd thought. "You're going to have to give me instructions—I mean detailed instructions. I'll ask Carter for a notebook and you can write them down. And it will be a couple hours before I can get there, at least."

"That's no problem. Most people start wandering in after dark."

"Okay. I'll drop by for the instructions on my way to the bar. If the state police show up before I get back, leave them with Carter."

His relief was apparent. "I really owe you. And I'll pay your PI rate for the work. The tips are all between you and the IRS. Should you choose to tell them about it." He forced a smile.

"Don't thank me yet. I might manage to burn the place down. I tend to get into trouble over there."

He shrugged. "Trouble is what bars are for."

CHAPTER EIGHTEEN

Ida Belle and Gertie managed to hold back their questions until we left the sheriff's department and climbed into Ida Belle's SUV. Then they both started.

"What was that yelling about?"

"I thought Carter was okay with the breaking and entering. Well, sort of."

"The yelling wasn't about the B and E," I said. "It was about something I promised to do for Whiskey. Actually, I was kind of hoping you'd help me with it."

"Of course."

"No problem."

I looked at them and grinned. "You don't even know what it is yet."

Ida Belle shrugged. "You agreed to do it, so I'm in."

Gertie nodded. "The only plans I had for tonight were laundry and cleaning the bird cage. I'm happy to postpone either or both."

"Okay. This isn't in our normal scope of duties," I said. "And I'm really hoping no firearms will be required."

Gertie looked disappointed. "That whole bird cage thing is looking better."

"Whiskey needs us to run the Swamp Bar for him," I said.

"No wonder Carter was yelling," Ida Belle said.

"Whoot!" Gertie yelled so loud that Ida Belle flinched. "This whole PI thing is the best job ever!"

Ida Belle looked a bit less enthusiastic. "This is well beyond our normal scope. Does Whiskey really want rank amateurs running his bar? Seems like he'd know people better suited."

I explained Whiskey's situation with his dad, the holiday money, and the stealing-him-blind thing. Ida Belle frowned and nodded.

"I can see his point," she said. "Well, I'm up for anything once. One more thing to add to the list of things I did before I died."

I stared. "I'm really hoping we add a lot more to that list before things take that big a downturn."

Ida Belle shrugged. "You never know."

Gertie rolled her eyes. "Now that the voice of doom has spoken, give us details."

"I can't yet," I said. "Whiskey's supposed to write up some instructions. We show up this evening and that's all I know for now."

"I hope it's bikini night or something," Gertie said.

"No bikinis for you," Ida Belle said. "We just got back from a vacation where Fortune and I and half of Florida saw more of you than any of us wanted."

"If there were any themes this week, I'm sure Whiskey would have mentioned them," I said. "I assume he'll put together a list of where to find things, how to run the cash register, what to charge, and the general rules for the patrons."

"You're assuming there are any," Ida Belle said, then looked at Gertie. "However, there will probably be rules for you.

Things like no causing a riot, discharging a weapon, blowing up anything from your purse, stealing a boat, or any of the other things you have a tendency to get up to. A lot of which happened at the bar."

Gertie waved a hand in dismissal. "Ancient history. This is so exciting! Fortune coming to town is like having a whole second childhood."

"You haven't completely made it out of the first," Ida Belle said. "So what time should I pick you up?"

"Actually, I was thinking we might want to take two vehicles," I said. "Just in case there's an accident or something."

Ida Belle glanced back at Gertie, who was car dancing. "Or something."

GERTIE INSISTED I stop by her house on the way to the Swamp Bar. She claimed she had something I absolutely had to have in order to do my job tonight running the bar. I figured it was either a weapon or some newfangled push-up bra. Regardless, I would be passing on the offer. I pulled up and hurried inside because it was getting late and I still needed to stop and get the instructions from Whiskey.

Ida Belle was in the living room giving Francis the side-eye.

"What's he singing now?" I asked.

"He wasn't singing," she said. "I don't know Latin, but whatever he was saying was intense. He started flapping and bobbing up and down."

"There is no telling what's stored in that bird's mind. Quite frankly, I'm surprised the cops auctioned him. Surely he knows some stuff they don't."

"Yeah, but it's not like he could take the witness stand."

"That would be totally cool if he could. I would pay to see that."

Ida Belle grinned. "I would too."

"Gertie wanted me to stop by. She has something for me?"

Ida Belle shrugged. "Her highness has been closed in her bedroom for over an hour. I thought about yelling for her, but then I think about what might come out and I'm scared."

"Might as well find out now," I said and called to Gertie that I was there.

A minute later, she bobbled into the living room, not quite balancing on the high heels she wore. And that was the best part of the outfit. The rest was so terrifying that Ida Belle actually made a sort of "eek" sound, as when normal women saw a mouse.

"You are not even getting into my vehicle dressed like that," Ida Belle said once she'd found her voice. "Much less going into the bar."

I stood silently, mouth slightly open. I was still trying to figure out what she was going for and drawing a complete blank. "What...?" I asked. "I mean..."

"This is my sexy chief look," Gertie said. "Isn't it awesome?"

Ida Belle shook her head. "No. 'Awesome' is not the word that comes to mind."

The outfit was typical Gertie and not in a good way. A short, tight brown dress made of something that looked like rawhide clung to every square inch of her body. Unfortunately, the clinging plunged deep at the breast line and was short at the booty line. Her boots looked like black leather and had a ridiculously high heel and fur around the top. A headband with feathers completed the clothes part of the outfit, but perhaps the most disturbing part was the spear she carried.

"Why can't you dress like normal people?" Ida Belle asked.

"Look at Fortune—jeans and a T-shirt. That's what you wear to the Swamp Bar. If you insist on holiday-themed dress, at least bat for the other side."

"Please," Gertie said. "Have you ever seen a sexy pilgrim?"

"No," Ida Belle said. "That's my point."

"Aren't you afraid that something will...you know, pop out?" I asked.

"I barely got everything in," Gertie said. "There's no way it's coming out without help."

Ida Belle gave her a look of dismay.

"Okay, well as your boss I have a couple of requirements before you're allowed to serve at the bar," I said. "First off, lose the spear. You'll be carrying drinks and it was a risk walking from your bedroom to the living room with that thing. I'm not about to let you stroll through a crowded bar carrying drinks with it."

She stuck the spear in the corner. "I was just showing you the entire getup. I didn't intend to bring the spear."

"Good," I said. "You're also not serving in those boots, so go put on some flats. If you fall and break a hip, we'll have to close the bar. If you fall with a tray on someone else, a fight could ensue and we'd have to close the bar."

"This is not going to look right with tennis shoes," Gertie said.

"That's not going to look right no matter what," Ida Belle said.

"I'm picking my battles," I said. "If you want to work the rest of the night without taking a deep breath, that's on you, but you'll do it in flats. Now, what did you want to give me?"

She reached into a bag on the recliner, pulled out a T-shirt, and tossed it to me. "One of the Sinful Ladies makes T-shirts for the sports teams. I had her make this up for you since I figured you'd be dressed in your usual gear."

The T-shirt was black with a dancing turkey on it. It looked absolutely absurd but still made me smile.

"I figured that gave you a holiday theme but might be silly enough to distract men from hitting on you," Gertie said. "If that doesn't work, I have a button that says 'I date the deputy,' but I was afraid that might be off-putting given the regular clientele."

Ida Belle raised one eyebrow. "That might be the best idea you've had in a while. Why didn't you get yourself one?"

Gertie rolled her eyes. "Because I *want* men to hit on me."

"You're a stone-cold fox," Francis said.

"See?" Gertie said.

"I'm going to take my shirt and go," I said. "I'll see you two in about thirty minutes."

I stopped by the sheriff's department and picked up the instructions and keys to the bar from Deputy Breaux. Carter was out, so I couldn't see Whiskey in person. I figured that might be the case, so I just thanked the deputy and headed out, praying that I didn't screw this thing up. It amazed me that I'd pulled off some of the CIA's most intricate missions and on foreign land without a qualm, but running a bar in what was now my hometown slightly terrified me.

Ida Belle and Gertie arrived right after I got the bar open and we'd barely gotten the instructions covered before vehicles and boats started pulling up. Whiskey was right. If the bar was starting to hop this early, the night would be a big moneymaker. Ida Belle headed outside to let everyone know the situation and to ask everyone to wait a minute until we could get set up inside. Gertie and I started checking the bar and refilling stock as needed.

Misty and Chloe, the two regular waitresses, showed up together and looked confused when they saw me behind the bar. They looked downright startled when they got a peek at

Gertie. I gave them the bare basics and a note that Whiskey had written. They read the note and both nodded, looking a bit frightened.

"You don't think Whiskey killed her, do you?" Misty asked.

"No," I said. "Or I wouldn't be here helping."

Chloe bit her lower lip. "He was so mad at Venus that night. I mean, not that I blame him."

"What did he expect getting mixed up with her?" Misty said.

"Did you know Venus well?" I asked.

They both shook their heads.

"We're not from Sinful," Misty said. "But everyone in a hundred-mile radius had heard about Venus."

"Her reputation precedes her," Chloe said. "Everyone knew not to have anything valuable around Venus, and that included your man. I don't know why Whiskey hooked up with her. He's smarter than that."

Misty shrugged. "He's still a man, and Venus *was* smoking hot. That makes a lot of smart men stupid."

"God, isn't that the truth," Chloe said.

"But still, Venus was a piece of work," Misty said. "That night after Whiskey fired her, she didn't even leave right away. I saw her a couple minutes later when I threw out a bucket of dirty water. She was just standing in the parking lot chatting with some of the regulars, like she hadn't done anything wrong."

"Do you remember which regulars she was talking to?" I asked.

"Bart Lagasse for one," Misty said. "Probably trying to take him for whatever he had in his wallet. She did that on a regular basis. Red was there as well, and the Lowery brothers."

"How long was she out there?" I asked.

Misty shrugged. "Don't know. I went out to smoke maybe thirty minutes later and she was gone."

"Were the others back in the bar?" I asked. "Or did they leave as well?"

Misty's eyes widened as she got my implication. "Oh! I hadn't thought...I'm sure the Lowery brothers came back in because one of them broke a pool cue later that night and Whiskey threw them out. But I'm not sure about Red or Bart. You don't think...?"

"I don't think anything," I said, although that was far from the truth. "I was just wondering, but all the same, you should probably tell that to Deputy LeBlanc when you get a chance."

"Sure," Misty said. "I'll call him tomorrow. I didn't even think..."

Gertie patted her hand. "Of course you didn't, dear. You're a good person. Good people don't think about things like that."

"Well, we're all good people here," I said, steering the moment back to the job at hand. "And we're going to do our best to make this work for Whiskey. So if you two see anything being handled wrong, please let me know. He really needs to keep the bar open."

They both nodded.

"And we need the jobs," Chloe said. "I know it doesn't look like much, but tips are pretty good. And Whiskey gives us some extra when we've had a really good week. He's a nice guy. I just don't think he wants people to know it."

"They'd all be asking for free drinks if they thought he was nice," Misty said. "Anyway, we're happy to help wherever you need it. There's a notepad under the cash register that has the mix for some of the more difficult drinks, but only a handful of customers deviate from wine, beer, or whiskey, so you should be good to go."

"Thanks," I said, and they headed off to prep the tables.

Ida Belle poked her head inside. "Are you almost ready? The natives are getting restless."

I looked over at Gertie, who nodded.

"As ready as we'll ever be," I said and sent up a silent prayer.

THE FIRST SEVERAL hours went smoothly, considering. Misty and Chloe managed the crowd nicely and I stayed behind the bar, taking money and pouring drinks as fast as possible. Ida Belle and Gertie shifted between helping me with drinks and helping serve. I made a couple things wrong and Gertie dumped a tray of beer, but at least it hit the floor and not one of the customers. I was beginning to think we had this.

But as the night wore on and people got drunk, I could see where the rest of my energy would be spent—in keeping the customers under control. Misty and Chloe were adept at handling most outbreaks of rowdiness with swift service and a bit of flirting to distract male tempers. But eventually, we had one that refused to comply. He was sitting at the end of the bar and as the night wore on and he got drunker but showed no desire to leave, I started mixing his drinks weaker. I didn't charge him less, of course. I figured that's what Whiskey would do for having to deal with the aggravation. Although in this case, I had a feeling Whiskey would have tossed him out on his ear given that the man was complaining about Whiskey.

When Misty made a run back for drinks, I asked her who he was. She glanced over and frowned. "Dean Allard. He's a nasty drunk, although to be honest, he's not much better sober. Walks around mad most of the time."

Ah, I thought as she hurried off with her tray. This was the man who cheated on his wife with Venus and got stuck with child support for six kids. I supposed that would lend to making one angry all the time, although the fault for cheating still lay entirely with him. After all, Venus was not the married one and he was capable of saying no and remaining clothed like the rest of us.

"Don't know why he had to bring that trash into the bar," Allard said. "Whiskey knew how much trouble she caused me and what does he do—hires her and then takes up with her himself. Stupid."

"Whiskey weren't married," the man next to him said. I recognized him as one of the locals, an old fisherman called Red. He was gray and balding now but apparently he'd once had a full head of bright auburn hair. "He was still a fool to take up with her, but at least he isn't a fool that'll be paying for it for a decade."

Allard snorted. "He'll be rotting in prison for killing her. How is that not paying? And for what? Throttling a piece of trash that we're all better off without? I should have throttled her myself. Lying skank was all she was. I gave her money, just like she asked, and she told my wife anyway."

"Shoulda kept it in your pants," Red said. "Then you wouldn't be out the money or the wife."

"For all I know, I did," Allard said.

"What do you mean?" Red asked. "Either you had it out or you didn't."

"All I know is I came here, got drunk, and woke up on the floor in Nickel's camp with my pants around my feet. That skank was naked on the couch and claimed we'd had a go at it most of the night." He tossed back another shot of whiskey. "Now here I am paying nine ways to Sunday and I don't remember any of it. Doesn't seem fair, really."

Red nodded. "If you're going to lose everything, you really should get to remember the good parts of your indiscretion."

"What's an indiscretion?" Allard asked, his speech now slurred. "You're using those big words again. Ain't nobody in Sinful got time for big words."

Red patted him on the back. "I think it's time for you to head out. Maybe grab a six-pack and watch some television. I'm leaving myself. I can give you a lift and you can get your truck tomorrow."

Allard nodded. "Being here is depressing anyway. Shoulda killed her myself is what I should have done." He frowned. "Hell, I might have. Can't remember that night either. Gotta piss before we go."

"Thanks," I told Red as Allard stumbled off in the direction of the bathroom. "I was trying to figure out how to stop serving him without him causing trouble."

Red nodded and shot a worried look in Allard's direction. "He's working up to it, that's for sure."

"You think he could have killed Venus? I mean, if he doesn't remember that night..."

Red shrugged. "I didn't see him in the bar that night. I don't like to think it was him, but somebody did it. And I don't want to believe it was Whiskey."

"Anyone you would like to believe in?"

"I don't know. I guess if I was going to bet on it, I'd go with Bart Lagasse."

I nodded. Bart was the guy Venus had dated in high school and stolen from when she cleared out of town. The guy who was rumored to knock Venus around.

"Any particular reason why?" I asked.

Red shrugged. "Venus done him wrong back when she lived here before and he ain't forgot it. Plus he's got a temper. Probably half the fights that get started in here go back to Bart."

"Was he in the bar the night she disappeared?"

Red snorted. "You might say that. He was the one that Venus grabbed up front like."

I stared. "Interesting. I'd never heard who the receiving party was."

"I don't know who was madder—Whiskey or Bart. Both of 'em looked like they was going to shoot her. All red in the face, jaws twitching, fists clenched. It's a wonder one of them didn't punch her."

"So I take it Bart was no longer interested in that sort of attention from Venus?"

"Shouldn't have been with the way she did him, but he's a fool." Red pointed to the corner where a table of young men sat. "Look at him now. He's the one wearing the shit-eating grin. Looks entirely too happy for a man whose old girlfriend was murdered. I don't care what he thought of her. That still ain't right."

"No, it's not. But I guess I prefer the truth to people pretending otherwise."

Red narrowed his eyes at me. "You're the CIA gal, aren't you? Didn't think your kind went in much for the truth."

I laughed. "We do when it's coming from others."

Red managed to get Allard out of the bar and things went back to normal...for about fifteen minutes. Then the next overly loud drunk made his presence known. He was a young guy, probably early twenties, and sitting at a table with two other guys about his age. I'd seen them all around town but didn't know who they were.

The loud one lifted his shot glass in the air. "To Whiskey! For doing what this town needed to rid itself of evil."

I took some money from Chloe and pointed. "Who's that guy?"

"Oh, that's Jeff Breaux," she said. "I've only seen him in

here once before. Apparently, he's not much of a drinker."

I took a closer look. Everything I'd heard about Jeff Breaux was that he was quiet and a nerdy type. Given he was married and his pregnant wife was probably at home planning Thanksgiving dinner, I was surprised he was in the Swamp Bar. Even more surprised that he was so drunk he was spouting off things better left unsaid, especially in public.

"What about the other two?" I asked.

"Um, I don't know the ginger," Chloe said, "but the guy with the dirty-blond hair is Bart Lagasse. He's a regular."

"Don't know why people are upset," Jeff continued to rant, even though it was clear that Bart was trying to get him to stop. "Ought to be giving Whiskey a medal."

I left the bar and moved closer to the table, just to make sure I didn't miss anything.

Bart glanced around and leaned in. "You shouldn't go saying things like that."

"What?" Jeff said. "You going to pretend you're not happy she's gone? After the way she did you? God only knows why Melanie insisted on being friends with her. She was only being used."

"That's not the point," Bart said. "You can't say things like that or the police will start asking where you were that night."

Jeff's face flashed with anger, then sadness. "Know exactly where I was. Lost my son that night. Nothing's been the same ever since."

Bart squeezed his shoulder. "Oh, man, I'm sorry. I didn't realize that was the night..."

Jeff shrugged. "Doesn't matter, I guess. Can't change nothing. That's why I figured I'd take up drinking."

"Maybe you need to reconsider," Bart said. "At least for a while. Melanie won't be happy if she finds out you were here. Going to be bad enough going home drunk."

"Not going home," Jeff said. "Can't be there. I keep seeing that night...the blood, the ambulance, that doctor with the long face. I can't do it anymore."

Bart stood up. "Let me take you home, man. I'll smooth things over with Melanie." He reached down to help Jeff up from the chair. I was expecting him to argue, but he just wobbled up and leaned against Bart.

"Can't fix it now," Jeff said.

Bart led him to the door and I headed back to the bar. Misty was grabbing some beers from the cooler. She looked up and shook her head as Bart swung the door open and half carried Jeff across the threshold.

"You don't see that often," she said.

"What? Bart being nice or Jeff being drunk?" I asked.

She laughed. "Both, I guess. But I was talking about Jeff. I've only seen him in here one time before with a bunch of guys from work. He's married to what the older gen would call a proper lady. Kinda surprises me him being in here drunk, but I guess we all lose it every now and then."

"Poor Jeff," Gertie said as Misty walked off with the beers. "All this stuff with Venus has brought that night back full force. I didn't even realize myself. The timing I mean."

I nodded. "When we talked to Melanie, I felt like she was putting on a happy face, but there was an undercurrent of something...sadness maybe?"

"You're very perceptive," Gertie said. "I didn't even notice. But it's no surprise. They had a lot of trouble conceiving. Jeff was injured on the job a couple years back and things didn't work quite right. Doctors were involved and just when everyone figured they'd try to adopt, Melanie finally got pregnant. She was an only child, and so were her parents. When they died, she lost all of her family."

"And then she miscarried. That's sad."

Gertie nodded and gave me a side-eye. "You ever think about having kids?"

I had just popped a cocktail olive in my mouth and choked before managing to spit it out.

Gertie grinned. "Never mind answering. Your reaction said it all. It's not for everyone. Heck, you're taking things further than Ida Belle and me just settling down with a man."

"We're not settled. We're dating."

"Exclusively. And I have no doubt you'll make it legal one day."

I looked over at Ida Belle, who was serving a table of roughnecks shots. "What about her and Walter? Any guesses on how that's going to go?"

"None. And if anyone would know, you'd think it would be me. I've poked at her a bit here and there, but she doesn't utter so much as a peep about it. I even called Walter with some made-up order and dropped a million hints, but he didn't bite."

"Carter knows Walter asked," I said. "He's not happy about it. It's going to be worse when he finds out she didn't say no right away. I'm pretty sure that's what he thinks happened."

"You two going to yap all night or are you going to pour drinks?" Ida Belle's voice sounded from the other side of the bar.

I poured up more shots, hoping it had been too noisy for Ida Belle to overhear our conversation. Gertie went to the other end of the bar to handle beer refills. Everything seemed to be running well. In fact, I was a bit surprised at how easy it had been so far. Given our past history with the bar, I'd expected huge drama, but then as we'd been the ones causing it, I supposed that was a bit unfair.

My phone rang. I waved at Gertie to cover for me and stepped out the back door to answer Carter's call.

"How are things going?" he asked.

"Surprisingly well. No fights, explosions, or gunfire."

"Maybe Whiskey should sell you the bar. You're doing a better job of keeping things quiet than he did."

"I think the reason it's calmer is *because* Whiskey is in jail. There's a general seriousness that I never saw before."

"Uh-huh. And just how many times were you at the Swamp Bar before that you have to compare?"

Crap. I'd forgotten that most of our forays into investigation that led to the Swamp Bar were supposed to be a secret. "Oh, you know," I said vaguely.

"I'm afraid I do."

"Any word on the motorcycle gang angle?" I asked, changing the subject. I expected him to tell me he couldn't talk about an ongoing investigation, but he surprised me.

"Yes. The front desk clerk at the motel remembered Starlight being there back in May, so I called a buddy with the New Orleans police to see if he knew anything about Catfish and his club. Boy, were we both surprised."

"Why?"

"Because my buddy is in charge of a task force that's trying to take the club down for drug trafficking. Venus had been busted for dealing in the French Quarter and agreed to flip for them in return for having her charges dropped. She was supposed to give them information on suppliers and dates and times of deliveries."

"I take it she didn't."

"No. She disappeared from New Orleans after another informant was killed. That's when she appeared in Sinful."

"So why didn't the cops look for her here?"

"He called Percy. Said a woman answered claiming she was a cousin living with him and that they hadn't seen Venus since she left the first time, nor had they heard from her."

"Venus. She's a quick thinker. But why didn't he think to check it out in person?"

"He figured if Venus was alive, she'd be contacting them to get her somewhere safe. I get the impression they were concentrating more on finding a dead body than a live one."

"Well, they've got one now. And I guess now we know what Catfish had Starlight looking for—evidence that Venus had collected on them. But if they packed up all her stuff, I'm assuming they went through it then. Why risk showing up now?"

Carter blew out a breath. "Yeah, the luggage in the trunk of the car is where things get weird."

"I agree. If Catfish was looking for notes or a USB or something, he would have taken the luggage with him and gone over it with a fine-tooth comb. And if we assume they didn't break into Percy's house that night to pack things up, that means they had to keep the car until the next day to put the luggage in it. Which meant sending the car over that overhang during the day. That's so many levels of risky."

"Risky or just plain stupid. My buddy says the gang has a steady, high-income business, and they think they've been at it a while. That doesn't say sloppy or stupid to me."

"I don't get this. I don't get it at all."

"That makes two of us."

We disconnected and I headed back into the bar. Despite the late hour, spirits were still lively and the drink orders were flowing in. Unfortunately, that meant the crowd was getting drunker and louder and I was beginning to worry that we might have an incident before the night was over.

That incident happened at 1:00 a.m.

CHAPTER NINETEEN

FOR ONCE, Gertie didn't start it. Ida Belle and I agreed that we might never get to make that statement again, but in this case it was true. However, that does not mean she didn't end up in the fat middle of it. It started innocently enough, with two of the regulars fighting over which one should get to spend the night with the token blonde at their table—the guy who was married to her or the guy she was cheating with.

I really wanted time to process that situation, especially given that the two men had been drinking together with the blonde all night and the cheating thing was a known fact, but I didn't have time to ask any pertinent questions because the fight started.

The blonde was the first casualty, but I had to admit I didn't really feel sorry for her. She kind of had it coming. Her boyfriend jumped up and flipped the table over, sending beer flying onto at least a dozen people. That prompted the husband and the patrons now doused in beer to also stand. I figured I would give the husband time to get in at least one good punch, because really, he needed to do something about the situation, but he didn't do as well as I'd hoped. First off, he'd been drinking for hours and was so wobbly that when he finally drew his arm back, he stretched it back to Mexico. If the boyfriend didn't see it coming, he was so drunk he was blind.

Oddly enough, he didn't see it coming.

But since the husband was sloppy drunk, it didn't connect with the boyfriend's face, which is what I assumed he was going for. As he swung his arm forward, he lost his balance and fell, striking the boyfriend right in the crotch. The boyfriend, who'd been mourning the loss of the table of beer, doubled over, banging his forehead right against the blonde, who flipped over backward in her chair and right into a table occupied by a group of women who looked like cage fighters and had just received a fresh round of shots.

The women all stood and stared down at the blonde as if she had personally started all the drama, and in a way, she had. In the meantime, the boyfriend stood back up, but the husband cocked another slugger and managed to get a shot right to his jaw. The boyfriend staggered backward and I had to give him points for not falling. Then I realized that the rest of the bar was about two seconds from erupting into a mass fight and I had to get back to the bar-running business instead of acting like an observer.

I yelled over at Ida Belle, who was at the other end of the bar. "Toss a bottled water above those idiots."

Ida Belle grinned, grabbed a bottled water, and flung it directly over the head of the warring husband and boyfriend. I pulled out my nine and shot it, sending a blast of sound through the bar and a shower of water over the people under the bottle. It had the desired effect. Everyone stopped what they were doing. Even the DJ turned off the music.

"I'm sure most of you know by now that I was a CIA agent," I said. "Anyone want to guess at my job with the agency? If you continue fighting in this bar, the next thing she flings for me to shoot will be made of glass."

I must have sounded impressive because everyone was still and quiet for several seconds, as if weighing their options. Then the husband waved one arm in the air.

"Then we'll take it outside," he said, and the other patrons started to clap. Half the bar stood up and headed outside.

Ida Belle looked over at me. "I don't know whether to care or not."

"Your SUV is parked outside," I said.

She frowned and pulled her keys out of her pocket. "Maybe I'll just move it to the far side of the building."

I looked over at Misty, who was putting some dirty shot glasses into the sink and didn't seem remotely concerned. "How would Whiskey handle this?"

She shrugged. "As long as they weren't tearing up the bar or his boat, or shooting, he'd let them sort it out. Nice shot with the water bottle, by the way. Never seen Whiskey do that."

"I probably shouldn't have done it either, but it seemed like a good idea at the time."

"Got their attention," Misty said. "Anyway, I need another round of shots for the table that Blondie fell into. Told them it would be on the house."

"I'll bill the boyfriend for it," I said. "Since I'm assuming Blondie never pays."

Misty rolled her eyes. "Why do you think she got the boyfriend? Her husband only works when he runs out of beer or cable money."

I poured up the shots and sent Misty off with her tray, then Ida Belle hurried back in, a worried look on her face. I stiffened a little. If she'd been angry, I would have assumed someone had touched her baby. But worried wasn't a look Ida Belle wore often and never without reason.

"What's up?" I asked.

"Apparently, the boyfriend came here by boat and the husband is threatening to leave with it in exchange for his cheating wife. The boyfriend said the boat's worth ten of her and he'd better throw in money for the deal. The husband is headed for the dock."

"Crap. The last thing I need is drunks stealing boats. We're supposed to be keeping this under control."

I motioned to Misty to watch the bar, then headed outside. Gertie was already standing in the parking lot, watching the mob move toward the dock. She was wiping a layer of dust off her face.

"What happened to you?" I asked.

"I tried to stop them, but I don't have my purse," she said. "I figured I'd throw some gravel from the parking lot. The pebbles didn't faze them and all the dust blew back in my face. I can't see crap now."

"You couldn't see crap before," Ida Belle said. "If the dust came back in your face, then based on wind direction, you threw the gravel directly behind where the action was."

"Let's get this handled," I said as I started toward the dock. "I don't want Whiskey's place shut down because we couldn't keep some drunks under control."

"You don't think Carter would do that, do you?" Gertie asked, bumping into me as she hurried to catch up.

"If it becomes a crime scene, he wouldn't have a choice," Ida Belle said. "And those two are stupid enough to get someone killed."

"I should have stopped serving them earlier," I said.

"If you were serving based on the ability to avoid doing stupid stuff, you wouldn't have served ninety percent of the customers when they first walked in," Ida Belle said.

"She's right," Gertie said. "One of my customers drove his

lawn mower here because he had his license suspended. Guess he knew that George Jones story."

"Who?" I asked.

"Country singer," Ida Belle said. "I'll explain later."

We reached the dock and spotted the husband and boyfriend arguing in a bass boat. They were only at the yelling point right now, but I had no doubt the blows were coming. And given that both were so drunk they couldn't even shout without losing their balance, I had no doubt a punch would send either into the bayou. No way was I fishing a drunk out of an alligator-infested bayou. There were limits to what bartenders should be required to do.

The wife was standing on the dock, yelling at the two men in the boat that she wasn't going home with either of them. Then as we walked up, she laid the real bit of news on them. She was leaving town with her husband's twenty-year-old nephew. She whirled around to walk away and the husband lunged for her at the same time, knocking the boyfriend into the bayou.

Unfortunately, his grab missed the mark. And got Gertie instead.

The husband was so drunk he didn't even realize he'd grabbed the wrong woman. He hauled Gertie into the boat, started it up and took off, one arm wrapped around her waist. Gertie was at a serious disadvantage. Her glasses, which were mostly useless anyway, had flown off when she was yanked into the boat. Her eyes were probably still full of dirt and there was only moonlight to see by, which must have made the dash in the boat all that more frightening. Without her purse in tow, and since screaming wasn't doing any good, Gertie resorted to the only weapon she had.

She bit him.

The husband yelled and yanked the steering wheel on the

boat hard to the left, which sent him careening straight for the dock. I pulled out my pistol and the crowd started to cheer.

"Shoot him. I never liked him!"

"Save me the trouble of a divorce!"

"Don't hit the old lady! She's cool!"

As the boat rushed toward the dock, I leveled my pistol, hoping to get a shot at the engine and stop the boat's progress. The husband, finally realizing he was headed straight for a solid object, turned the wheel but didn't let off the gas. Drunk people are not good at multitasking. The turn put the dock out of the boat's path, but now it was headed directly for the boat ramp, and the engine was completely out of my line of sight. I shoved through the crowd, trying to get my sight line back, but couldn't manage it in time.

The boat struck the ramp and continued up it as if it were performing at one of those extreme shows where people on mopeds jump tractors and stuff. It was carrying so much speed that when it reached the top of the ramp, it got airborne. I heard Ida Belle gasp as the boat left the ground, and we both took off running.

The boat flew off the ramp at an alarming rate of speed and height, but at least managed to stay right side up. Finally, it crashed into the back of a pickup truck, the bow running clean through the cab. Ida Belle and I dashed up to the crash site and climbed onto the truck, praying that Gertie had hit the deck. We spotted her in a heap in the bottom of the boat and my heart caught in my throat as I jumped inside.

"Gertie!" I yelled as I reached to check for a pulse. "Are you all right?"

"Good God, stop hollering," Gertie said as she rolled over. "I'm fine."

"You're sure?" I asked. "Can you move everything? Nothing broken?"

She sat up and moved her limbs around. "Everything seems to be good but boy, I bet I'm going to be limping around tomorrow."

"What about your head? Is it okay?"

"Loaded question," Ida Belle said.

Gertie gave her the finger and Ida Belle grinned.

"She's okay," Ida Belle said and helped me get Gertie to her feet.

Unfortunately, her outfit had not fared as well. Sexy chief had become X-rated chief.

Ida Belle's eyes widened. "Good Lord, woman. You're flashing the entire bar!"

"Just part of the bar," one of the patrons said. "She's not bad for an old broad."

I grabbed a life jacket that had fallen out of a storage box and pulled it over her head, covering her misdemeanors. Some of the crowd started to boo and I made a note to check and see exactly what was in the shots we'd been serving.

The husband crawled out of the cab and stood up, not a scratch on him and all his clothes intact. He surveyed the damaged, then his expression went from somewhat impressed to dismayed.

"This is my truck!" he yelled.

"Serves you right," I said as Ida Belle and I helped Gertie down from the truck.

"He totaled my boat," the boyfriend said. "You gonna do something about that?"

"Darn right I am," I said. "I'm calling the cops on both of you."

"Go ahead," the boyfriend said. "The cops don't bother much with things out here."

"Oh," I said. "Didn't I mention that I'm dating Deputy LeBlanc?"

Both the husband and boyfriend looked as if I'd shot them, and I almost wished I had.

"Get her inside," I said to Ida Belle. "And find her something to wear—even a tablecloth will do. As for the rest of you, the bar's closed. I've had quite enough fun for the night. And if you want this place to remain open, you might consider keeping things more civil because I'm not Whiskey. Understand?"

There was a lot of grumbling and shuffling of feet, but everyone started to walk away. There was even more grumbling by the patrons inside when they found out the idiots outside had shut down their evening a bit early.

"It's only an hour," I said. They grumbled some more but no one made an active protest.

"They're scared you're going to pull out your pistol again," Misty said.

"They should be," Ida Belle said.

"I'm sorry to cut your night short," I said to Misty and Chloe.

They both smiled and Chloe shook her head. "Don't be," she said. "I've made a ton tonight and I'm dog-tired anyway. They really kept us running."

Misty nodded. "You did a really good job. If that gunslinging thing doesn't work out, you should look into opening a bar."

The thought dismayed me so much I couldn't even respond. Just waved my hand and headed for the cash register to collect the take for the night. I'd already told Whiskey I'd take the money home with me and get it to the bank the next morning.

"I present Toga Turkey," Ida Belle said and waved her hands at Gertie, who was now sporting a tablecloth wrapped around her.

Gertie sighed. "Looks like I ended up being a pilgrim anyway."

"You're lucky you weren't the Headless Horseman," I said. "And your right elbow looks swollen. Are you sure it's all right?"

She moved her arm up, extended it, then bent it back in. It didn't go all the way easily. "I guess it's a little stiff. But nothing's broken."

"Then let's get this place closed up and get out of here so you can ice that thing. And I'm afraid you can't hit the sheets yet. Emergency meeting at my house about my phone call earlier with Carter."

They both perked up and along with Misty and Chloe, we set about putting the bar straight, then we all headed out. At my house, I popped leftover lasagna in the oven to reheat, served up some beers, and got Gertie an ice pack and some aspirin.

"I don't know about you guys, but I'm starving," I said. "And I ate two turkey sandwiches before I left tonight."

They both nodded.

"I had no idea you worked off that much energy tending bar," Gertie said.

"You probably don't at regular bars," Ida Belle said. "But waiting tables at the Swamp Bar means serving, negotiating guys trying to slap your butt, and playing bouncer. It's a lot to cover."

"Guys tried to slap your butt?" Gertie asked, looking somewhat confused and a little dismayed. I assumed the dismayed part was because she hadn't been pursued by the butt-slapping crowd herself.

"A couple did," Ida Belle said. "But a quick twist to the wrist had them both keeping their hands to themselves the rest of the night."

"No one tried to slap my butt," Gertie grumbled.

"How would you know?" Ida Belle asked. "That outfit is so tight your butt probably went to sleep on the ride over there. You probably won't feel anything in it until Christmas."

"Possibly true," Gertie said. "Hey, you don't have another ice pack that I could sit on, do you? Just in case it was injured in my boat ride and I can't feel it?"

I grabbed a pack of frozen peas from the fridge and tossed them to her. "Use these. I'm not going to eat them."

"Then why do you have them?" Ida Belle asked.

"Walter slipped them in my food order," I said. "I think he worries about my diet."

Gertie stuck the peas on her chair and wriggled up her dress, exposing her bright pink underwear with turkeys on them. Then she flopped down on the peas.

"That was wholly unnecessary," Ida Belle said. "I've seen more of your bare body in the past few weeks than I have of my own. Why didn't you go upstairs and change? Not like we don't keep spare clothes here."

"Too much effort," Gertie said. "And I don't think this dress is coming off without scissors and some assistance."

Ida Belle cringed.

"Bare bodies and cold peas aside," I said, "let me tell you the latest."

I filled them in on my conversation with Carter. When I was finished, they both stared at me, not saying a word.

"Well?" I asked.

They both shook their heads.

"I've got nothing," Gertie said.

"As much as I hate to admit it," Ida Belle said, "I don't have a clue either. That doesn't make any sense. If Venus had some sort of evidence about the gang's illegal business, then that's even more reason why Catfish wouldn't have sent her luggage over the embankment with the car."

"We're missing something," I said. "Carter can probably gather enough evidence to push Catfish to the top contender in the murder suspect pool, which definitely helps strengthen Whiskey's defense, but it doesn't eliminate him from contention."

"We need to solve this," Ida Belle said. "It's the only way to ensure Whiskey is off the hook for this permanently."

"Great idea," Gertie said. "So how do we do it? Because we have a lot of clues that don't fit together right. We all agree that there's no good reason for Venus's suitcase to be in the trunk of the car. Catfish might be an arch criminal, but no way he sneaked into Percy's house and packed those bags without waking him, so it had to be done the next day."

I frowned. The luggage-car disposal thing had always been a huge sticking point for me. The timing simply didn't make sense, and I couldn't imagine Catfish taking the risks required to have the two things line up the way they did.

"What if Catfish isn't the one who packed the luggage or sent the car over that cliff?" I asked.

"You're thinking it was Starlight?" Ida Belle said. "I don't get how it would be any easier for her than it would for Catfish. You saw the way Percy reacted to her showing up at his doorstep. There's no way he'd allow her in his house, much less let her pack up Venus's things and haul them out."

"I wasn't thinking of Starlight or Catfish," I said. "Maybe we're making this too complicated. Maybe the simplest explanation is the right one."

They both stared at me for a moment, then Ida Belle's eyes widened. "You're thinking Percy?"

"He would have the easiest time getting the luggage out of

the house," I said. "And it was his claim that Venus sent him a text saying she'd left. Did anyone actually see it?"

"But why would Percy kill his own daughter?" Gertie asked. "I know there's no love lost between them but he could have just kicked her out."

"I don't know," I said. "I'm just throwing a scenario out there that fits the facts better. Since she was sleeping with husbands and demanding payment to keep her mouth shut about it, Venus obviously had no problem with blackmail. Maybe while she was living there, she found out something about Percy that he didn't want to be public knowledge."

"Like what?" Gertie asked.

"I have no idea," I said. "Maybe he visits prostitutes or cheats on his taxes. Maybe he's really a serial killer. My point is, we don't really know people like we think we do."

Ida Belle nodded. "And if Percy had a weakness, Venus would have tried to exploit it for her own gain."

"So how do we figure out if that's what happened?" Gertie asked. "It's not like Percy is going to offer up his secrets, especially if it was big enough that he killed his own daughter over it."

"Maybe it was someone else completely," Ida Belle said. "Bart Lagasse is still in the running as far as I'm concerned. I know he seemed all nice tonight handling Jeff, but I think he was more interested in getting Jeff to stop talking about Venus's murder than worried about his safety."

"And he was outside with Venus after Whiskey fired her," Gertie said. "And Misty can't recall if he came back in the bar."

I nodded. "There's Dean Allard, too. He had a lot of reasons to hate Venus and claims he can't remember the night she was killed." I told them what I'd overheard Allard say in the bar about his night with Venus.

"I don't like Allard and would love to go with him, but he

can't be our guy," Ida Belle said. "I had Myrtle do a check for me on our local suspects and she texted me tonight to say that Allard was in jail the night Venus was killed."

"And he doesn't remember?" I asked. "That's a serious drinking problem."

Ida Belle nodded. "Doesn't remember sleeping with Venus. Doesn't remember being in jail. He really needs to lay off the whiskey. Apparently his body keeps going long after his mind checks out."

"Well, crap," Gertie said.

"Don't be disappointed," I said. "This just helps narrow down our list. Then we don't waste time investigating someone who isn't the killer."

"For all we know, it could be someone we didn't even have on our list," Gertie said.

"Let's not go there just yet," Ida Belle said. "We have enough to contend with already. I got another bit of information from Myrtle, but I don't think it helps us any. She overheard Carter on the phone saying that Venus was killed by a blow to the back of the head. Given the lack of tissue, the ME can't say what it was, but I don't think it matters. Tire iron, bat...something hard enough to crack a skull."

"You're right," I said. "It doesn't necessarily help, but it's nice to know anyway. And it does support our theory of this being an unplanned kill."

"Which leaves Percy in the running," Gertie said. "Assuming he has something to hide."

"Percy was never completely out of the running," I said. "At least not in my mind. But I'll admit that Starlight and Catfish looked better for it." I sighed. "Maybe we're overthinking it. Maybe Catfish is the one who killed Venus and he sent her luggage over the cliff in that car figuring if he hadn't found what he was looking for, it would be destroyed by the water if he'd missed it."

"Then why are they here now?" Gertie said.

"Because they didn't find what they were looking for?" Ida Belle suggested. "Now that Venus's body surfaced, the cops will be taking a hard look at everything, unlike before when people just thought she'd left on her own accord."

"Exactly," I said. "And they couldn't have taken their time packing up Venus's things. They had to hurry. Maybe they concentrated only on her room. But if Venus had evidence, she might have hidden it somewhere else in the house."

Gertie's eyes widened. "Which means if Percy didn't kill Venus, he could be in danger."

Ida Belle gave me a worried look. "I know we can't give him details, but we need to warn him."

"It's the middle of the night," I said.

"Let's drive over, at least," Ida Belle said. "If lights are on, we'll knock. If not, we'll wait until tomorrow."

"I suppose it couldn't hurt," I said.

"Cool!" Gertie said and jumped up. "Can I bring the peas?"

CHAPTER TWENTY

IT TOOK a bit of effort to cut Gertie's dress off. That leather was really thick. Then once she had changed into clothes that weren't ripped or cutting off her blood flow, we headed out to Percy's house. The lasagna was long forgotten on the counter. It was close to 3:00 a.m. and the entire town was asleep. Aside from streetlights, only the rare lamplight shone through cracks of blinds. When we turned onto Percy's street, it was completely dark.

"Looks like everyone's out for the night," Gertie said.

"I'm just going to pull up in front of the house," Ida Belle said. "He might have a light on somewhere."

She parked at the curb and all three of us stared at the house as if willing a light to come on. Unfortunately, given our luck, it would probably be in another house, and they'd be calling the sheriff's department to report a suspicious vehicle parked outside their home in the middle of the night. We waited a good ten minutes, but nothing stirred.

"Looks quiet," Ida Belle said. "I guess we'll have to wait until tomorrow."

She put the SUV in gear and was just pulling away when I grabbed her arm.

"Wait!" I said. "I saw something inside."

She slammed on the brakes. "A light?"

I nodded. "But small."

"A lamp?" Gertie asked.

"I don't think so," I said. "There!"

I pointed to a window on the far-right side of the house. "Did you see that?"

"Barely, and then it was gone," Ida Belle said.

I nodded. "Flashlight. And given that there's no power outage, I can't see any reason for Percy to be prowling around his own house with a flashlight."

"We have to get in there!" Gertie said. "If Percy wakes up, Catfish might kill him."

"If we rush inside a sleeping man's house, he might kill *us*," Ida Belle said.

"She's right," I said. "And since there are no other cars parked on the street, that means Catfish came through the woods. Starlight or another member of his crew could be on lookout in the back. We can't assume whoever is in there is alone."

"So what do we do?" Gertie asked.

"First, I call Carter," I said and dialed. He sounded half asleep when he answered but as soon as I explained the situation, he came alive cursing.

"Do *not* go into that house," he said. "I'm on my way!"

"Are you going into the house?" Gertie asked.

"Of course," I said. "But you two need to wait here. I need a sharpshooter and someone with a cell phone watching my back."

"I have dynamite," Gertie said. "Although I'm not sure of the application in this case."

"Maybe later," I said.

I pulled out my nine-millimeter and headed for the front door. Percy couldn't have good locks or someone wouldn't already be in his house. Then I drew up short. He'd never changed the locks. Ida Belle and Gertie had said when Percy came home from work, Venus had moved in because she still had a key. Jeez Louise. That explained how Starlight and Catfish had such easy access. Starlight probably still had her key or she'd copied Venus's back when she was running with the gang, figuring you never know when things might come in handy. Typical criminal mind-set.

I'd noticed when we visited Percy before that the back door had an interior dead bolt on it. But the front door only had one of those silly chains that didn't provide any protection at all but gave people a false sense of security. I was going to hazard a guess that Percy didn't bother to use the chain, which meant whoever was in the house had probably gotten there through the woods but had likely entered through the front door. I was willing to bet it was still unlocked.

I inched onto the porch, pausing every time the boards creaked, and put my hand on the doorknob. It turned easily and I pushed the door open and slipped inside. The room was pitch-black, so I gave my eyes a couple seconds to adjust. Since I'd been there before, I remembered the layout, at least to the main rooms, but the bedrooms were a different story. When I could see a dim outline of the objects in the room, I crept to the hallway and listened. I could hear rustling in one of the rooms on the right side.

The light had been in the last room on the front, so I eased down the hallway, pausing at the first room to listen. It was quiet but I could still hear the faint sound of cloth rubbing together. A single person was walking in the last bedroom. I moved close to the wall and inched toward the bedroom door, pistol in the ready position, even though I knew I couldn't fire it. Technically, at the moment I was just as big a criminal as whoever was in the bedroom.

But if I could get the jump on them then the pistol should be enough to keep them in place until Carter got there. Assuming the person in the bedroom was the only one in the house. I hadn't heard any indication that anyone else was there, but I couldn't be sure. The one thing I couldn't risk was Percy waking up. That could set off a chain reaction where no one came out the winner.

I stopped at the door and listened, trying to pinpoint where in the room the person was. It sounded as if the noise was coming from the exterior wall on the front of the house. Mentally calculating the risks, I decided to go with the plan that would likely eliminate the option of flight. I reached around the wall with my left hand and located the light switch. Then I flipped the switch on, whirled around the corner, and leveled my pistol at a very surprised Starlight.

"Put your hands up and don't even think about taking a single step," I said.

She held one arm in front of her face, blinking in the bright light.

"You were here the other day with the old ladies," she said. "You're not a cop."

"Do you think that gives me more or less reason to shoot you?"

She hesitated for a second, clearly not expecting the question. Then she let out a yell.

"Police!"

I heard a crash from the bedroom across the hall and someone bolted down the hallway. Crap! There had been two of them. When I turned to look at the hallway, Starlight launched at me. Fortunately, hand-to-hand combat was not her strength.

I dodged to the left and gave her a shove as she tried to grab me. Her foot caught one of the bedposts and she went tumbling headfirst into the dresser. I heard the thud as her head connected with the hard wood, then she slumped onto the floor, not moving. I paused only long enough to check her pulse, then took off down the hall. The front door was standing open so I ran out and saw Ida Belle sprinting for the side of the house.

I ran past her and saw the man ahead of me about to enter the backyard. When he reached the edge of the house, a large object struck him directly in the face, and I heard Gertie let out a battle cry. He yelled, then stumbled and fell. I jumped on him, trying to get control of his arms, but he was twisting around like a snake and he was strong. Finally, I managed to grab his arm and flipped over, twisting it backward. As I looked up at Gertie's enormous handbag, I realized what had connected with his face.

"Arm bar!" Gertie hollered. "Better tap out before she breaks it."

"Police," Carter said, stepping up to me as I held the cursing man in place. "You should probably listen. I've seen her do worse."

The man stopped struggling, any hope of getting away dashed by the two people standing above him with guns trained on him, one holding a stick of dynamite, and me about to break his arm. Not surprisingly, his gaze lingered the longest on the dynamite.

Carter holstered his gun and leaned over to cuff him. "Catfish, I presume?"

The man flashed an angry look at Carter but didn't say anything.

"Starlight's in the back bedroom," I said as I hopped up. "She knocked herself out."

"I'll get her," Ida Belle said and headed off.

Carter pulled Catfish to his feet and looked at me. "She knocked herself out?"

I put my hands up. "I swear. She rushed me and I just dodged her. Well, maybe I gave her a little shove."

"Uh-huh," he said. "Didn't I tell you not to go into the house?"

"Yes, but I was worried about Percy. Oh my God! Where is Percy?"

Gertie and I took off running for the house and met an upset Ida Belle at the front door.

"I found Percy tied up in his bedroom," Ida Belle said. "Those fools had his mouth taped and part of his nose. It's a wonder he didn't suffocate."

"But he's okay?" I asked as Carter hurried up, dragging an angry Catfish along.

"He's fine," Ida Belle said. "Just mad as a hornet."

"Got that right!" Percy said as he walked into the living room. I could see red marks on his face from where the tape had been, and it made me want to turn around and punch Catfish dead in the face. Then I figured, what the heck?

I whirled around and clocked him so hard in the jaw that he fell to his knees.

Gertie hooted and Ida Belle grinned.

"What the hell?" Catfish yelled.

I gave a stunned Carter my best innocent look. "I thought he was trying to escape."

"Bull—"

Carter yanked Catfish back up before he could continue. "If you try to escape again," he said, "I'm going to let you just so I can watch her come after you."

"You people are crazy," Catfish said. "You can't do this. You're the law."

"I'm not the law," I said. "I operate under a completely different set of rules."

"Really?" Carter asked. "What are those?"

"I'll let you know when I figure them out," I said. "Where's Starlight?"

"She was starting to come around, so I tied her up with a lamp cord," Ida Belle said.

"For future reference," Gertie said, "I have fuzzy handcuffs."

We all stared.

"Someone needs to explain to me what's going on," Percy demanded.

"I wish we knew," I said. "They were searching your house for something that Venus might have hidden inside." I looked at Catfish. "You want to tell us what you were trying to find?"

He glared at me but didn't utter a word.

"Any idea where Venus might have stashed something?" I asked.

Percy shook his head, clearly angry. "I got no idea what the girl was up to and I don't care to know. If she hid something in the house, I don't know what it is or where it is. But feel free to look yourself. I'd prefer to have it out of here, especially if it means more of Starlight's friends are going to pay me a visit in the middle of the night."

"I appreciate that," Carter said. "And I'll get back with you about a search. Do you need me to call the paramedics?"

"No. I'm fine," Percy said. "Just need to put something on these tape burns. I assume these two won't be out to terrorize me again?"

"I don't think they'll be out anytime soon," Carter said.

"Breaking and entering, assault...should hold them long enough to find even more things to charge them with."

Percy nodded and looked over at me. "What were you doing here?"

"I'm a private investigator and I'm working this case," I said, figuring the basics without mentioning my client would do. "Ida Belle and Gertie work for me. Given certain things we've discovered, we were afraid you might be in danger, so we drove over to check on you."

Percy was confused but only shrugged. "None of that makes sense, but thank you."

I figured we'd done all we could for the night and pretty successfully, I might add, but as I turned to Carter to tell him we were taking off, I noticed a bulge in Catfish's waist.

"He's got a weapon," I said and yanked up his shirt. But it wasn't a gun that I found stuffed in his pants. It was a paper bag.

I pulled it out and opened it up, figuring maybe we'd lucked out and found what they'd been searching for. I peered inside, expecting to find documents or a murder weapon, as it was too heavy to be just a flash drive, and was stunned to see a stack of cash inside.

"It's money," I said. "Hundreds. Lots of hundreds."

"Don't touch it," Carter said. "You want to tell me where you got this?"

Catfish just glared.

"You are in a heap of trouble," Carter said. "I suggest you start answering my questions. Did you steal this from Percy's house? Is this what you've been looking for?"

More silence.

"My buddy with the NOLA PD is going to love hearing about your arrest," Carter said. "He'll love it even more when I tell him that given the way you taped up Percy, he could push for an attempted murder charge."

Catfish finally came alive. "Man, I ain't trying to murder nobody. Can't nobody pin that on me."

"Can't they?" Carter asked.

Catfish stared at him, trying to figure out whether or not he was bluffing. But Carter didn't bluff. Finally, Catfish blew out a breath.

"I found it on the floor at the front door," he said.

"A bag of money?" Carter asked. "Just sitting on the floor next to the door. And you expect me to believe that?"

"It's the truth!" Catfish insisted.

Percy frowned and stepped closer, studying the bag. "Is there something printed on the bottom of that bag?"

I turned the bag over and saw a stamp. "Says *Calico Feed Store*."

Percy's jaw dropped. "That's my money. I knew she'd done it!"

"Done what?" Carter asked.

"Venus," Percy said, his teeth clenched. "I had ten thousand dollars in that feedstore bag tucked in my safe-deposit box. When I went to add some to it earlier this year, it was gone. That bank manager tried to tell me that no one could access the box but me. But given that my money was gone and I didn't take it, I don't see how that's the case."

I remembered the gossip Dorothy had been spreading about Percy getting sideways with the bank manager. Apparently, it was true, and now we knew why.

"Was Venus on your account?" Carter asked.

"Hell, no," Percy said. "But that don't mean she couldn't find the key. There was this guy who worked down there... maintenance or something. He was always sniffing around. He could have helped her."

"You know his name?" Carter asked.

"Bart something," Percy said.

"Did you ask the manager to check the security tapes?" Carter asked.

"Of course I did," Percy said. "She said the thing was broken and hadn't been recording. That all the tapes were static. I had to push her but she finally admitted that no one had checked them for a month. Some manager she is. I'll see her fired over this."

"Let's not jump to conclusions just yet," Carter said.

"That's easy to say when it's not your money," Percy said. "And I can prove it's mine. Never trusted banks. I wrote down the serial number of every bill in there. Should have buried it in the backyard."

"Bring me that list of numbers tomorrow," Carter said. "And I'll see what I can do to expedite getting your funds back to you."

Percy gave him a nod, then turned around and stalked off. I could see his jaw flexing as he turned and figured Catfish was really lucky that Percy wasn't armed.

A vehicle sounded behind us and we turned to see Deputy Breaux hurrying over. "I'm so sorry," he said. "I was on another call."

"Anything important?" Carter asked.

Deputy Breaux hesitated as he glanced at us. Then he gave Catfish a good once-over, clearly confused about what had happened here.

"Let's get this guy in your car," Carter said, noticing the deputy's hesitation. They secured Catfish in the patrol car before they both headed back over to where we were standing.

"So?" Carter asked Deputy Breaux. "The other call?"

"Jeff Breaux tried to kill himself," he said.

"What?"

"No! Is he all right?"

"How?"

Ida Belle, Gertie, and I all spoke at once.

"Took a bunch of sleeping pills, looks like," Deputy Breaux said. "Musta changed his mind, because he called 911 but passed out before he could say anything. I startled the heck out of Melanie, banging on the door in the middle of the night, but the paramedics got him sort of conscious. They're taking him to the hospital."

"He was in the Swamp Bar tonight," I said.

"Really?" Carter said. "That doesn't sound like Jeff."

"He was drunk," Ida Belle said. "Really drunk. And saying that Whiskey should be getting a medal and such. I think the discovery of Venus's body brought back some bad memories for him. The night she disappeared was the night Melanie miscarried."

Carter sighed. "He was really torn up about that."

"They both were," Gertie said. "Anyway, Bart Lagasse took him out of the bar and said he'd get him home."

Carter frowned. "That's two times Bart Lagasse's name has come out of people's mouths tonight. I know he did maintenance at the bank for a while. They fired him, of course. He can't hold a job for any length of time."

"Maybe you should talk to him," Ida Belle said.

"Oh, you bet I'll bet talking to him," Carter said. "About Jeff. About this money. About a lot of things."

"There's something else you might mention," I said and repeated my conversation with Misty about Venus and Bart talking in the parking lot after Whiskey had fired her.

Carter's jaw clenched and I could tell he wasn't happy that someone else was looking good for Venus's murder. Especially when he had Starlight and Catfish all wrapped up in a neat little bow.

"Did Melanie go with the ambulance?" Gertie asked.

Deputy Breaux nodded. "She didn't look so good. I asked if there was anyone I could call but she said no. I just waited until they left, then hurried over for this call. What exactly happened here?"

"All I know," Carter said, "is that this guy and Starlight broke into Percy's house, tied him up, and taped his mouth shut. I need you to get Starlight out of the bedroom. Bring your handcuffs. She's currently tied up with a lamp cord."

"Sir?" Deputy Breaux looked confused.

"We'll figure it all out later," Carter said. "Let's just get these two into jail and then we'll sort it out." He looked over at us. "I'll need to talk to you guys first thing in the morning."

I nodded and we headed for Ida Belle's SUV.

"Okay, so that wasn't weird at all," Gertie said as we pulled away.

Ida Belle nodded. "That was out there, even for Sinful. You'd think it was a full moon with all the crazy behavior going on."

"What about the money?" I asked. "You think Venus got Bart to help her steal it from the safe-deposit box?"

"Stranger things have happened," Ida Belle said. "And since you're not supposed to keep cash in there, Percy didn't have a leg to stand on with the bank."

"When he coughs up those serial numbers and proves Venus managed to get her hands on his money, there's going to be hell to pay down at the bank," Gertie said. "Rumor has it that manager's been on thin ice for a while now."

"I wonder where Venus had the money hidden," Ida Belle said. "Clearly somewhere good enough that they didn't find it last time."

"That Catfish doesn't strike me as all that intelligent," Gertie said. "We're supposed to believe he found a bag of cash on the living room floor? He should have just said it was his."

"And probably would have if Fortune hadn't spotted it," Ida Belle said. "I mean, I don't think for a minute that Carter or the DA or anyone else with a brain would buy that Catfish stuffed a bag of hundreds in his pants and then went to do some breaking and entering, but like Gertie said, clearly, he's not all that intelligent."

"We knew that as soon as we heard he'd hooked up with Starlight," Gertie said.

"True."

Gertie sobered. "You better call Marie and see if she can help with Melanie and Jeff tomorrow at the hospital. Jeff's parents are still out of town, right?"

Ida Belle nodded. "I'll call her first thing in the morning. Assuming the hospital releases him, they'll need a ride home. If they decide to keep him, Melanie will still need to come home and get some clothes and she'll need company. We're a little booked with giving police statements and running bars."

"I had no idea Jeff was so depressed," Gertie said. "I just thought he was having a drunken pity party and he'd work off his headache, then move on. I guess he still hasn't gotten over losing the baby."

"He was a wreck that next morning when we picked them up at the hospital, remember?" Ida Belle said.

"How could I forget?" Gertie asked.

"He doesn't have any other family nearby?" I asked, remembering that Melanie didn't have any left.

"Jeff's family isn't that big and the rest gravitated off to college and jobs in the city," Ida Belle said. "His parents moved to New Orleans when their import/export business took off and they travel out of the country a lot."

"I really hope this stress doesn't cause Melanie any problems with her pregnancy," Gertie said. "I'd hate for her to lose this baby too. Maybe the overdose was accidental. I mean, Jeff was really drunk and he's not much of a drinker."

Ida Belle nodded. "I think you're probably right, especially since he called for help. I can't imagine him taking his own life with the new baby on the way. He probably just didn't realize how many he'd taken."

"I almost took a handful of blood pressure meds once when I was working on a new batch of Sinful cough syrup," Gertie said. "Lucky for me, it was a box of Tic Tacs. Had fresh breath for days."

Ida Belle looked over at me. "You're awfully quiet. You should be happy. Tonight's debacle should be enough for the DA to let Whiskey go."

"Probably," I agreed. "But he's still not completely off the hook. Not until a case is built against Starlight and Catfish. And I'm not sure that's going to be a slam dunk."

"Why not?" Gertie asked.

"Because something doesn't feel right," I said.

"You don't think they did it?" Gertie asked.

"I'm not convinced they did," I said. "That ten thousand dollars gave Percy a lot of reasons to throttle Venus. And since we've already agreed that no one had better access to pack up her things and ditch the car that night, I still can't eliminate him."

Ida Belle frowned. "I don't want it to be Percy, but I agree it looks sketchy. Especially now that we know about the money."

"I want it to be Catfish," Gertie said.

"I think we all want it to be Catfish," Ida Belle said. "But we can't do business based on what we'd like. The truth is the only thing that sets Whiskey free for good. Otherwise, this whole mess just hangs over everyone's head. I hate to speak ill of the dead, but that girl caused so much trouble when she was alive. I really don't want her lingering forever from the afterlife."

Gertie sighed. "So what's our next step?"

"Shower and bed," I said. "We try to sleep, have breakfast, and go give our statements down at the sheriff's department. Then I guess we have to take a closer look at Percy and Bart Lagasse. If Bart helped Venus get Percy's money, then he knew what she had. He might have killed her for it, then couldn't find it."

"He's definitely foolish enough to make the mistakes we've seen," Ida Belle said. "But if he got the money out of the box, he could have just kept it then."

"And Venus would have turned him in," I said. "My guess is she said she'd give him a cut, but if all 10k is in that bag, then it's just another scam she ran. A man with his temper has limits. She might have hit his."

Ida Belle dropped me off at my house and I gave them a wave as I headed inside. For the first time in a long time, I was utterly exhausted. Running the bar had been both easier and harder than I'd thought it would be, but combine that with hunting down potential murderers in the middle of the night and I was done in. I thought briefly about the uneaten lasagna, but couldn't bring myself to care. Instead, I headed upstairs, took a hot shower, and poured myself into bed.

I was asleep before my head hit the pillow.

CHAPTER TWENTY-ONE

GIVEN ALL the activity the night before, I figured I'd be able to sleep in, but by 8:00 a.m. my mind was racing and wouldn't allow my tired body to lie still any longer. Plus, I was starving. I threw back the covers and headed downstairs to fix up a quick prebreakfast snack before my real breakfast at the café. I got a text from Ida Belle while I was eating toast over the sink—less cleanup that way—letting me know that she and Gertie were awake and ready to meet whenever I was.

I texted back that I'd be at the café in fifteen minutes and headed upstairs to dress. Ida Belle and Gertie were already at our usual table in the corner when I arrived, and Ally stuck a cup of coffee in front of me as soon as I sat down.

"I heard you guys ran the Swamp Bar last night *and* foiled a robbery at Percy's house," Ally said. "That's a lot to put into a single night. Do you want me to run an IV of this stuff? Or, if you don't like needles, Francine is stocking energy drinks now."

I smiled. "I think the coffee will do for now."

We ordered breakfast and Ally went off to the kitchen.

"Did you guys hear anything about Jeff?" I asked.

Ida Belle nodded. "Marie said he's awake and told the

doctor he thinks he remembers taking a bunch of aspirin. That's the best possible explanation for a bad scenario. He could have died, but at least it wasn't intentional."

"So he says," Gertie said. "But according to Marie, Melanie is still worried. She said he hasn't been himself lately, been sleeping a lot, not interested in watching sports or fishing."

"Sounds like a classic case of depression," I said.

Gertie nodded. "Marie said Melanie is feeling responsible as it was her sleeping pills he took. She didn't think keeping them in the same cabinet would be a problem."

"Hopefully, the new baby will shake him out his funk," Ida Belle said. "Anyway, Marie said they're releasing him this afternoon so he'll be home for Thanksgiving. His parents fly back in Thanksgiving morning. I think that will do him some good."

"It's a relief to know he's okay," I said. "I felt somewhat responsible since he got drunk at the bar. Maybe he'll lay off the alcohol for a while. He doesn't seem a good candidate to take up serious drinking."

"Definitely not," Gertie agreed. "So, did you solve this mystery in your sleep?"

"I'm afraid not," I said. "I'm not sure I even solved lack of sleep in my sleep."

Ida Belle nodded. "I never did get into a deep slumber. Everything was surface level. I feel like I dreamed all night but I can't remember them. Just tiny bits of anxiety and frustration are all that remain."

"Yeah. Same for me," I said. "I think we have so many angles to consider right now that our minds are finding it hard to sort it out. I was thinking after we talk to Carter that maybe we should take a break from investigating and put everything on paper. Maybe tack sheets with different points on my kitchen wall. I read somewhere that seeing things in writing sometimes prompts a different line of thinking."

"Sounds interesting," Ida Belle said. "Why not."

"I'll try anything to get better sleep," Gertie said. "Between running the bar, clobbering bad guys with my purse, and Francis citing the Florida penal code all night, I am beyond scattered."

"You were beyond scattered before," Ida Belle said. "But that bird is going to be the death of you."

"At least I'm keeping up on Bible verses and Florida criminal law," Gertie said.

"Neither of which help in our current line of work," Ida Belle said. "Unless you have the opportunity to pray for someone who's being extradited to Florida for prosecution."

"It's better than me taking up singing with him," Gertie said.

"True," Ida Belle agreed and then looked at me. "Have you heard anything from Carter this morning?"

"Not even a text," I said. "I imagine he's as busy and as exhausted as we are. Maybe more. I wonder if he's even been home since arresting Catfish and Starlight."

"He hasn't," Ida Belle said. "Myrtle sneaked outside and gave me a call earlier. He's been there all night. Catfish and Starlight aren't saying much that she can tell and Carter looks frustrated as heck. And apparently, Catfish and Whiskey tried to go at each other between the bars when Whiskey figured out why they were in jail. Carter had to shift them around and put Starlight in the middle."

"Seems appropriate," Gertie said. "If there's trouble, Starlight was always in the middle. Venus definitely didn't fall far from that tree."

"What about the New Orleans police?" I asked.

"Carter called his buddy early this morning, but when he realized Myrtle was in the break room, he closed his door," Ida Belle said. "She climbed on the counter to get closer to the vent but couldn't make out what he was saying. Apparently, he also knows to keep his voice low."

"He's figuring out all our tricks," Gertie said.

"What I do know is that Percy was down there at 7:00 a.m. with his list of serial numbers," Ida Belle said. "And they all matched. Myrtle could hear him yelling all the way down the hall."

"Was all the money there?" I asked.

"Yep," Ida Belle said. "Which lends credence to your theory that if Bart helped Venus steal the money he got shorted in the deal."

"Is Percy still on the suspect list?" Gertie asked.

"He's not off of it," I said. "When the money came up missing, you have to figure his first thought was Venus. If he accused her of taking the money, what do you think her response would have been?"

"Knowing Venus?" Ida Belle said. "She would have told him to call the police with his crazy idea and see what they had to say about him keeping cash in a safe-deposit box."

"So she would have challenged him on it," I said.

"Or outright mocked him," Gertie said. "Especially if she knew he wouldn't or couldn't do anything about it."

"Definitely not off the list then," I said.

"As much as it pains me to think it," Ida Belle said, "I'm going to have to agree with you. I was willing to count Percy out before this money thing, but now...I don't know."

"It would help if we knew when Percy found out the money was missing," I said. "If he went to the bank after Venus was killed, that's a whole different story."

"Yeah, but if he went before, the smartest thing he can do is say he doesn't remember," Ida Belle said. "Carter can subpoena the bank records, but it will take some time. And even if he was there before Venus was killed, we don't know when the money was taken."

"So what we really need is for the manager to remember the exact day that Percy yelled at her," I said and sighed. "Half a year after the fact."

Ida Belle shook her head. "That is not looking like a good angle to pursue. At least not first, anyway. Maybe that visual thing you were talking about doing will help us out."

Ally arrived and put our breakfast in front of us. I stabbed at my blueberry pancakes as if they owed me money. Frustration was getting the best of me and I needed to take a step back and try to get perspective. But it was hard to do when a man's future, his business's future, and his dying father's life were riding on my success.

"He didn't make a mistake in hiring you," Ida Belle said quietly.

"Can you read minds?" I asked.

"Sometimes they're not all that hard," Ida Belle said. "If this was a cut-and-dried situation, Carter would have already figured it out. He's smart, has experience, and has access to more information than you do."

I thought about that. "You're right. But he also has the government bureaucracy tying his hands, and that's something we don't have. Plus, he doesn't have the two of you."

"Got that right," Gertie said. "No one has seen or heard more than Ida Belle and me. Our combined memories cover the history of this town for the past...uh, for a lot of years."

I grinned, feeling better already. "You're right. We've got this."

CARTER WASN'T at the sheriff's department but he'd asked

Deputy Breaux to take our statements. We had discussed it a bit at breakfast, but ultimately saw no reason to hide anything that we'd done. Percy wasn't going to press charges against the people who'd saved his life, and the DA wouldn't touch it with a ten-foot pole, lest he get ostracized by the community at large, who had already decided we were heroes.

A couple at the café had insisted on paying for our breakfast. One of the Sinful Ladies had bought us each a loaf of banana nut bread for later, and Pastor Don had required the entire café to stop eating and join in a prayer of thanks for us. All the attention was making me itchy. I was beginning to long for the days when everything I did had to be a secret. Even Deputy Breaux had insisted on giving us all high fives.

I would have liked to talk to Whiskey, but with Starlight and Catfish locked up in the next cells, I knew it was out of the question. And with the New Orleans police due to arrive at any time, Deputy Breaux couldn't risk letting me back there.

When we were on our way out, I got a text from Carter.

Working on getting Whiskey released. Will call later.

Finally, some good news. I read the text to Ida Belle and Gertie and they both smiled.

"I hope he's out in time for Thanksgiving," Gertie said.

"I hope he's out in time to open the bar tonight," Ida Belle said.

Gertie looked dismayed. "Maybe if he's out, we can still help. You know, until he gets back in the swing of things."

"He was gone one night," Ida Belle said. "I'm pretty sure his swing is fine."

"But I have another outfit," Gertie said.

"If we have to work tonight, you are not going as sexy anything," Ida Belle said. "You darn near became the Headless Boatman last night and that's not a good look on any holiday."

"Yeah, but in all fairness, that whole potentially headless thing wasn't due to my outfit," Gertie said.

"She has a point," I said.

"Whose side are you on?" Ida Belle asked. "The side of propriety or the side of unplanned nakedness?"

"I'm only for unplanned nakedness if Carter stops by without calling first," I said.

"There you go," Ida Belle said. "If we bartend tonight, we're all wearing jeans, T-shirts, and tennis shoes. Maybe even chain mail."

Gertie smiled. "I have sexy chain mail."

WE SPENT the rest of the morning and into the afternoon trying to diagram the case. I'd removed the pictures of fruit hanging on my kitchen wall and now it was covered with paper and sticky notes. We were all sitting in chairs, staring at the notes, drinking our third round of coffee, and hoping that inspiration would come.

So far, all the paper hadn't clarified anything at all except that I really didn't like the fruit pictures.

I rose from my chair to put on another pot of coffee and sighed. "This didn't help one bit."

Ida Belle shook her head. "It's great information, and I can see how this type of thing might shake something loose. But yeah, I'm still not convinced on any one over the other. I can still make arguments for and against Bart, Percy, and Catfish."

"And Whiskey," Gertie said. "Which is the problem. I mean, yeah, we definitely found some credible suspects to take the heat solely off Whiskey. Enough so the DA might never bring up charges against him. But he's already been arrested, and people will never stop talking. Stop wondering."

Ida Belle nodded. "Whiskey's business doesn't necessarily depend on the goodwill of the most stellar of Sinful's residents, but a murder rap hanging over his head could still cause problems. And not just with the locals, but with his suppliers."

"I get it," I said as I flopped back down in my chair. "But I don't know how to fix it."

"Maybe the forensics team will come up with something on Venus's body," Gertie said. "A hair or something."

"A hair belonging to who?" I asked. "She lived with Percy, was in a relationship with Whiskey, and grabbed Bart's privates the night she disappeared. Unless that hair belonged to Catfish, we'd still be in the dark."

"Crap," Gertie said. "Then I'm going to hope they find one of Catfish's hairs."

"Me too," I said. "But we're being paid to do more than hope."

Ida Belle patted my shoulder. "You can't create answers when there aren't any. We've assessed this nine ways to Sunday and the reality is any of them could have done it, but none of them make complete sense."

My phone rang and I checked the display. "It's Carter," I said and answered. He sounded exhausted.

"I just got done going over everything with the DA," he said. "Between the break-in and attack on Percy and what the New Orleans police have on Catfish, he's happy to bring them up on those charges. He's itching for a murder charge for Venus but wants to put everything together—timeline, all the evidence, statements—before he moves forward. We did find a USB drive in the pocket of one of Venus's bags but it's too damaged to get anything off of."

"Have Catfish and Starlight said anything else?"

"They've flapped their gums plenty but haven't said anything of merit. They're still insisting they never found

Venus when they came to Sinful in May. Whiskey gave me the names of some regulars and two have identified Catfish as someone they talked to in the Swamp Bar on the night Whiskey kicked Venus out. They remember that he asked about her, but they can't remember whether he was there before or after Venus left."

"Has to be after she left the bar. If Catfish had shown up while Venus was there, she would have taken off right then," I said.

"I'm sure," he said. "But he could have pulled up while she was in the parking lot. He might have seen her leave. I'll talk to Misty and get her statement, then I'll probably spend the next week talking to everyone who ever graced the front door of the Swamp Bar."

"Sounds like fun."

"Not the word I'd choose. But I'm glad to have Catfish and Starlight up on charges. I should be able to spring Whiskey late this afternoon."

"What about the money?"

"Percy had the serial numbers all right, so he should eventually get it back. He might face some tax issues if the IRS gets wind of it. Apparently, it was cash payments for some off-book work. He was saving it for a new bass boat."

"I bet he's fit to be tied that the money was in his house the whole time. Did Catfish ever tell you where he found it?"

"No. That idiot is still sticking to his story that it was on the living room floor. I have no idea why he insists on that stupidity. It's theft whether it was on the floor or hidden in a mattress. But then, nothing he says sounds all that normal. I think he's more than a little off."

"You know, since I've been dealing with the general public, I am constantly amazed at what people get away with given the lack of logic applied to their criminal enterprises."

"I talked to my buddy again and he doesn't think Catfish was running the show. They're leaning toward thinking he was the muscle, not the brains."

"That makes a lot more sense."

"Well, I've got to run. I've got a mountain of paperwork to do on this and need to follow up on Whiskey's release. I would tell you I'd see you later, but honestly, I'd rather have a date with my bed so that I'm not falling asleep in my fried turkey tomorrow."

I laughed. "Get all the sleep you want. I'll be right here tomorrow. Probably too stuffed to move or maybe even breathe, given the menu, but we can go into a diabetic coma together."

"That's what Thanksgiving is all about."

CHAPTER TWENTY-TWO

I TOSSED my cell phone on the table and filled Ida Belle and Gertie in on the conversation.

"You don't seem satisfied," Ida Belle said.

"I am. I mean, I guess I am." I sighed. "I know I should be happy. Whiskey is off the hook and the bad guy wasn't a local for a change."

"But?" Ida Belle asked.

"But there's still things that bother me," I said. "Like the USB in a zipped pocket. Why didn't Catfish and Starlight find that? It should have been simple."

"Like you said before," Gertie said, "maybe they figured any evidence would be destroyed by submerging the car so they just hauled it all out and let it sink."

"But wouldn't they want to know what Venus had on them?" I asked.

"You would think," Ida Belle agreed. "But if Catfish was the muscle and not the brains, then that might account for the stupidity of the choice."

"Okay, so if they thought they sank the evidence, why did they come back?" I asked.

"Because the brains of the operation told them to make sure?" Ida Belle said. "We might not ever understand their reasons, especially if we think differently."

I shook my head. "I know you're right. I have to stop attributing skill sets to people because I think they ought to have them."

"Give it some time," Ida Belle said. "With the CIA, you were dealing with highly skilled and intelligent enemies. Their actions would have been logical and deliberate. You had to assume your target had the same ability as you because that's what kept you safe."

Gertie nodded. "When Ida Belle and I came back from Vietnam, it took us a long time to adjust back to civilian life. And this was our hometown. Everything seemed slower, less thought out, less important but more dramatic. But finally, we settled into the knowledge that average people do and think average-people things. That's all they know."

"And then there's the below-average people," Ida Belle said. "And Sinful has its share of those. Some people just don't have the sense God gave a goose but they never seem to know it. That's why so many criminals are caught."

"Carter says the same thing," I said. "I guess I just need to wrap my mind around it."

"While you're wrapping," Gertie said, "let's get to the General Store and pick up those last-minute supplies that Walter is holding for us. Maude Perkins got a glimpse of the condensed milk cans in our bag and there was a small stampede over them. Walter had to threaten them with the fire extinguisher."

"Over condensed milk?" I asked.

"Thanksgiving is serious business when it comes to food," Gertie said.

"I'll drive over," Ida Belle said, "but if you two could pick up the order, that would be great."

Gertie and I gave each other a knowing look. Ida Belle had avoided any mention of Walter ever since she'd made her optional marital announcement. Physical avoidance wasn't surprising, but it made me wonder if she'd made up her mind and was just waiting until after Thanksgiving to say no, not wanting to ruin the holiday. I wondered for the millionth time why she hadn't said no right away, but I was afraid to broach the subject with her while the answer to Walter was still pending.

The General Store was packed full of people and the half-empty shelves reflected it. Walter stood at the cash register, looking harried and trying to explain to people that he could not produce eggs when he didn't have them. And no, he did not have chickens to lay them either. There were collective groans when he suggested they drive to the nearest supermarket up the highway. I would have added something about planning better for next year but that probably wasn't good for business.

As we walked in, I caught sight of Bart Lagasse standing in the frozen meal section. I told Gertie to go get our order and motioned toward Bart. She nodded and started squeezing her way toward the counter. Given that most people were fixing big meals from scratch for the holiday, there was plenty of space at the freezer section. I walked up next to Bart and stood, pretending to inspect a microwavable chicken potpie.

He looked over at me, giving me the up-and-down, which I expected. Then he focused on my face and narrowed his eyes.

"You're that chick that was running the Swamp Bar last night," he said.

"That's me," I said and stuck out my hand. "Fortune

Redding. Thanks for taking Jeff home. I felt bad that he got that drunk on my watch. Especially given what happened."

Bart shrugged. "Wasn't your fault. Jeff's not much of a drinker. I heard he took sleeping pills thinking it was aspirin. Talk about feeling guilty. I just opened the front door and let him in. I didn't even think to go inside and get him to bed."

"His wife was there. You figured she'd handle it."

"Actually, she wasn't. I called out but Jeff mumbled something about a meeting. I was hoping he'd sleep off the worst of it before she got home."

"You couldn't have known, and taking the sleeping pills was an honest mistake on Jeff's part. But maybe he'll reconsider drinking as a way to deal with his issues."

"I'm guessing he will. I heard they arrested Starlight and some motorcycle guy for Venus's murder. Does that mean Whiskey's getting out?"

I nodded. "Hopefully late afternoon."

"That's great. Whiskey is a good guy. I mean, he was stupid to hook up with Venus, but I can't say much about that. She took me for a ride more than once. I wasn't surprised when it finally caught up with her, but it sucks that her own mother was involved. Although I guess that shouldn't surprise me either."

"Why not?"

"Look at the way she took off and left Venus when she was a baby. Even gave up rights. What kind of woman does that? Venus hated her. Always told me when she got old enough, she was going to New Orleans to find her and make her pay."

"I guess that didn't work out like she'd planned."

He shook his head. "First time for everything. Usually Venus came out on top. Look at what she did to Allard."

"It's not like he was innocent. He did cheat on his wife."

"I don't know about that. His wife's been complaining

about his nonworking parts for years now. More likely, he passed out and Venus told him that's what happened to get money out of him."

"You really think she'd take it that far?"

"She didn't like it when people were happy. Before Venus, Allard and his wife had a decent thing going, even with the nonworking parts. And I'm pretty sure Venus hated men."

"Why do you say that?"

He shrugged. "Just thinking back on all the things she pulled. I know she didn't respect Percy. Thought he was weak for letting Starlight get the best of him. I ain't no head doctor, but even I could see that Venus thought she'd got cheated with her life and she was intent on punishing anyone she thought had better. I think she played with people for fun."

"That's a dangerous game," I said.

"Got her killed, didn't it?"

"I heard she stole money from Percy right out of his safe-deposit box."

I watched him closely, looking for any shift in the eyes, any twitch that might indicate he had something to hide. But he just shook his head. "Doesn't surprise me. It was nice talking to you, but I have to pick up some fishing tackle up the highway before the store closes. Have a nice Thanksgiving."

"You too," I said and watched him inch his way toward the cash register.

Gertie was pushing back through the crowd and I took the bag from her as we headed outside. I put the bag in the back of the SUV and we climbed inside.

"Looks like a madhouse in there," Ida Belle said.

"It was," Gertie said.

Pastor Don rode up on his bicycle and leaned it against the wall of the store. He caught sight of us and lifted his hand to wave. We waved back as Ida Belle pulled out of the parking space and as we headed for my house, I filled them in on my conversation with Bart.

"You think he knew anything about the safe-deposit box?" Gertie asked.

I shook my head. "If he did, he was really good at hiding it."

"Playing ignorant is one of Bart's many talents," Ida Belle said. "Especially since he's not the most diligent on the job."

The entire drive, I rolled the conversation with Bart around in my mind. Nothing stood out, but something about it bothered me. I held in a sigh. Maybe I was just being stubborn, refusing to accept that the simplest answer was likely the right one. Venus had tried to get revenge on her mother and it had cost her the ultimate price.

I leaned my head back and closed my eyes, trying to calm my restless mind. But it didn't work. Things came in pieces, flashing in completely random and weird assortments—Bart Lagasse's comments, the USB drive in the luggage, the luggage in the car, Venus's overwhelming desire to destroy people's lives, Catfish claiming the money was on the living room floor, Pastor Don riding a bicycle.

No man for her to sleep with.

Haylee's words echoed through my mind like a gunshot and my eyes flew open.

"Has Jeff left the hospital?" I asked.

"Yes," Ida Belle said. "Marie took them home a little while ago. She said Jeff looked a little exhausted but Melanie said they were going to take a boat ride and see if that would lift his spirits. Jeff really loves his boat."

I grabbed Ida Belle's arm so hard, she yanked the steering wheel to one side. "We have to find them. Now! We got it all wrong."

"What are you talking about?" Ida Belle asked, now looking as anxious as I felt.

"I think Melanie killed Venus," I said.

"What?"

"No way!"

They both sounded off at once.

"Just trust me on this. I'm still missing some pieces but everything else fits. We have to find Jeff right now."

"Why?" Gertie asked.

"Because I think Melanie's going to kill him."

CHAPTER TWENTY-THREE

IT REALLY PAID to have friends who trusted you, even when you sounded like a crazy woman. Five minutes after my declaration, we were in my airboat and headed down the bayou toward the lake. I'd asked Ida Belle to take us to the deepest known bayou where no camps were located and where people were unlikely to fish. She'd launched the boat without question and soon, we were speeding along the top of the water.

I had my binoculars in place, scanning the water for any sign of a boat. So far, I'd spotted several fishermen but none of them were Melanie and Jeff. Ida Belle went straight to the center of the lake and stopped so I could cover the entire thing from one place. Nothing. Not that I'd expected anything to be going on in the middle of the lake.

She pointed to a large channel on the left side. "That channel is deep and wide, but the fishing isn't very good. I'll pull up next to those fishermen closest to the opening and ask if they saw them."

We headed out and stopped to question the fishermen who said they were pretty sure it was Jeff and Melanie who'd entered the channel about ten minutes before. I barely got a thank-you out of my mouth before Ida Belle took off. The width of the channel allowed us to move at a good clip but I could only see as far as the bends in the bayou would allow. And there was no way we could sneak up on them. They would have already heard the airboat echoing across the water.

But none of that mattered. All that mattered was that we got to their boat before Melanie finished what I was certain she'd started the night before. I didn't believe Jeff had accidentally taken sleeping pills. I believed Melanie had given him sleeping pills, telling him they were aspirin. Or maybe she'd filled a bottle of aspirin with sleeping pills and handed it to him. But he hadn't taken a lethal dose and he'd been lucid enough to call for help.

"There!" I saw them at the same time as Ida Belle and she cut the throttle on the boat, bringing it down to a cruising speed. I zoomed in on them with my binoculars. Two people. But my relief was short-lived when I realized that Jeff was standing in the bow of the boat and Melanie stood at the rear with a pistol trained on him.

"She's got a gun on him," I said.

"What the—?" Gertie said. "I'm sorry. I guess I didn't want to believe..."

"Time to start," I said, and pulled out my pistol as Ida Belle inched us closer to their boat.

Melanie dropped her arm to hide the gun next to her side, but I knew it was there. Jeff stared at us as we approached, his eyes wide with fear.

"Careful," I said to Ida Belle, my voice low. "But if she makes a move, don't hesitate."

Ida Belle cut power to the boat and we began to drift closer, now maybe twenty feet away.

Melanie tried to force a smile. "Are you ladies out for a boat ride too?"

"No," I said. "We're here to keep you from killing your husband."

She flinched a bit but the outrage that would have flooded the expression of an innocent person was nowhere to be found.

"What?" she said finally. "Are you crazy?"

I glanced over at Jeff, who was clearly panicked.

"You killed Venus, didn't you?" I asked Melanie. "You work at the bank and managed access to the safe-deposit box. You stole Percy's money. Was that what she told you it would take for her to leave town? To stop pursuing your husband?"

Realizing the gig was up, Melanie lifted her arm, pointing the gun at Jeff.

"Venus never wanted anyone to be happy because she was never happy," Melanie said. "She knew Jeff didn't want her but she got him drunk and tricked him. Then she bragged about it to me to get me to help her. She wanted the money and her sister's legal documents."

And suddenly it hit me. The twin sister who had died weeks after birth. She'd already been issued a birth certificate and a Social Security card, and Percy had kept them with other legal documents in his safe-deposit box. Those documents would have given Venus an entirely new identity, and the ten thousand would have allowed her to easily disappear.

"It was Venus who packed her things into the car, right?" I said. "She was going to meet you to get the money, then she was leaving town. So why did you kill her? Why not just let her go?"

Melanie's face twisted in anger. "She mocked me. Said I was so ugly and plain that Jeff would never be faithful. That people like me didn't deserve a family. Then she talked about how good he was in bed...and I slapped her across the face.

She laughed at me. Laughed. And when I went to hit her again, she shoved me. As soon as I hit the ground, I knew."

Tears began to stream down Melanie's face and the truth of what had happened washed over me.

"She killed my baby!" Melanie said. "She'd taken everything I loved from me. Then she turned around, holding that bag of money, and started to walk away. She was just going to leave me on the ground clutching my stomach. So I pulled myself up, and I grabbed a piece of rebar and hit her as hard as I could. She deserved it!"

"Maybe she did," Ida Belle said. "But Jeff doesn't deserve it."

"He cheated on me," Melanie said. "He slept with her. I called him at work after I hit her. He helped me hide the body and then I went to the hospital and the doctors confirmed what I already knew. But we could have been fine. With Venus gone forever, we could have gotten pregnant again and had a family. But Jeff couldn't handle it, especially after Venus's body was found. He felt guilty. He wanted to tell the truth but I couldn't let that happen."

"You're going to have to let it happen," Ida Belle said. "When everyone hears your story, they'll go easy on you. You didn't plan to kill her. It was a fight gone wrong. But if you shoot Jeff, that changes everything. Just put the gun down and we'll all go talk to Carter. You know Carter will do everything he can to help you."

I watched Melanie's face, looking for a sign that she was buying into Ida Belle's plan. Ida Belle was doing an excellent job trying to talk her down from the ledge. She'd hit on all the right cylinders and the fact that Melanie had known and respected her for her entire life should weigh in.

But it didn't appear to.

Melanie stared at Ida Belle for several seconds, then finally she shook her head.

"I can't."

She looked at Jeff and as her finger tightened on the trigger, I squeezed off a round.

It was a direct hit.

The bullet caught her right in the biceps, which is what I'd been aiming for, but reflex caused her to fire anyway. The shot hit Jeff in the shoulder and sent him careening backward into the bayou. Melanie screamed in pain and dropped the gun as she fell into the bottom of the boat. I shoved my pistol into Ida Belle's hand and dived into the bayou. Jeff's shoulder was out of commission and he was probably still weak from all the sleeping pills. I couldn't be certain he could swim for the surface.

The bayou water was too dark to see in, so all I could do was swim for the spot where Jeff entered the water and dive down. The tide was slowly moving out, so I moved forward a bit with it, waving my arms as wide as I could get them, trying to lock onto Jeff. I had my eyes open, but it did no good. Seconds ticked by and I found nothing. Ida Belle had been right. This section of the bayou was deep.

I dived deeper, still searching, but if I didn't find him soon, I was going to have to surface for air. And that would seal Jeff's fate. My lungs began to burn and I struggled to control them, pushing for that few extra seconds that could make the difference between life and death. But when I started to heave, I knew I had to get to the surface.

As I repositioned myself to swim up, my hands brushed something solid. I grabbed onto an arm and swam as hard and fast as my stressed lungs would allow. I opened my mouth to breathe right before breaking the surface and a rush of bayou water flooded into me, causing me to choke. I heard yelling, and then someone grabbed my arms and I felt the hard metal of the boat. As I grabbed the side with one hand, I felt Jeff being lifted away from me.

I coughed up the water and blinked, trying to clear my eyes. I could hear Ida Belle calling CPR instructions to Gertie and I grasped the side of the boat with both arms and gave one last tremendous kick to pull myself up. Adrenaline must have been working overtime because I managed to haul myself over the side and fall into the bottom of the boat, still choking. Ida Belle and Gertie were performing CPR on Jeff, who didn't look responsive. I crawled over and looked down at his pale face.

That's when the first shot flew right by my head and struck the side of the boat.

Melanie!

Ida Belle and Gertie ducked at the sound of the blast and I scanned the boat for my pistol. I spotted it next to Jeff and grabbed it as the second shot rang out on the bench. Without hesitation, I rose up and fired.

This time, my aim was a permanent solution.

The bullet struck Melanie center mass. Her eyes widened and she stared at me for a second, her expression shifting from fury to surprise. Then she took one staggered step and fell forward, collapsing in a heap.

I heard a cough and looked over to see Jeff spitting up water. Ida Belle and Gertie rushed back into paramedic mode and helped him onto his side so he could rid himself of the rest of the water. I grabbed the anchor from the side pocket of the boat and tossed it into Jeff's boat, then pulled it over to us.

I jumped into the boat and checked Melanie's vitals. "She's gone," I said.

"She didn't give you a choice," Gertie said. "She was too far off the deep end. She would have kept shooting until we were all dead."

I nodded as I slumped down into a sitting position. I'd done what I had to do to save four other people. And even though Melanie was guilty of killing Venus and trying to kill her husband, I still felt horrible. She had been a normal person with normal wants and dreams until Venus had targeted her. Had taken from her the only things that mattered.

Melanie had handled everything wrong. But I still felt sorry for her. Sorry for Jeff. Sorry for lives cut short and dreams banished.

CHAPTER TWENTY-FOUR

THE AFTERMATH of our bayou showdown took well into the night to unwind. Getting Jeff to the hospital was the first priority, and Carter had paramedics waiting on the dock as soon as we arrived, acting on the fast and confusing phone call I'd made to him. Once Jeff was off, a second round of paramedics had to collect Melanie. Given all the chaos at the dock, a crowd had gathered, but Carter had forced them to disperse and finally gotten us inside the sheriff's department to explain what had happened.

We were separated immediately, per protocol, and each gave our statements to Carter and Deputy Breaux. Hours later, we were finally allowed to go. Carter gathered me into his arms as I rose to leave and hugged me so hard it hurt just a bit.

"I could have lost you," he said. "Next time, call me instead of trying to apprehend a murderer yourself."

"It was a wild idea," I said. "I couldn't be certain."

"But your instincts told you that you were right. I appreciate and respect your abilities, but you have to trust that I'll believe you when you put forth something that sounds crazy."

I leaned into his chest, the warmth of it coursing through my exhausted body. "I love you," I said.

"I love you too."

IDA BELLE and Gertie insisted on staying the night. And although I would never have admitted it, I was glad for the company. Being alone would have allowed too much time for reflection and regret, and I needed to move past the emotional high I was on and into a logical assessment of everything that had happened. I knew I'd had no choice but to shoot Melanie, but it still weighed on me. It would take time to get past it.

We all took a shower and trudged downstairs. I'm sure we were all hungry, but no one felt much like eating. After several minutes of silence, Gertie heated up some canned soup and put crackers on the table. We managed to start on the soup while we talked.

"I still can't believe it," Gertie said. "I mean, not that I doubted you, but how in the world did you figure it out?"

"I don't know that I did," I said. "Not completely. There's still a lot that I'm guessing at and we won't know for sure until Jeff talks."

"Take us through it," Ida Belle said. "Because I'm with Gertie. I still don't see how you made the connection."

"For starters," I said, "there were a several things that bothered me. The first was the luggage in the car. It didn't make sense for Catfish and Starlight to leave it in there, and it didn't make sense that someone had waited until the next day to get rid of the car. But if Venus had packed the luggage herself, intending to leave town, but was killed before she could, then it made perfect sense."

"So you think that was the plan?" Gertie said.

"I think it was always her plan," I said. "She fled New Orleans after the other informant was killed. I think she came back here because she knew that her twin's legal documents were in the safe-deposit box and she probably knew Percy kept off-the-books cash there. She just needed to figure out how to get to it and then she was going to disappear for good."

"So sleeping with Jeff was just her way of getting Melanie to do her dirty work at the bank," Gertie said.

"Not only that," I said. "Remember what Haylee said—that Jeff was the only guy who'd ever turned Venus down? I think that stuck with her all these years. I think she was someone who could wait for revenge for a very long time. And seeing Melanie happy didn't make it any better. She didn't like for people to have the life she felt she got cheated out of."

"You think she got him drunk?" Gertie asked. "Drugged, maybe? So she could get him to sleep with her?"

"I'm not convinced he did sleep with her," I said. "I absolutely think she got him unconscious somehow. Then she made sure he woke up naked and she told him they'd slept together, but I wonder if they actually did. Remember what Bart told me about Dean Allard—that Allard's wife had complained about certain parts not working? And Allard himself said he couldn't remember having sex with Venus. It's because I don't think he did. I think she just set him up to get money out of him."

"Happily married guy," Gertie said. "Big family."

Ida Belle shook her head, clearly disgusted. "You know, the more we find out about that girl, the more I wish she'd left and never come back. I don't wish anyone dead, but Venus was a plague on everyone who knew her."

"So Melanie arranged to meet Venus at the schoolyard after Jeff left for his night shift," Gertie said. "But why did Venus go to work that night if she was going to get the documents and the money? Why not sit around and wait for her exit?"

"Because Venus was never one to sit around and wait," Ida Belle said. "She probably figured she could lift a good bit of cash off of customers that night—maybe even out of the register—giving her more cushion for her escape."

"Not to mention taking a swipe at Whiskey before she left," I said. "Bart Lagasse said Venus hated men. I don't think that was far from the truth."

"And that's why she went around crotch grabbing," Gertie said.

I nodded. "Melanie told us what happened at the playground. Melanie called Jeff afterward and he hurried out of work, later claiming it was because of the baby. They buried the body in the construction site and Melanie took the money, documents, and Venus's phone. Then they hurried home and called the paramedics for Melanie."

"But Jeff went to the hospital with Melanie," Gertie said. "We picked them up the next day because he didn't have a vehicle. So when did he have time to get rid of the car?"

"This is where I'm guessing," I said. "But I'm thinking Jeff didn't ride with Melanie."

"Neighbors saw him get in the ambulance," Ida Belle said.

"Then I'll bet he rode a block or so, then said he forgot something—wallet, phone—and would meet them there."

"So he got out and went back for the car," Gertie said. "But how did he get from Nickel's camp to the hospital?"

"Melanie's bicycle," I said. "Remember the one you said she used to ride everywhere? The one she claimed she got rid of? Jeff sneaked back to the house to get the bicycle, put it in Venus's vehicle, and that's what he rode to the hospital after dumping the car."

"Nickel's camp is only a couple miles from the hospital,"

Ida Belle said. "That's completely doable and it wouldn't have taken long to execute. I bet you're right."

"So they got away with it," Gertie said. "And chances are they would have continued to if you hadn't put it all together. Starlight and Catfish would probably have gone down for the crime or at least been the biggest suspects for the rest of their lives. But how did we get from everything contained so well to Melanie trying to kill Jeff?"

"Guilt," I said. "I think Jeff was having a hard time dealing with the fact that Melanie had killed Venus and that he'd helped her cover it up. Their marriage was strained already and Jeff was exhibiting signs of depression. Jeff said in the bar that nothing was the same since that night, and then he said he couldn't do it anymore. People took that to mean his marriage but I think he meant keeping their secret."

"So when Venus's body was found, his guilt was multiplied by a thousand," Ida Belle said. "That's why he was drinking in the Swamp Bar, even though he rarely drank."

"Yep," I said. "I think after Bart dropped him off, he took the money to Percy's house and stuck it through the mail drop. Catfish insisting he found the money on the living room floor and refusing to change his story is the second thing that really struck me as odd."

"That makes total sense," Ida Belle said. "Returning the money to Percy was one of the few things he could do to make things right."

"He was going to tell," Gertie said. "That's what happened. He returned the money to Percy, then went home and told Melanie that he was going to the police the next day to tell them everything."

"I think so," I said. "So Melanie managed to dose him somehow with sleeping pills so it would look like he killed himself, but she didn't get the job done. At some point, he was conscious enough to know something was wrong and call 911."

"Why didn't he tell the doctors that?" Gertie asked.

"Because he probably didn't remember," I said. "My guess is he repeated whatever Melanie told him. He was drunk and the drugs would have affected his memory. But there's a good chance he would have eventually remembered. Melanie couldn't afford that, and since her initial plan didn't work, she took advantage of it by acting like she wasn't sure his overdose was accidental."

"So when he took a dive headfirst into the bayou and didn't resurface, no one would question it because a pattern of behavior had been established," Ida Belle said. "That's beyond devious."

"My guess is she was going to shoot him, weight the body with the anchor, and dump it in the bayou," I said. "Then she was going to drive somewhere else and claim that's where he jumped in."

"And her being pregnant, no one would question why she didn't go in after him," Gertie said.

"If she was even pregnant," Ida Belle said. "I wonder now if that's just another lie she told, trying to keep him in line."

"But eventually, that lie would catch up with her," Gertie said.

"I think she'd been teetering on the brink of sanity for a while," Ida Belle said. "When Gertie unearthed Venus's body, it just pushed her over the edge. Her decisions beyond that point were no longer rational. She was just scrambling to keep her secret."

Gertie sighed. "Even if it meant killing Jeff."

"In her mind, she'd already lost him," Ida Belle said. "When I tried to reason with her, she didn't even look like the same person. I think the Melanie we knew was long gone. What a tragedy, all the way around. It's amazing that a single person could incite so much sadness."

"But there is a silver lining," Gertie said. "We saved Jeff and solved the case. Whiskey will be free and clear of any doubt or suspicion."

"She's right," Ida Belle agreed. "We did an excellent job, and Fortune proved that she has excellent analytical abilities. You're going to make a fine detective. Not that I ever doubted it."

Before I could reply, there was a knock at my door. I knew it wasn't Carter but I wasn't expecting anyone else. I swung open the door and was pleased to see Whiskey standing there, smiling. I waved him in and led him back to the kitchen where Ida Belle and Gertie gave him enthusiastic hellos.

"I know you've had a bitch of a day," Whiskey said. "And I won't keep you. But I had to thank you in person, and it couldn't wait. I have no idea how you figured all that out, but it impressed the heck out of me. I knew you were smart when I hired you, but you've blown my expectations out of the water."

"I'm just glad you're out and that it's all over," I said. "And mostly, that we won't be tending bar again."

"I'm kinda sad about that part," Gertie said.

"You guys are welcome to work the bar any time you'd like," Whiskey said.

Ida Belle and I groaned.

"Don't encourage her," Ida Belle said. "She was almost beheaded in a boating incident."

He grinned. "Heard about that. Always some excitement at the bar. That's why I love it." He looked at us and sobered. "You ladies risked your life today and though I'll be forever grateful that you figured all this out, it's a sobering thought to know I could have sent you into the ground."

"Not you," I said. "Melanie. You didn't do anything wrong and none of this was your responsibility. You were just one more casualty slung from Venus's orbit."

"All the same," he said, "I hope you ladies are more cautious going forward. I knew Venus was a bad one but the talk I'm hearing tells me I didn't know the half of it. And that's bad enough. But when people like Melanie Breaux become killers, then it's time for all of us to take a hard look at everyone in our lives."

"We've been doing a lot of that lately," Ida Belle said.

"Well, I'm going to let you ladies get back to it," Whiskey said. "Goes without saying that you've got free drinks for life at the bar. Anytime you want. Just stop in."

After Whiskey left, Gertie looked at Ida Belle and me, her expression animated. "I might take him up on that work thing. I made two hundred bucks last night and even got a phone number."

"Who gave you his phone number?" Ida Belle asked.

"Some cute guy sitting by the dartboards," Gertie said. "I might just give him a call."

"Let me see that number," Ida Belle said.

Gertie reached into her purse and pulled out a bar napkin with a number written on it. I leaned over and took a look.

"That's the number to the bar," I said.

Ida Belle laughed.

"Well, crap," Gertie said. "I guess that means I'll have to go find him myself. I don't suppose—"

"No!"

We both answered at once.

Ida Belle wagged her finger at Gertie. "You and I don't have enough lives left to hang out at the Swamp Bar. Besides, you have fishing and that ridiculous bird to occupy your time."

"And working for me," I said. "I bet solving this case gets us some clients."

Ida Belle frowned. "The question is, with Whiskey giving out the accolades, what kind of clients will they be?"

"The kind that aren't boring?" Gertie suggested. "Are you sure we can't bartend just one last time...I have this naughty elf costume."

CHAPTER TWENTY-FIVE

My house was hopping with activity the next day. I'd insisted on hosting my very first Thanksgiving in Sinful but had made it clear that while tables, chairs, and drinks were on me, everyone else needed to cover the cooking thing. For the first time in my life, I had a houseful of people and was loving every minute of it. Carter was there, of course, and his mother, Emmaline, her boyfriend, Carlos, Ida Belle, Gertie, Ally, and Walter.

There was enough food to feed all of Sinful for a week but I had every intention of putting a major dent in it. The fried turkey alone had my mouth watering as Carter and Walter supervised the frying in the backyard. Since the day was so pleasant and sunny, I'd forgone formal dining inside and opted for folding tables and chairs outside. Everyone seemed pleased with the arrangement.

I leaned over the fryer, taking in the awesome smell of the turkey cooking, and Carter grinned. "Just you wait," he said.

"I saw Sheriff Lee at the store yesterday," Walter said. "He finally took my advice and saw a dentist about his dentures. Ordered a pile of steaks."

"Thank God," Carter said. "If he was on soft foods for Thanksgiving, I was afraid I was going to have to shoot him. He's been on a tear for over a week now. Even threatened to arrest Celia for crossing the street while glaring. Deputy Breaux and I have been covering double shifts because we didn't want him on the clock."

I smiled. Another mystery solved.

It took a bit of assembly, but finally, our Thanksgiving meal was ready for consumption. We all took our seats at the table and I asked Walter to sit at the head. Before we dug in, I stood and looked at everyone.

"Before we launch into this incredible feast, I just want to tell you all that being here with you, like this, is something I never pictured for myself. After my mother died, all semblance of family went with her. People tried, of course, but staging an event with others isn't the same as gathering with those you truly care about. I never thought I'd have this. Didn't even know I wanted it, to be honest. But now that I'm here, I can't think of anywhere else I'd rather be. Or anyone else I'd rather share my life with. Thank you all for making me a part of your family."

As I sat, Carter reached over and squeezed my hand. There was a good bit of sniffling and Ally had tears in her eyes, but everyone was so happy that it made my heart clench.

"Praise the Lord and pass the turkey," Walter said, breaking the silence.

Everyone laughed and reached for dishes. We all talked and ate, several different conversations going on at once. The food was incredible, especially the fried turkey. Everyone had been right. I would never eat turkey any other way again.

No one mentioned Venus, Melanie, or Jeff, and I was glad. There would be plenty of time to talk about the bad things that happened. Today was a celebration of everything that was good. Everything that we were thankful for, and for the first time in my life, I had a very long list. Good community, great friends, an interesting and challenging profession, and a boyfriend who made my heart flutter.

When the last fork had been placed on an empty plate and the last chair had been pushed back for more breathing room, the sun was just starting to set over the bayou. Walter cleared his throat and rose.

"Before we all retire to our homes to drop into a food coma, I have something I'd like to say. And it's best said here, with all my family together."

I glanced at Ida Belle, but she was staring directly at Walter. I looked over at Gertie, who shrugged.

"This past week," Walter continued, "I asked Ida Belle to marry me. Now, we all know I've been down that road many times, and the result has never been what I'd hoped for."

He motioned to Ida Belle to join him.

I held in a gasp as she walked to the head of the table and stood next to Walter, smiling up at him.

Walter looked down at her and I could see the vast amount of love he felt for her now, before, and would always. He looked out at us and grinned.

"This time, she said yes."

WILL Walter and Ida Belle finally tie the knot? Will Fortune and the girls have a new mystery to solve? Find out in the next Miss Fortune series book, coming end of year 2019.

SIGN up for Jana's newsletter at her website to receive notification of new releases.

. . .

janadeleon.com

MORE MISS FORTUNE FUN

Did you know that Jana created a publishing company that allows approved authors to pen their own stories in the Miss Fortune World? For a different take on Sinful and its residents, check out J&R Fan Fiction.

jrfanfiction.com

Sinful, Louisiana has its own website! If you want to escape to a bit of hilarity, check it out!

sinfullouisiana.com

CPSIA information can be obtained
at www.ICGtesting.com
Printed in the USA
FSHW012237160819
61145FS